On a lush, secluded island, one passionate adventure leads to another....

Diana Fletcher means business. The beautiful, innocent, reverend's daughter has traveled all the way to a tropical island off Madagascar on a mission: To find her brother—and to punish the man who drove him to a life of piracy. But when she comes face to face with the enemy in question, the handsome, powerfully seductive man is not at all what Diana expected...

Tristan Kent never intended to harm Diana's brother. A man of humble origins, Tristan claims he tried to save him from another ruthless captain. Diana is desperate to believe he is telling the truth...and that the intoxicating desire that escalates between them is true as well. But can she trust him? Or is Tristan's story—and his heart—nothing more than fool's gold? Amid the haze of sensual delights and soaring ecstasy Tristan has in store for her, all will be revealed...

Visit us at www.kensingtonbooks.com

Books by Tina Donahue

Dangerous Desires
Loving Lies
Wicked Whispers
Passionate Pursuit

Pirate's Prize
First Comes Desire

Published by Kensington Publishing Corporation

First Comes Desire

Pirate's Prize

Tina Donahue

LYRICAL PRESS
Kensington Publishing Corp.
www.kensingtonbooks.com

Lyrical Press books are published by
Kensington Publishing Corp. 119 West 40th Street New York, NY 10018

First Electronic Edition: February 2017
eISBN-13: 978-1-5161-0062-0
eISBN-10: 11-5161-0062-X

First Print Edition: February 2017
ISBN-13: 978-1-5161-0065-1
ISBN-10: 1-5161-0065-4

Printed in the United States of America

To my street team, Tina's Romance Rebels, and my team leader, Pamela Leonhardt. I couldn't have done this without you ladies. You rock!

Author's Foreword

From the moment I read Shanna, I fell in love with historical romances and tropical locales. Nothing is more seductive than lush island nights and a hero who not only commands but also cherishes. Falling in love with Tristan was easy. How I envy Diana in having his passion. How I raged against those who wanted to separate them. Enter the world I created in First Comes Desire and be swept away.

Acknowledgments

To Penny Barber, an exceptional editor.

Chapter 1

Madagascar—1717

Harsh breathing pulled Tristan Kent from sleep.

Snores rose from his crew, his men having collapsed earlier from rumfustian, a potent mixture of sherry, gin, and beer. If their past imbibing served as evidence, they'd remain unconscious until dawn, sprawled on the isolated beach.

He inhaled deeply and relaxed.

Whispers intruded. Heated murmurs followed, drifted close, and stopped abruptly.

"On your feet, Kent. Do it now, coward." A young woman had spoken, her British accent refined, tone decidedly heated.

His pulse jumped. Eyes closed, he lay motionless against his bed of felled mangroves. At any other time, he would have murdered the person who dared insult him. Not now. What he'd heard made no sense. He hadn't been in an Englishwoman's company in more than four years. Those females had never used cultured speech or their mouths for anything other than delivering the most wanton pleasure.

Pretending sleep, he stretched his legs lazily over the sand and hit an obstacle.

The thing kicked back. "Do as I've ordered or die where you are."

Sweat prickled his neck. He inched his hand from beneath his book to the brace of pistols across his chest. Like other pirates, he was never without his weapons. Unlike most, he never overindulged in drink, as his occupation hardly ensured a long and pleasant rest or life. Even so, he never believed an educated Englishwoman would challenge him.

He couldn't fathom who she might be, what she wanted, or how she'd come to this particular spot. The hidden beach offered protection against attack or capture while his crew careened the Quest, the sloop he commanded. Brimstone and tallow antifouling reeked on the balmy night breeze.

She kicked his foot harder.

He touched his pistol and opened his eyes. Firelight danced in the muggy breeze casting the exposed hull and mast in a hellish orange glow.

Her rapier point nearly rested on his throat. "If you're incapable of moving, my blade shall."

It already had. Any closer and she'd shed his blood. Before he died or they both did, Tristan looked up.

She was young, surely no more than twenty or so, skin fair and flawless, eyes lushly lashed, though he couldn't determine the color. They seemed too dark to be blue, too fair to be brown. Her features were elegant, lips full and rich, overall surprisingly exquisite.

His mouth went dry.

Only her clothing disappointed. A cap covered her hair, though a few dark tresses had escaped. She'd hidden her womanly form in canvas trousers, a patterned shirt, and short blue jacket. The mild breeze ruffled her clothes, pressing them into the alluring swell of her unbound breasts.

Despite his disquiet and confusion, he smiled.

Bewilderment swept her face, and then she frowned. "On your feet now or I'll run you through where you lie."

He settled his fingers carefully against the flat part of her blade. Only his thumb rested directly on the cutting edge. He pressed. Steel sliced into him. Blood ran down.

She made a face.

"Go on, run me through." He pressed harder. "I'll assist you in keeping your blade steady."

She remained perfectly still, not even breathing.

He guessed she wasn't prepared to murder him after all, though what she would do remained a mystery. He eased the point from his throat, held the flat part, and reeled her in. Her wrist was tantalizingly close. A quick move, along with a firm grip and he'd have her beneath him.

Panic swept her features. She tugged.

He put on a show and gasped loudly.

Mewling like a wounded kitten, she looked at his hand.

His fingers were intact, rather than severed. He'd released the blade in plenty of time, proving she was an innocent at this and foolhardy for having challenged him.

He chuckled.

Three men hurried from behind and raised their blades to his chest. A fourth man strode into view. He removed Tristan's pistols, cutlass, and dagger.

The men said nothing and made no move on their own, appearing to serve rather than using her as a decoy. Each looked to be in his late twenties, dressed like mariners or pirates. In the Indian Ocean, there was little distinction.

To Tristan's knowledge, there had never been a genteel Englishwoman on the account and surely not one functioning as ship's captain. However, he'd been absent from his homeland since seventeen-twelve. Perhaps in the last five years, beautiful young women had taken to bolder goals than being a pleasure source to men. "Pity."

"Pity?" She looked down her nose at him. "Because you've yet to lose your fingers to my blade?"

He closed his book. His men weren't in a position to help him. None ordered to keep watch. He'd left the task to his friend and quartermaster, James Sullivan. Most likely, James was still alive, since the young woman wasn't brutal. However, he wasn't here nor had he sent out an alert as to these intruders.

Tristan lifted his face to her men. "Who is she?"

Before they could answer, she directed her blade to his throat. "I said, on your feet."

"State your purpose and I may consider your sweet request."

The man next to her snickered.

She gave him a withering look. "Quiet."

He fell silent but didn't lose his smile.

Poor girl handled this badly. A man would have killed the fool to warn the others. In this part of the world, it often took violence to secure obedience and respect.

She withdrew her blade. Her glare, however, didn't soften. She wanted Tristan quite dead, even if she wasn't the one who would spill his blood. Odd.

"My ship has no valuable cargo." He gestured to the vessel. "It's not yet fit for sea, so what could you possibly want other than to have me on my feet?"

"I'll see you back in England and hanged."

"You want to send me to the gallows?" He couldn't hide his shock. "Why?"

"Tell me what you've done with Peter."

Ah, she searched for a man. Her long throat and satiny flesh showed no signs of Peter's mark in the recent past. Despite her loose clothing, Peter's seed wasn't growing inside her, unless she had yet to swell with the man's child.

Her eyes filled. "Where is he?"

Her distress surprised Tristan. There were six men named Peter in his crew, none worthy of her. She was young, lovely, and apparently educated. Too good for those beasts.

"Montgomery." She gestured to the man who'd previously snickered. He was her largest crewmember, his weight in jiggling fat.

She stepped aside. "Make him talk or you'll answer to your master."

"Yes, miss." Montgomery clamped Tristan's shoulder.

Miss? Master? This was odd. Once Montgomery felt comfortable in his superior role, Tristan offered a swift punch to the man's jaw.

He staggered back on the sand.

The other men pressed close.

Before they ran Tristan through, he spoke to her. "If you want to know what happened to Peter, order your men to back off. Do it now."

She gestured for them to withdraw.

"What's Peter's last name?"

"Fletcher."

Another surprise. "Peter Fletcher, my cabin boy?" The lad was fourteen and innocent when it came to women. "How do you know him?"

"Coward."

Tristan bristled, but tempered his anger. Youth and inexperience had caused her careless words. When he'd been her age, he'd also despised pirates. Going on the account hadn't been his choice or James's, but a man did what he had to in order to survive. "There's no need to fear for the lad's safety. He's quite well."

"Where is he? What have you sent my brother to do?"

Everything fell into place, her outrage and sorrow making sense. Peter had spoken of a mother who'd died from the pox when he was quite young and a clergyman father who'd succumbed to the fever three years ago. The boy might have also mentioned a sister.

She must have come to take Peter back to England after finding him here, of all places. The ship and crew she used certainly weren't hers. Presumably, the vessel belonged to the man she referred to as master.

Tristan longed to ask for particulars but guessed she wouldn't answer a pirate she wanted hanged. With her, he wanted to comfort. A woman's distress was never a small matter. "No need to worry. Peter's task won't put him at risk."

"To whose way of thinking, yours or those in the civilized world?"

"Everyone's. I'm fully aware he's not yet a man and requires protection."

She opened her mouth and closed it, cheeks flushing.

Good. He'd won their first battle. Threats moved men. Women needed civilized behavior and a kind word to bring them to a man's side. He wanted her at his, so he could teach her what pleased him. There would be much she'd learn and enjoy.

Heat pooled in his groin.

She stepped back and gestured to the man who stood next to the still-moaning Montgomery. "Reeves, restrain the captain."

Tristan stood. Her men lifted their blades to his chest. "What's the meaning of this? I've done you no harm. Stay where you are." He pointed at Reeves, who'd edged closer, then turned back to her. "Hear this, Miss Fletcher. No matter what transpires, I'll never do you harm."

Firelight danced over her milky complexion. Her eyes reflected the flames.

Enticed further, he held up his hands. "Call off your men. You're safe here. So is Peter. No one's hurt him."

She stiffened. "No one? Not even you, especially you? How can you say such a thing? You abducted him."

"No."

She advanced a step. "You'll hang. I'll see you hang."

Not likely. He had other plans for them and kept his peace.

* * * *

Tristan's composure rattled Diana, his demeanor at odds with what she'd heard about him being a ruthless pirate. For nearly a year, she'd pursued him. Upon capture, she'd expected him to curse her and struggle fruitlessly against her men while she watched with great satisfaction. Instead, he'd smiled. He also seemed to care about Peter.

Impossible. No matter Tristan's dignified manner or him claiming innocence, he was still a pirate, Welsh in the bargain, and strangely enough, liked to read. His book lay forgotten on the sand, its title embossed in gold on the cover. Homer's *Iliad*, a classic far above what common folks would enjoy.

Her confusion grew. He was more than he should be, as tall and athletic as a young noble, clean too, hair and face washed, his crimson waistcoat, dark breeches, and white shirt well cared for. Moist wind separated the linen to bare his muscular chest. Perspiration glistened within those crisp curls. They begged for a woman's touch, and later him pleasuring and protecting her in his strong embrace.

Something stirred within Diana. She pushed her foolish reaction away and met him eye-to-eye, wanting to see the devil.

He waited patiently for her next move, searching her gaze, puzzling her further.

He was an undeniably handsome man. Blond hair fell in thick waves over his forehead, and curled around his ears and on his neck. Firelight turned his bronze skin a deeper gold. Only his eyebrows were dark, same as the stubble on his upper lip, chin, and cheeks.

He smiled softly.

Her belly clenched. She needed him to be afraid, not playful or aroused, to know the suffering he'd caused. When he'd taken the merchant ship Peter served on, he'd nearly ruined her brother's life and surely destroyed hers. It was heartache enough to have Peter foolishly run away to sea as if it were a game. Tristan's actions had forced Peter into piracy and put the child at even greater risk. Boys younger than him had gone to the gallows for crimes that were serious or not.

Helpless with outrage, she lifted her hand to strike Tristan.

He didn't curse or try to defend himself from her coming blow.

Unsettled, she lowered her hand. "Go on. I know you want to strike me, so why haven't you? Are you afraid what my men will do?"

"As they're armed and I'm not, taking caution merely shows good sense. But might I also remind you, Miss Fletcher, I wasn't the one with the raised hand."

Her cheeks burned. "A necessary defense against the likes of you."

He sighed loudly. "Yes, the likes of me. I'm nothing in your eyes. You've made yourself quite clear. However, before you take to insulting other men in this part of the world, ones who are far less understanding than I, and those who wouldn't hesitate to treat you quite brutally, it's best you remember words have power. They should be used with great care."

She opened her mouth but found no acceptable retort, the same as when her father had been alive. To him, she'd always been wrong and expected to apologize, beg his forgiveness. There wasn't a chance in hell she'd do so with Tristan. She hardly forgot what he'd done to Peter and who waited for her at her journey's end.

Benedict Bishop made her physically ill. He was twice her age, her father's friend. In return for Bishop's ship and crew, she'd pledged her flesh to him. Once she arrived in Mozambique, she'd share his bed without marriage or the decency any woman deserved. A living hell she'd endure when they arrived in England. One made possible by Tristan.

Her outrage flared. "What's the real problem, Captain? Not man enough to stand the truth?"

He bowed his head slightly. "Your truth is flawed, which compels me to prefer your hand. Go on. Do your worst."

Her skin stung, but she wouldn't back down. "Very well." She brought her hand to his cheek to strike him, but couldn't, and delivered a gentle caress instead.

Her men mumbled to each other.

Tristan looked at her questioningly.

He above all should have known seduction was a woman's greatest weapon, forcing men to their knees, even one as alluring and confident as him. His skin was warmer than she'd expected, his stubble oddly exciting in how it bit her palm. She enjoyed touching him, until she recalled he was no more than a murderous pirate.

Tristan parted his lips.

Before he could speak and surely lie, she stroked his bottom lip, heated and achingly soft, the same as how he treated her. For now. And only because her men offered protection. If she and Tristan had been alone, Diana sensed he would have demanded her mouth and used her as he pleased. Just as he'd abducted Peter without giving the boy a voice in the matter. No more.

She raked Tristan's cheek, wanting him to feel the pain he'd caused her, relishing his coming shout and oaths.

He kept his tongue.

Furious, she dug deeper.

He didn't even blink.

"Damn you." She ached to pummel him, to make him bellow. "I want you to hurt."

"As you do." Blood trickled down his cheek.

She lowered her face, frustrated tears welling in her eyes. "I hate you."

"You've yet to know me."

"I've no desire to know you."

"In time you will." Longing radiated from him, rather than insolence.

She should have backed away. His presence held Diana, baffling and intriguing her.

"I did not abduct Peter." He glanced past. "If you refuse to believe me, ask him."

"Diana?"

She turned so quickly her cap slipped off, releasing her braid. The fire silhouetted a man. "Peter?"

He stepped into the light. The boy she recalled was no more, a stranger facing her.

Sun had lightened Peter's dark hair and baked his once pale skin as bronze as Tristan's. He was nearly as tall too.

Her chest cramped at changes she hadn't expected. The last time she'd seen Peter he was twelve years old, smaller than she, and far too thin.

Even with his new height, he was still more boy than man, all arms and legs, no fat. Only marks from work he'd done or beatings he'd endured.

She winced at the cruel bruises, the horrible cuts on her brother's bare chest and arms. "Turn around."

Peter looked at Tristan.

He nodded. "Go on. Show her your back."

She pressed her hand to her throat. Scar after scar crisscrossed Peter's skin. She whirled on Tristan. "Liar. You claimed no one had harmed him. You did that."

"I never touched the boy."

Then his foul crew had, and he hadn't stopped the assault. "You'll pay for this." She sheathed her rapier and spoke to her men. "Restrain Kent and his crew."

Peter gaped. "What?"

Diana struggled over the sand to reach him, ready to hug.

He sidestepped her and marched toward Tristan.

Her other men arrived to help their mates fetter the prisoners.

Peter stopped and growled. "What do you think you're doing?"

He shoved Reeves away from a pirate. To the man, they were drunk and swearing at having their slumber interrupted, but offered little fight.

"Stop it." Peter grabbed another man, who easily pushed him aside.

"Peter." She gripped his wrist to keep him from drawing his pistol, snatched it instead, and flung it into the sea.

He gasped. "What are you doing?"

She clasped his upper arms and forced him to face her. "I'm saving you from being hanged. This isn't a game. If you'd been captured with these animals, you would have faced the gallows as surely as they."

"You can't fetter them and leave. They'll starve. It ain't right."

But him being whipped and driven to work like a man was. Rubbish. "Peter, love, we—"

"Don't call me that. Why are you doing this to me?"

"To you? This was done for your safety and freedom."

"I ain't exactly in irons."

Diana had no idea where her sweet, proper brother had gone. "I was speaking of your future freedom. In exchange for it, I've promised to bring these men to England where they'll hang."

His blue eyes nearly popped out. "You have no bloody right to do this to me or them."

"Enough, Peter." Tristan's rumbling voice cut through the other noise. "Your sister deserves your respect."

Peter lowered his face and stood silent as a statue, obeying Tristan far too readily.

Even with his hands bound behind his back and facing certain death, Tristan was quite relaxed, his stance belonging to one who ruled and seduced.

Unnerved, she stepped back. "Reeves."

The muscular seaman finished restraining a pirate. "Yes, miss?"

"If Captain Kent's unable to hold his tongue, gag him."

Peter inhaled sharply. "No."

"Quiet." Tristan gave the boy a hard look. "Not another outburst, understand?"

Peter nodded obediently.

She frowned. "You just gave your final order, Captain. You're no longer my brother's master to whip and beat him as you see fit."

"You're making a great mistake about what truly happened."

"I'm warning you."

He lifted his dark eyebrows. "Against what? I have no desire to do anything except to please you while you please me."

Her pulse raced. "Please you? I'd rather die."

A smile played across his sensuous lips. "You want the same as me. You've much to learn. I look forward to teaching you."

Heat flooded her chest and throat. She took Peter's arm to hurry him along. "We must go."

He wouldn't budge. "To where?"

"I'll explain further once we board the Lady Lark."

"I can't leave these men or me captain."

"It's my, not me, as you well know. Please stop speaking like a common pirate."

"Why? It's what I am."

"No. Never say such a thing again." She tugged his arm, but couldn't pull him more than a few steps. "Will you move, please?"

"Not from here."

She'd risked everything to save him and received this behavior in thanks? She wanted to shriek. "Be grateful for my rescue. Don't you understand? Your time with Kent has come to an end."

"And yours, Diana, has only begun." Gone was Tristan's patient manner and seduction. He was determined and dangerous now, befitting the pirate he was.

She tingled with fear and an emotion she didn't want to identify. Something akin to excitement, which was mad. She pushed her feelings aside. "It would be best you heed your own advice, for words do have power. They should be used with great care."

"They have been."

Chapter 2

Diana stared, then lifted her chin.

Tristan fought a smile. Her trembling mouth and lingering gaze proved her uncertainty and interest. She didn't understand him, was determined to hate him, but wanted him nonetheless. As he did her. His cock strained against his breeches, craving her inner heat. The reverend's courageous and honorable daughter would bring him endless pleasure. He had yet to touch her, but already she belonged to him, no other.

She pivoted. Her braid swung, its dark color making her complexion seem even paler. In the future, he wanted her clothed in nothing except her glorious mane and two jewels he'd have her wear. Hopefully, she wouldn't fight him too much on his fantasy.

She pulled Peter toward the Lady Lark. At her endless words and flailing hand, the boy wilted. He'd met his match in her, but he wasn't yet a man.

The sorry souls who were men had paid the price for their drunkenness, the situation past control.

"Captain." Henry Wells staggered across the sand, lost his balance, and toppled over. "What in the hell is going on?"

Reeves hauled the pirate to his feet. "You're going to hang."

Henry wailed.

One of Diana's men grabbed Tristan's arm. He made no move to fight. Yet. "My book, if you please." He inclined his head to Homer's tale. "I would never forgive myself if I left my mother's most prized possession behind."

The man squinted at the cover. "That the Good Book?"

Even from where he stood, Tristan could read the title. His captor could not, no different from other illiterate mariners. "It remained with her till the very end."

The man's rough features softened. "Mine died in Newgate."

"A terrible place." Tristan's mother had spent much of her brief life in the prison. During his visits to her, he'd endured the stench from too much humanity caged like animals, and had been horrified at the prisoners' endless screams. They convinced him never to exist in filth, nor let anything or anyone steal his self-respect and hope. He would live and die clean. He'd always be free. "When I'm there myself and surely when I hang, I want her book with me."

The man trudged through sand to fetch it.

In the confusion and activity, no one watched Tristan. Inside a mangrove stand a doubloon flashed, the gold coin reflecting the firelight. The coin glinted repeatedly, spelling out James Sullivan's message.

Good man. Tristan suspected James hadn't kept a proper watch because he'd helped Peter collect the crew's water. Upon their return, the boy had probably stumbled unknowing into camp while James, who was far more experienced, had held back.

Tristan inclined his head to where Diana had pulled Peter.

The coin flashed in answer. James understood what to do.

Tristan's captor strode back. He shoved the volume beneath Tristan's arm and led him across the sand.

To the promise of freedom and the reverend's wondrous daughter, Diana Fletcher.

* * * *

Despite a chair in the great cabin, Peter sat on the floor, legs pulled to his chest like a common pirate, not the proper boy Diana loved and had raised. Holding back sorrow, she stepped around him to get a better look at his back. He shifted, hiding it. She hurried to his other side. He twisted away.

She stilled. "Please let me see your injuries."

"Ain't got none." He scooted back and slumped against the wall. "Them's scars."

Good Lord. This wasn't what she'd expected from their reunion. Peter should have been weeping, clinging to her as a frightened young boy would, grateful for his rescue.

She sank next to him, wearier than she'd ever been. "Why did you run off to sea?"

He shrugged.

"Talk to me, please."

"Why? Won't change nothing."

"Anything. I want us to be like we were before, sharing our woes and happiness."

"Ain't going to happen. I'm a man now."

She wasn't certain whether to laugh, cry, or rail at him. "Even men talk."

He muttered an oath.

Diana fought for calm. "Please?"

"Very well, have it your way. You was having trouble enough getting food for yourself, much less me, so I had no other choice except to run away, all right?"

She slumped. "I would have starved before you went without. Surely you must know that."

"Why do you think I left? I wanted you to have enough."

"Oh, Peter." She threw her arms around him and prayed for a kind response.

He finally hugged her.

Diana's sorrow broke free, tears rolling down her cheeks. He'd suffered cruel beatings, most likely starved, and God knew what else because he'd looked out for her. "I had Father's old room rented a week after you left, and then I had tenants in the others. There was enough for both of us, even some money left to educate you properly. I kept telling you I'd see to your welfare."

He released her and squirmed away. "I can take care of meself."

"No, you can't and it's myself." She swiped away tears. "You're with me now so you don't have to pretend to be uneducated like the crew. Once we return to England, everything will be better than it had been. I promise."

"I ain't going. I have to stay with me captain."

She resisted shaking him. "Are you mad? He beat you."

"Did not. He never laid a finger on me."

"Then who did? One of his filthy crew?"

"None of them touched me, neither. It was just a whipping. If me captain can take it, I can too." He pushed to his feet and crossed the room.

Diana followed. "Are you saying your captain was also whipped? You can't possibly believe it. The man put your life at risk. He abducted you."

"Did not. He ain't never been mean to me excepting for when it comes to his books."

She recalled Homer's *Iliad* on Tristan's lap. A large volume and a gentleman's read, or a brute's weapon. "He beat you with his books?"

Peter laughed.

She kept herself from shouting. "Stop that at once. If he beat you, I want to know."

"I've been trying to tell you. He forces me to learn Latin, Spanish, history, and no end of boring things even when I told him I have no use for it."

Good heavens, Peter was more deluded about Tristan than she'd guessed or he'd become a superb liar during their separation. "He educates you, yet doesn't notice how poorly you speak?"

Peter rolled his eyes. "He's just like you, always telling me to talk properly. I learned not to around the other men. When I spoke like you, they pushed and punched me asking if I thought I was better than them." He shoved both hands through his hair, dragging the locks off his shoulders. "I even told the Captain what they said, but did he listen? No. He still gives me lessons to do every day and helps me with them unless he's with Canela."

"Canela? A crew member?"

"Of course not. She's a beautiful island woman he fancies."

Diana's belly twisted.

Before she could recover her indifference or dislike for Tristan, Peter took in the cabin. "Where'd you get this vessel? Are you having to pay for its use?"

Once they were in Mozambique, she would. She lowered her face. "No."

"Because you intend to get me friends hanged?"

"They are not your friends. And no, I'm not going to get them hanged. They did it on their own by committing piracy without my help. The Lady Lark belongs to Benedict Bishop. If it weren't for his kind assistance, I wouldn't have had the means to come here and rescue you. Once we're home, he's promised to pay for your schooling as he worries about your safety and future."

Peter stared. "That makes no sense at all."

"What doesn't?"

"Mr. Bishop told you he wanted to help? Why? What does he get out of the bargain? Oh my God." He put up his hands. "You haven't promised to wed him, have you?"

To hide her shame, she focused on smoothing her clothes. "No. The man's old enough to be our father. He knew how worried I was about you, so he helped willingly as he's also concerned for your safety."

"What makes you so sure he ain't the one who put me in harm's way?"

She frowned. "What do you mean?"

"I've heard things about him from me shipmates."

"They're pirates, Peter. Crude, vicious beasts without courage. Listen to them now."

Several wailed below from where her men had taken them. One made a coarse noise. Something crashed.

Another man cried out. "Captain, help us!"

"My men are having difficulty negotiating the ladder." Tristan spoke as a noble born to a manor rather than a pirate in a ship's hold. "They need time to get down the steps. Especially Cook. He's missing a limb. Allow me to assist him."

She rubbed her temple, not knowing how to react to such thoughtfulness, from a pirate no less. One who fancied a beautiful island girl and had claimed Diana wanted the same as him.

Not likely. She needed him to hang.

* * * *

Tristan found the accommodations abominable but expected no better since Diana believed he and his men were going to die, anyway. Her crew had pushed them inside the hold unconcerned as to the stuffy air and stifling heat. Or where they might land. He was lucky, his book safely beneath his arm, even after he'd stumbled over a small cage and came to rest against a barrel holding something solid but slightly fetid.

Given the splashing sounds and his men's snarls or curses, Tristan guessed their beds weren't as nice. He had no way to know, the space so dark he might have been blind.

The others panicked, the new situation pushing them toward quick sobriety. One even prayed.

Tristan kicked the barrel for their attention. "Quiet."

They grew still. The hull's groans and slapping sea filled the silence.

"Captain." Henry Wells kept his voice low. "What do you want us to do?"

A curious question. Although Tristan was in charge, his power wasn't absolute. True rule lay with his men. Each had a voice and vote on what action to take. If they didn't like the outcome or anything he suggested, they could easily replace or kill him.

The prospect of facing Newgate and the gallows made them eager to leave him with this mess. He used his shoulder to wipe sweat from his face. "I don't intend to sail to England, nor do I intend to hang." He spoke as quietly as Wells had. "Are you men with me?"

Whispered "ayes" filled the space.

"Then keep quiet."

When they were relatively still, he lifted his face. Diana's light footsteps sounded in the cabin overhead. She was either dressing for bed or undressing. He preferred the latter and having her clothed in nothing more than what he desired.

Right now, he had to be patient and wait.

Above, someone cried out briefly and softly, followed by a thud.

One of her men had fallen to James's forceful blows.

* * * *

Diana craved a bath, clean clothes, cool air, and conversation, needing to talk the most. Peter still hadn't rewarded her for his rescue. If anything, his behavior had gotten worse. He laid on his mattress, his scarred back to her, and feigned sleep.

There wouldn't be any rest for her tonight. She dreaded closing her eyes, fearing the moment she did he'd leave the cabin and help the others escape so they could return to piracy. Never in her wildest worries had she considered Peter would want to remain with those animals.

She rested her arm over her eyes and tightened her fist at the noise below. The pirates alternately swore and moaned like men facing certain death. Served them right. At least their misery would end. Hers, on the other hand, was about to begin.

Every time she considered Bishop's carnal demands, her stomach rolled. Enduring his attention would be hideous. Refusing wasn't an option. He'd made it quite clear he'd deliver Peter to the authorities if she didn't obey immediately, wantonly, willingly. A fourteen-year-old boy would hang because she hadn't done everything Bishop wanted.

Bloody beast. Same as all males. They always wanted, expecting women to submit.

No different from her father, a cold, indifferent man. His church had meant more to him than his own son, while his daughter had meant nothing at all. Her only good, he'd once said, was the comfort she could bring to his home by cooking, cleaning, sewing. Once she'd finished those dreary tasks, he'd expected her to work for his church and deliver her will to his.

Diana had obeyed but never agreed with his beliefs. Women hadn't been born to yield. Women could yield. They might even enjoy doing so, but only with the right man. One they desired. First came desire. Respect and love followed.

She could only deliver her heart to a man like that.

Even if Tristan wasn't facing the gallows, he wasn't the one she needed. His skin was warm against hers but what of it. He was handsome as the devil, yet there was the rub, because he was also brutal, violent, taking what he wanted. His mouth on hers was something she refused to consider, though she could hardly forget how he'd spoken calmly when she'd railed. She insulted and he smiled. He claimed she wanted the same as him. Diana did not. She wanted to be home. She needed to be free.

Her eyes flew open. A sound or voice had awakened her. Reclined on her side, she faced away from the door. An oil lamp had gone out, telling her she'd slept far too long, recklessly too.

Oh my God. Peter.

Diana rolled onto her back but didn't check his mattress, knowing he wasn't there or in the cabin.

Tristan was. His long legs, muscular calves, and thighs blocked her view of the door. He'd placed his precious book on the table. The volume was safe. She was not.

Before she could push to a sitting position or think to fight, he straddled her, his hands circling her wrists, holding her arms to each side. His touch didn't harm, at least not yet.

Her heart pounded.

He offered a smile.

How dare he be so smug. "Release me at once."

He tightened his grip slightly and studied her mouth, then her eyes. "Violet." Awe flooded his face. "I wondered about your eye color but never expected this."

She pushed and writhed but did no good against his strength. Breathless, she stopped. "What have you done with Peter?"

Tristan stared at her eyes. "Amazing color, quite beautiful. Fits your dark hair and pale skin perfectly."

She rammed her thighs into him.

He held her more firmly. "Stop that."

"Not until you tell me what you've done with my brother." She slammed into him.

He scooted down and trapped her legs. "Peter's on the main deck with the other men."

"He's a child and proved it by helping you escape."

"This wasn't his doing, and you've no reason to fear for his safety. I have James, my quartermaster, looking after him."

"A bloody pirate, you mean. The same as you. Perhaps even worse than you."

"No. James is a good man." A haunted look touched Tristan's features before he shook off whatever had troubled him and became casual. "He saved my life. He'll take great care to watch your brother."

She wanted to retort but couldn't reconcile her indignation with Tristan's previous anguish and the mean scratches she'd left on his cheek. Dried blood had gone black, the surrounding skin swollen and red. "What do you mean he saved your life?"

"Just that, ask no more for I'll give you no other answer."

"The only thing I want from you is my freedom."

He stroked her wrists. "You want the same as me."

She pushed against him, straining with the effort.

He tightened his grip, proving she wasn't a match for his strength. If he chose to take her now, she'd have no choice except to allow him what he willed.

She didn't beg. Wouldn't. Not to him or any man, including Bishop. They could conquer her body but not her spirit, never her heart. Reconciled to her fate, she grew limp as she could, pulse racing. "Take what you've come for and be quick about it."

"I shan't be quick, Diana. With you, I'll never be quick."

Heat stung her face and throat. "You won't be the last, either."

His gray eyes darkened as storm clouds do, danger building in them. "What do you mean?"

"When you're finished with me, I go to the man to whom I truly belong. Nothing will change that no matter how long you intend to take raping me."

Despite her harsh words, he didn't flinch or frown.

"Who is this man with whom you'd willingly lie?"

"Willingly?" She laughed. "You believe I've chosen him any more than I've chosen you? The fact is you've driven me to him."

"What do you mean? Who is he? Tell me."

She turned her face away.

Tristan brushed his lips over her cheek and buried his face in her hair.

Her scalp tingled. She could scarcely draw enough air to speak. "I said, be quick about it."

He took his time, his lips soft and warm against her temple and ear, breath heated and sweet.

She tensed even more, determined to resist.

"Why do you fight me when you want this as much as I do?" He kissed her jaw.

Pleasure rushed through her, delight making her come alive as she never had, the feelings new, troubling, far too exciting. Her lids slid down.

"Tell me who the man is."

Tristan's scent surrounded her, surprisingly clean, tinged with musk.

"Tell me, Diana."

"Why?"

He suckled her neck.

She trembled, an unfamiliar ache building between her legs, tension mounting within her. Flustered, she fought his hold and failed, growing weak from his imposing size. However, she refused to surrender, wanting him to know what he'd done to her. "He's a wealthy merchant who agreed to help me find Peter if I promised to become his mistress, which I shall."

"Never." His breath skipped over her skin. "No one will have you but me."

She fumed, her previous weakness gone. "You'll take me. You'll never have me."

"Nor will the wealthy merchant. He owns this ship? Is his name Benedict Bishop?"

Tristan kept surprising her, giving her no defense. She pushed against him. He eased back. "Is that the merchant's name?"

"Yes. He's the man to whom I belong."

"Not any longer."

* * * *

Tristan brushed his lips against hers, teasing, testing. Diana softened beneath him, proving what he needed to know.

Gently, he eased his tongue into her mouth. The world spun, her thrilling heat snatching his breath and thoughts. He explored her intimately, deepening his kiss. Her taste soon belonged to him, his to her. They were no longer separate. He hoped she'd suckle him and deliver pleasure.

She resisted briefly, then coaxed his tongue deeper into her mouth. Pleased beyond belief, he released her wrists, slid his hands over her palms, and laced their fingers.

She yielded fully, her rigid nipples pebbled against his chest. She smelled like an English spring, soft rain mixed with fragrant flowers. He didn't finish their kiss until she smelled of him. Slowly, he withdrew his tongue, lifted his head, and struggled for breath. "Open your eyes."

Arousal brightened them, her mouth still wet with him, lips slightly bruised from his impassioned kiss.

His spirits soared. "You desired that."

"I did not."

As a clergyman's daughter, she was a poor liar and would never fool him. "Then I'll have to continue until you do."

He kissed her, tenderly at first, then hard and greedy. She whimpered in what sounded like pleasure but held back, not giving herself fully. Finally, she tore her mouth free.

He pressed his lips to her neck. Her breath spilled out on a contented sigh, telling him what words never could. "I'll not deliver you to Bishop. You belong to me."

She went rigid. "I'm not yours to give. I'll go to Bishop myself. I'd lie with the devil to save Peter from the life you've forced him into."

She still believed he'd abducted the boy, refusing to listen to what really occurred, the monster Bishop was. Tristan wasn't going to argue the point now. He trailed kisses from her throat to her cheek to her temple, tasting her dewy, achingly soft skin.

She whimpered. "Stop it."

He did, though not because of her words. Diana wanted him, had from the start, her desire evident in her kiss. Contempt didn't fuel her resistance, but worry over Peter's safety, the boy's future. Tristan wasn't about to cause her more pain. She was his to protect. "No harm will come to Peter."

She laughed, the sound remarkably derisive and cruel. "Indeed, as he'll be away from you."

"He'll remain with us."

Diana scowled. "I'll not have Peter become a common criminal. You believe reading a fancy book makes you a gentleman?"

"You believe wealth and position makes Bishop one? You'll not return to him. You're coming with me. I've had enough of this life, and a ship's no place for a woman and children."

Her eyes rounded. "You think I'll bear your bastards?"

His chest tightened. He strained to breathe. "If you were a man, you'd be dead for saying such a thing."

"Whether I die here with you or with Bishop matters little. Do your worst, Captain."

To what end? Tristan craved her pleasure and acceptance, not heartless disdain. He loosened his grip. "Do you need to wound me so badly, Diana?"

Embarrassment flooded her features. She averted her gaze.

He squeezed her hands gently. "You'll not bear my bastards."

His children wouldn't go through what he had. They'd have a name, respect, and her as their mother. He couldn't do anything less.

"Why won't I be bearing them?" She looked at him. "Has the task already gone to the island girl you enjoy?"

So, Peter had told her about Canela. Pity the boy didn't know Canela wasn't a rival for Diana.

"I have no children, legitimate or otherwise. I've taken great pains to avoid them. Peter's been telling you things, hasn't he? It appears you've been listening. Good. Proves your interest. Or would it be desire?"

"Neither. But believe what you will. Whatever I say won't change matters."

Only because he already knew her better than she did. He unlaced their fingers, straightened, and eased Diana's shirt up, baring her breasts. The soft mounds were ripe and snowy, her nipples pale pink. A deep flush stained her throat and face, but she didn't stop him.

Delighted, he cupped her exquisitely soft flesh. Primal need gripped him. He fought for control against taking her, what should have been an easy matter, but was far more complicated because he wanted her desire, not obedience. Better to wait. If frustration didn't kill him first. Her nipples were erect against his calloused palms, skin heated and moist, her arousal undeniable.

She struggled for breath, color tinted her cheeks, and lust hooded her eyes.

He squeezed her breasts and thumbed her nipples.

Her lips parted. She blinked slowly, looking drugged.

He was beyond intoxicated. "I see you desire this."

She blew out a breath. "No."

"Pity. You'll have to go through this and far more. The acts delightful, I can assure you. How else will you ever bear my children, with them having my last name the same as you?"

Confusion, then surprise flashed across her lovely features. "Wed you? Never." She cuffed his wrists as well as she could but didn't shove him away. "You'll hang the moment you return to England."

"We're not going there. We'll remain here."

"No." She pushed.

He captured her wrists in one hand, kept them above her head, and stroked her nipples. They couldn't get tighter. He drew one into his mouth and reeled at its faint salty taste, her musky skin.

She moaned. He suckled, then enjoyed her other nipple. She arched her back, delivering herself to him, approving his intimate attention.

He could have kept at this for days, but needed air, and eased back. "Look at me."

She stared at the wall behind him, lingering arousal, then dismay on her face. "Do what you want in this cabin. I haven't the strength to fight you. But know this, I'll not allow Peter to grow up in this barbaric land."

Her trust wouldn't be won easily, though he had to try. "I offer my word I'll have him educated as a gentleman, even providing the tutor, while you give me what I've missed most during these last years. A taste of home. An Englishwoman. Pure, virginal. You are a virgin, are you not?"

She blushed worse than before.

He didn't dare smile. "It would appear you are. So rare in these parts, the same as your lovely eyes and pale skin. I'm not about to deliver you to Bishop, nor allow you any freedom from me. You'll wed me, lie with me, bless me with many children, and never know another man's touch, save mine. You'll not only desire that, you'll surely be lost without it."

Something slammed into the door.

Diana flinched. Tristan looked over.

On the other side, feet shuffled, men muttered.

Chadwick Vincent's voice stood out. "She must be in there."

Tristan pulled down her shirt, pushed to his feet, and helped Diana to hers.

Voices rose. "Captain better not think he's getting all of her."

Vincent chuckled. "We each get fair shares in this prize, just like any other."

Someone kicked in the cabin door. Ten faces looked inside for Diana, the prize, Tristan's other men joining them.

Chapter 3

Diana locked her knees to keep from collapsing.

Pirates crammed into the cabin, leaving little room and not enough air.

A short man sporting a huge belly squeezed past the others. His front teeth and left ear were gone, his cheeks pockmarked. "We're here for our share."

Another man and then the rest demanded her flesh, everyone talking at once, each new pirate more horrible than the last.

Her legs went watery at what the coming moments would bring. No matter what Tristan had said about her never knowing anyone else's touch, he couldn't fight his entire crew.

She'd vowed to hate him, but didn't, couldn't, not even with his piracy and her belief he'd abducted Peter. Tristan could have easily raped her earlier. He'd offered marriage instead. He was a curious man, good and bad, hard yet tender. She didn't understand the paradox, but no longer wished him dead. A distinct possibility given how these animals leered, shouted, laughed, and jostled each other.

She shrank back and grabbed his arm.

"What are you doing?" He pried her hand off. "Hope you don't think I'm going to save you." Laughing, he pulled her in front of him. His hands fell so heavy on her shoulders she swayed. His fingers trailed casually to her nipples. "We take a vote on who gets her first."

Horrified, she looked over. Tristan shook her roughly, forcing her to face his men.

Her skin prickled at his unexpected betrayal, her foolishness in having believed in him after a few kisses and kind words. He'd proved he was no different from any man, caring only about himself.

Her throat ached at the painful truth, her rage mounting. "Coward."

He pulled her into him, making certain his stiffened shaft pressed against her buttocks, letting her know the male power he'd use to bring her to her knees.

"Best you watch what you say, Miss Fletcher." He stroked her neck.

She jerked away.

He yanked her back into him. "I say James Sullivan gets her first."

The crew complained loudly.

A pirate wearing a bright yellow scarf on his head shoved the others away. "Why him?"

Tristan dipped his hands lower, touched her nipples, and then held tight so she couldn't move. "He saved your necks. If not for James, we'd still be in the hold, not preparing to have our pleasure with this woman."

Some grumbled. Most laughed, then voted James the first share with Tristan getting the next, as captain. After him, the others would draw straws to decide their turns.

The pirate with the pocked face shook his head. "Excepting for young Peter. He's her brother."

"That right?" This man smiled wide enough to show his rotted teeth. "Well, miss, best you not scream. If Peter was to find out how much pleasure you was bringing us, we'd have to kill him. Understand?"

Bile rose to her throat, but she nodded.

Another man, near Tristan's height, worked his way through the others to where she stood. His hair was longer than Peter's, dark red threaded with gold. Freckles covered his bare chest and face. He appeared slightly younger than Tristan, but wore the same hard look in his brown eyes.

"I'll be taking her in here." He regarded his mates. "Clear out. Now."

The others streamed from the room.

"Enjoy yourself." Tristan pushed Diana into James Sullivan.

She wheeled around to strike Tristan.

He caught her wrist easily and glanced over her head. "Do her well, James, so some of her fight's gone when it's my turn. Miss Fletcher." He lifted her hand to his lips.

She yanked free and scratched his cheek.

He gave her a rough look. "You will regret that." On the way out, he slammed the door, leaving her to James.

He crowded her before she could blink.

She kicked his shins, clawed his neck, and tried to ram her knee into his groin.

He tightened his arm around her waist and finally slammed her onto the mattress.

Her breath whooshed out.

He trapped her beneath him, his hand over her mouth.

She bit him hard and tasted blood.

"Goddamn." He yanked his hand away, slapped his other one on her mouth, and pressed his lips to her ear. "Keep still, damn you. If Tristan sees one mark on you, only one, he'll have my head. Understand?"

Diana did. Tristan wanted this first act to go smoothly so she'd be unmarked for him, yielding and meek. Like bloody hell. Still, she nodded.

James gulped air and withdrew his hand slowly.

She dug her nails into his neck.

"Damnation." He twisted and squirmed against the scratching and her knee ramming into his inner thighs, heading for his groin. "To hell with this. You draw another drop of my blood or hit me where it truly hurts, and I'll not help you escape."

She stopped clawing and kicking him, though she didn't let go of his hair. "What are you saying?" She yanked hard to make certain she got an answer. "What do you mean?"

He pulled his hair from her fists and rolled off her. Sprawled on the mattress, he stared at the ceiling. His clawed chest pumped with his rough breaths. "No one on this ship will have you, except for Tristan, of course."

She'd been ready to kick James's ribs. She pulled back her foot and pushed up, uncertain how to react, bombarded by too many emotions. Relief because Tristan hadn't betrayed her after all. Shame for having doubted him. Confusion as to what this meant.

She wanted to believe Tristan's decision to trick the men went beyond carnal desire. He'd begun to like her as a woman and person. Good sense told her he probably didn't want any man taking her before he did, his pride not allowing such a thing.

Hopelessly confused, she squeezed her fists so much they hurt. "He wants me for himself? Like bloody hell."

"My duty's to protect you from the crew, not from Tristan. With him, you're on your own. Though I would advise you not to fight your husband. It ain't right. It surely ain't natural."

"I'm not wedding him."

"You are. Quit resisting what's going to be, whether you want it or not. Tristan's bringing Peter down here as we speak. When the time's right, we'll leave the ship."

"Why are you helping him?"

"Tristan?" James smiled. "He's my friend. Even if he wasn't, he saved my life. I'll owe him forever."

Diana lifted her face. Footfalls and loud laughter sounded from the main deck. The pirates possibly drinking as they had on the beach, egged on by Tristan.

He'd saved James's life, yet earlier Tristan had said the man had done the same for him. "How did he save you?"

James spit on his fingers and wiped blood off his chest. "No time to get into it now."

"Then how did you save Tristan? He told me you had."

"He would. That's the kind of man he is." Finished with cleaning his chest, James grabbed her arm.

She pulled back. "What are you doing?"

"Checking for marks." He shoved up her sleeve, studied her forearm, and nodded. After examining her other arm, he tugged her shirt over her right shoulder, exposing her breast to the edge of her nipple.

She squirmed away. "Stop it."

"Quiet. You want the others to come in here to watch?"

"No, only Tristan so he can see what you're doing."

James's face flamed bright red. "I'm not trying to rape you. Now be still."

Wasn't easy. He pulled her shirt over her shoulders and viewed her bare skin as a physician might.

At last, he nodded. "No harm done."

To her. The scratches she'd left on him were deeper than the ones she'd given Tristan. "I suppose I should apologize for what I did to you."

He shrugged. "I've known worse."

She believed him. "Who lashed my brother?"

Footfalls neared the door. James glanced over.

She tapped his hand. "Who harmed him?"

"Ask Tristan. It's his place to tell you, not mine." He stood and faced the door.

Peter slipped in first, followed by Tristan. He stared at the claw marks on James's chest and neck, then frowned at Diana.

She deserved his anger for doubting him but wasn't in the mood to ask for his forgiveness. She padded to Peter. "Are you all right?"

"Peter's fine." Tristan pulled her to the other side of the room.

"Let go of me."

He tightened his grip, not enough to bruise but enough to imprison.

She yanked her arm. "I want to speak to my brother."

"Speak to me. You've yet to thank me for saving you."

"I shall when you promise to return Peter to England."

Tristan released her arm and looked over. "Peter, come here."

He did so without pause.

"Even if it would be safe for you, do you want to go back to England?"

"No." Peter glared at her. "You ain't making me, neither. You try, I'll run away to be with me captain."

This was a nightmare she couldn't awake from. "You can't be serious about staying in this uncivilized land."

"I'm a man, Diana. You'll not tell me what to do." He made a face like a petulant child, but lost his nasty expression before he faced Tristan. "Anything else?"

"Stay in here until I tell you otherwise. Keep close to James at all times."

"Aye." He joined the man.

Diana strode to the cabin's windows.

Tristan followed and touched her arm.

"Don't." She pulled away. "You're not my husband."

"I will be." He spoke as a pirate would but there was also yearning in his eyes.

Her frustration warred with desire until she recalled what Peter had said about Canela. Diana had no idea whether the girl was the only woman Tristan had or if there were a dozen more. Nor did she know the life he led, except as a pirate. She doubted marriage would make him want her and no one else. She wrapped her arms around herself. "How right you are."

"About what?"

"That you'll be my husband. However, only because you've given me no choice in the matter. By poisoning my brother's mind against his own country and taking over my crew, you've forced me to remain here. I've no means of returning to England without this ship. I'm quite certain your mates intend to take or scuttle it. So, I will be your wife, Captain Kent. But by no means will you have me. You will never have me. Take what you wish, use me as a husband uses a wife, for it will surely be your right, but it's all you'll get."

He lifted her braid and kissed the ends. "If I demand more?"

Her belly fluttered when she should have been immune to his charm. "You'll be sorely disappointed."

"Is that what you think?" He stroked her bottom lip. "Know this. I'm never discouraged because I never give up until I get exactly what I want."

Warmth flooded her.

"Tristan." James motioned him over.

He crossed the room.

* * * *

Tristan huddled close to James who had his ear to the cabin door. "What is it?"

"Some of the men are back and drawing straws to see who'll have Miss Fletcher after we're supposed to." He spoke as quietly as Tristan had. "Best you herd them to the main deck and get as many spirits into them and the others as you can. Otherwise, I may have to put my back into this."

"Allow me a moment with the lady first." He joined Diana. "In my absence, do whatever James says. He's helping us escape. Don't fight him, and no matter what he does to the others, don't scream."

She looked appalled. "What is he planning to do?"

"Just follow his orders and keep quiet. Now give me a fond farewell." Without waiting for her to obey, he slanted his mouth over hers and slipped his tongue inside, enchanted at her glorious heat and wondrous taste.

Soft moans escaped her. Their tongues danced. No matter how close she was to him, she was still too far away. Her scent captivated, making him long for more than a simple kiss. When he angled his head for greater access, she pressed against him, her mouth willing and wanton beneath his, denying him nothing.

His ears buzzed.

At last, Tristan needed a full breath and so did she, their mouths parting. His cock was painfully hard, his balls so tight they ached. She stroked his chest like a woman born for the task.

He kissed her velvety cheek. "Well done."

She fought a smile. For him, the first of many.

He released her and motioned Peter over. When the boy was at his side, Tristan clamped his shoulder. "Guard your sister well."

* * * *

The moment Tristan left, his loud laughter sounded outside the door. Whoops and hollers from the men followed, along with crude comments.

She leaned close to Peter. "What's he up to?"

"Fixing this mess you put us in."

"Miss Fletcher." James spoke softly. "It would be best if you wait on the mattress with the blanket over your trousers and your shirt pulled off your shoulders, baring them."

"What?"

"You need to look as if we've had you. Unwind your braid and muss your hair too. No matter what happens, don't scream."

Peter grabbed a shirt off the floor. "Should I gag her?"

She frowned.

James smiled. "No need. She'll keep quiet if she wants to escape."

Although Diana longed to flee this wretched ship, she feared what would happen next. Fighting panic, she loosened her hair, bared her shoulders, and perched on the bed.

The cabin door flew open. The pirate wearing the yellow scarf reached her in an instant and grabbed her shirt, ready to tear it from her.

James slammed his pistol butt against the man's skull with a sickening crack. The pirate crumpled without a fight, or words, or even a cry. After James had bound and gagged him securely, he and Peter pulled him to the far corner from immediate view.

Another pirate staggered inside, drunk but offering more fight, throwing wild punches, kicking and scratching as she had.

Peter swore and hit him soundly in the jaw.

He collapsed.

James slapped the boy on his back. "Well done."

"I'll do even better with the next one."

Diana shuddered. "I thought you said these men were your friends."

"Not him."

James chuckled. He and Peter gagged and fettered the pirate, then returned to their posts. The next man and the next came inside.

Soon, felled pirates filled the cabin to near overflowing.

Joining them, Tristan viewed the carnage and nodded. "Good work." He tucked his volume beneath his arm, helped Diana with her shoes, then to her feet. "Peter, her jacket."

He tossed it.

Tristan handed the garment to her. "Put this on. Time to go."

He led her through the ship and across the moon-washed deck littered with bound-and-gagged men, all unconscious.

She stepped around their bodies the same as the others. "You plan to leave them here?"

Tristan stopped. Moonlight silvered his eyes and hair, turning his eyebrows and stubble even darker, making him look like a dangerous angel.

He glanced around. "Would you prefer to take a few with us?" He made an elaborate bow and gave her a roguish grin. "Your wish is my command."

She nearly laughed. "I was wondering if you're leaving them here to die."

"Hardly." He pulled her toward the rail and a skiff.

She held back. "Are we taking this to the beach and your ship?"

"No."

"Then where?"

"You'll see."

* * * *

With three strong males to work the oars, they made swift progress away from the Lady Lark.

Diana twisted in her seat, trying to determine their destination, since they appeared to be putting out to sea. Surely, Tristan hadn't planned to row to the African coast. That would be madness. The skiff was far too small for the journey.

James and Peter kept their peace, seemingly unconcerned.

Diana wished she could trust as easily but wanted answers, and faced Tristan.

He regarded her.

Her pulse quickened and her limbs grew heavy with desire. When they'd been on the ship, she had no trouble denying he'd ever wed her. Now, the notion seemed inevitable and far less disturbing than living out her days with Bishop. Arousal blunted her caution at the man who would soon be her husband.

He rowed with grace and power, his face damp from sea spray, neck and shoulders tensed. Hard labor had sculpted his strong arms and body. His direct, unashamed gaze spoke of things he'd seen that she could only imagine and might very well fear. Yet he still fascinated her, and she wasn't certain why.

She'd always hoped a quiet, unassuming man would woo, then bed her, pleased to have her make the decisions. Tristan would have great difficulty doing so. Yielding wasn't in his nature. Ruling was.

The wind pressed her shirt against her breasts. She didn't bother to hide what he'd already seen. Soon, he'd be intimately familiar with her flesh, while she'd know his male passion.

Carnal hunger crossed his face. "Best you get some sleep."

No need to ask why. Once they arrived at their destination, he'd take her, expecting her full desire and participation in every act. A dull ache settled between her legs, same as earlier. The feeling was frustrating yet oddly pleasant.

Shaken from desire and uncertainty, she turned away.

Moist air laced with salt pulled at her hair. The heavy moon sparkled on water that held more lights than the star-splashed sky. Sea and air stretched forever, one touching the other, making her feel too small and ache for the familiar.

She had no idea where England was from here. Perhaps her homeland no longer existed. Her quest didn't. She'd failed to rescue her brother whom she no longer knew or recognized. She'd offered her own happiness and freedom in exchange for Peter's safety, protection he refused. Soon she'd be the wife of Captain Tristan Kent, a dangerous angel who caused her to want him so easily. Her passion was already his. Her heart, though, would have to resist.

He'd said he wanted a taste of home, an Englishwoman, not necessarily her, since they didn't know each other.

Despite the longing she'd seen in his eyes, lasting love might not matter to him. She'd always yearned for someone to cherish her. Not likely in a marriage that had come about as theirs would. She'd know a few sensual nights followed by too many lonely days that she was afraid to face. The hours ahead were as unfathomable as where the sea touched the sky, as out of reach and unknown. She hadn't an idea of where she'd be a day from now, much less a year, or when the moment would arrive when she no longer recognized herself, as she no longer knew her brother.

Heartsore and weary, she slid from the plank seat to the hull, curled up, and escaped into sleep.

* * * *

Tristan pulled in his oars and rested them to the side. He removed his waistcoat and draped the garment over Diana.

She stirred a hunger in him he found nearly painful, as any man would, yet she didn't flaunt her beauty. As a reverend's daughter, she'd probably learned to be quiet and plain.

Imagining Diana in either role was impossible. Her loveliness was undeniable, her courage nothing short of a miracle. Never had he known a woman to take the risks she had. Although her strong will rankled at times, her spirit mostly impressed.

He captured a lock of her hair. Her tress whispered across his palm, then floated on the wind, black as night, smelling fresh and flowery, like a proper Englishwoman.

Everything he'd left behind was here now with Diana, but only because of Peter and her sweet rescue. Back home, she would never have looked Tristan's way. Circumstances wouldn't have allowed a reverend's daughter to wed a man who'd had nothing, once made his living as a mariner, and then was a pirate. Of course, no one expected more of someone who came from poor beginnings. He'd surely had the humblest.

He lifted his face to the stars, knowing them far better than he had his father, a man who'd given him a name and nothing else. Best not to recall what his mother had done to fill their bellies. Most times, they hadn't food or a place to live. They'd left Wales, which had been misery itself, and came to England and found the new land far worse. Going to sea at ten hadn't posed a hardship for him. Working on ships was a way to eat and survive.

In those early days, his shipmates hadn't thought him strange for not being able to read or write, since most also lacked the skills. Eventually, he'd taught himself those things, craving knowledge only books could offer and wanted to use his newfound talents to get a better life. That's when the men thought him odd.

Tristan hardly cared. He wanted to be educated and clean. He needed to be free. He craved respect.

Once, he'd even hoped for love.

Diana's delicate profile was to him, her lips parted in sleep, hands pillowing her head.

She'd agreed to be his wife, nothing else. He could take what he wished from her, but she'd offer nothing freely. She considered him uncivilized and without redemption, certainly not a man she would have chosen for herself.

James cleared his throat. "You all right?"

Tristan nodded. He picked up his oars and rowed hard. No matter Diana's initial appraisal of him, he would change her mind and have her desire.

Chapter 4

Gentle heat awakened and disoriented Diana. She wasn't certain where the warmth came from, unless she'd brought an oil lamp too close to her mattress. She reached out to push the thing away and touched something much larger instead, quite solid and muscular.

Her eyes snapped open. She snatched her hand from Tristan's calf and squinted at the sun trailing white light across a flawless blue sky.

Tristan's hair was tangled and damp. Whiskers shadowed his face but didn't hide her scratch marks. She regretted her assaults and should have apologized but was too ashamed to bring up the subject. "Have you rowed the entire night?"

"Rested some. We all did." He winked. "But I appreciate your concern."

He was so gentle and disarming she smiled.

He flushed and reached down.

She went weak, expecting him to touch her.

He removed his waistcoat from her lap.

Her heart turned over at him having covered her. She should have thanked him for his kindness but was now too shy. She pushed up and looked over. Beyond the rising mist, a faint outline signaled land. "Is this another part of Madagascar?"

"A series of islands, one of which is mine."

Surprise raced through her. "We're to live on your island?"

"The one to the far left. The only habitable land in these parts."

Evergreens carpeted the isle. A small section to the right was rocky and same reddish color as Madagascar. There was also a brief beach dotted with palms and other trees, the long, flat leaves swaying in the wind.

No buildings, though.

Pink patches floated up. "What is that?"

"Birds." He raised his face, watching their flight. "We call them flamingoes."

They trailed across the sky creating a lovely scene, but didn't answer where she and Tristan might live, not to mention Peter and James. There wasn't even one hut on the sand.

Close to shore, the men jumped out and pulled the skiff onto the beach. James and Peter faced the land and raised one arm as they might in greeting.

Tristan offered Diana his hand.

His palm was oddly comforting, his youth and vigor evident in how easily he lifted her into his arms, his embrace strong yet tender. There were blue flecks in his gray eyes and lines at the corners, proving he'd laughed often and well.

His heat warmed more than the sun had. His heart's impressive thundering encouraged her to snuggle close. She melted into him, their mouths near enough for a kiss. Diana wanted that badly, even though she shouldn't have.

Voices sounded in the distance.

Tristan looked over, carried her to the shade, and put her on her feet.

Two riders approached on horseback. Their geldings were magnificent, both men young and handsome. Their long, straight hair was dark brown, features a blend of islander and European, though she couldn't determine which group or nationality. Each wore breeches and a brace of pistols over his cinnamon-colored chest.

The man on the right stared at Tristan, his scowl deadly.

Alarmed, she touched Tristan's hand. "Who are they?"

"Island men loyal to me."

"Are you quite sure? The one on the right appears angry."

"Adamo's most likely thinking about Canela."

Diana's heart caught. Canela surely lived here and was either Adamo's sister or would-be-lover.

Diana couldn't blame him for whatever resentment and jealousy he harbored. Tristan was a splendid man, tall, strong, commanding. Canela must have thought so too, unless she was blind.

Tristan spoke to Adamo and the other young man in fluent French.

Diana had studied the language but had little command and didn't recognize this dialect.

They wheeled their horses around and departed. Surely, not to get Canela and bring her here.

Diana ached with worry. "I need to ask you something."

Tristan regarded her, his manner accepting, attention complete.

Nothing like what she'd expected. Most men simply ignored women or look annoyed when interrupted for any reason not centering on them. She was reluctant to ask him about Canela, not wanting to challenge his honor or fidelity, but also afraid to learn the truth.

She slumped. "Are we staying on the beach?" After saying a few words over them as ship's captain, he could pronounce them wed and take her here.

Tristan smoothed her hair. "Adamo and Phillipe left to fetch the priest. After the vows we'll ride to my plantation."

Surprised, she wanted to ask what he meant, but he'd already crossed the sand to James and Peter. They discussed something in low tones, then looked at the sea.

She fought anxiety and excitement in equal measure at the prospect of Tristan's plantation, Canela, marriage, coupling. Exhausted, Diana rested against a palm.

The men returned with three geldings. Phillipe handed a small sack to Peter. Adamo tossed a pouch to Tristan. A short, swarthy man, who wore a long brown tunic and a crucifix, joined them. After Tristan greeted him in what sounded like Portuguese, they strolled away.

Peter stopped at her side. "Here."

She recognized the bananas and grapes her brother had taken from the sack, but not slices of a yellow fruit or vegetable that glistened in the sun.

She touched the rough edge. "What is this?"

"Pineapple. Quite tasty." Juice flowed over his mouth and dripped onto his chest.

"Good heavens." She slapped his arm lightly. "You were taught better manners than that."

"We ain't in England, all right? You want this or not?"

Her belly's insistent growling answered for her. She gobbled pineapple slices, two bananas, and grape clusters, then sucked her fingers clean, something she would never have done back home. After less than a day on this island, she'd already forgotten her proper English training but didn't have time to dwell on the matter.

Tristan and the priest approached.

The holy man faced her and Tristan. James stood at his captain's side, Peter at hers. She felt wholly surrounded and completely alone.

Gently, Tristan took her hand.

His touch was so reassuring she lifted her face to his, loving his tender smile. The priest spoke. She had no idea what he said. Tristan's eyes held her. They possessed. He seemed to care if she accepted him.

At last, the priest wound down and fell silent.

Diana couldn't breathe. "Is it over?"

They were now man and wife and he'd take her?

"Not yet." He squeezed her hand. "The priest wants your answer as to whether you'll have me or not."

"Oh." Pushing caution aside, she nodded. "I will. I mean, I do."

Tristan kissed her knuckles and spoke to the priest. The man resumed the ceremony only to stop again. "Now, it's my turn." Tristan bumped her arm. "Should I say yes?"

She enjoyed his playfulness more than she should. "I believe you say I do."

"As you wish." Grinning, he spoke his vow in English and Portuguese. The priest said something she guessed was a blessing.

"Nearly over." Tristan faced her. "Lift your hair."

"Why?"

"Because I asked you to do so and quite nicely too."

He had, rather than demand as many men would. Pleased, she did as he wanted.

From the pouch, Tristan removed a narrow silver band studded with diamonds. He fastened the necklace around her throat.

She touched the dazzling but odd piece.

Peter leaned in. "Now you're wed. You're wearing your marriage collar. On this island it shows a woman's been taken."

So another man wouldn't dare touch her. "I see." Tristan wore nothing to prove he belonged to her, not another, especially Canela. Foolish jealousy raced through Diana, heating her skin. "What shows your vow to me?"

He gathered her in his arms and claimed her mouth, delivering heavenly warmth and true affection, not mindless lust. She opened herself to him willingly, welcoming his tongue, savoring his taste as he enjoyed hers. His kiss grew heated not cruel, passionate not vulgar. She wreathed her arms around his neck and molded to him. Woman to man, wife to husband, lover to loved.

Tristan deepened his kiss, pleasuring her beyond reason, his stiffened shaft pressed against her mound. Her cleft grew even damper and wanting. He gave her such a sense of being cherished and protected she would have been content to kiss him for days on end.

Too soon, he eased his mouth from hers.

James and Peter cheered. The priest laughed.

She'd forgotten about them. "Enough."

Tristan smiled. "Well put. Now we ride to my plantation."

Peter snickered. "Wait till she sees it."

She was afraid to know what he meant. "Is it dreadful?"

Tristan lifted his eyebrows. "I'll let you be the judge."

Peter and James laughed.

She hoped they were teasing. Even if they weren't, she should be able to clean Tristan's house, hut, or whatever he and the others lived in. Three men couldn't mess things up that much.

Tristan led her to the blackest gelding. With Diana astride on the saddle, he mounted behind her, his muscular thighs pressed close, rigid rod against the seam between her buttocks, arm wrapped securely around her waist.

She blushed hotly.

They took the lead, the others falling well back. With no prying eyes on them, he rested his hand on her belly and brushed her mound. Her heart stalled, then beat far too quickly. The horse climbed a narrow path through the forest and onto a rise. Tristan slipped his hand beneath her shirt, cupped her breast, and drew his thumb over her taut nipple.

She sagged into him.

He pressed his lips to her ear. "Do you find pleasure in this?"

His breath was hot, his touch unbearably pleasant. She struggled to think and speak. "Do you want me to?"

He stopped playing with her nipple.

She shouldn't have toyed with him as men often did with women, but couldn't help herself. Their days together had only begun, and she wanted him to take their vows seriously. To have their feelings grow, binding them to each other for all time so no other woman, not even Canela, would ever come between them.

He reined in the horse, wound the leather straps around the horn, and eased her face to his. She met his gaze as a reverend's daughter should, with studied innocence.

His smirk said she hadn't fooled him. "Already you crave my touch."

"Already you crave my flesh."

He laughed and kissed her quite hungrily. She smiled. He did too, their mouths still joined. Teasing gave way to passion, her desire as lusty as his growls and grunts. He cupped her mound, wordlessly stating she now belonged to him, no other man.

She didn't want anyone else.

After he was sated and she still hoped for more, he unwound the reins and prodded the gelding. At the highest point, forest still surrounded them, sweetly scenting the air, but in between the vegetation, there was a glorious view of the sea and surrounding valley. Pastures where countless cattle grazed and flooded rice fields.

Stunned, she gestured. "Everything here is yours?"

"It is." He wheeled his horse to the left and rode a short distance before reining in the gelding.

A brief clearing opened within the forest. Within it stood a sprawling stone structure that glistened white beneath the sun, its design similar to classical Greek buildings she'd seen in books. "My word. Did you build this or did you have it built?"

"I killed the man who once owned it."

Diana twisted to look at him.

As they rode closer, several shouts rose in French and another language she'd never heard. Thankfully, the tone was friendly and came from a large group of adult males and females along with a sprinkling of young children. The men approached first, wearing naught except breeches. Their smiles were wide and welcoming. So were the women's.

Diana could hardly believe their beauty, their complexions light brown, features exotic, dark hair hanging straight to their waists, their lush breasts quite naked. Some had leather marriage collars decorated with brightly tinted beads. All wore colorful silk cloths tied low on their hips, the fabric fluttering above their bare feet.

Tristan helped Diana from the horse.

The others reached them and dismounted.

A young woman ran up and threw herself into James's eager embrace. Laughing, he swung her in a full circle, then very nearly devoured her with his kiss. Two other young women sprinted to Peter.

The taller girl reached him first. Holding her hands behind her back, she regarded him shyly. "*Bonjour*, Pierre."

The other one pushed her aside and gave him a sultry smile.

Before they could touch him or he could do the same to them, Diana hurried their way.

Tristan grabbed her arm and pulled her back.

She fought him. "What are you doing?"

"Stopping you from interfering with Peter. It's not your place."

"Of course, it is. He's my brother. He's just a boy."

"Soon to be a man. Besides, you have your husband to please. After you've been washed and prepared by the women I intend to have you."

Diana went hot, cold, then back to hot, desire warring with her fear of the unknown. "As is your right, but I can surely wash myself."

"They can do so much faster."

He led Diana to the oddly designed mansion. Walled off on the outside, it opened into an interior courtyard before leading to the living areas.

They entered a cool, darkened hall.

Feet slapped the marble floor. "Tristan!"

An island girl ran up and threw herself into his arms.

He released Diana's hand.

Her stomach fell. So this was Canela, simply gorgeous and bare-breasted, looking to be no older than twenty.

The girl showered kisses on his cheeks and mouth.

Diana wanted to tear her apart but couldn't sink to playing the jealous fool, and stepped back.

Tristan grabbed her wrist and finally extricated himself from Canela. She promptly hung on to his arm, her cheek pressed to his biceps.

Diana pushed away hurt. "So this is how it is."

He gave her an odd look, then spoke to Canela in French.

Shock swept over her exquisite features followed by anger, her dark eyes blazing. Despite her outrage, she kept her tongue and stared at the diamond marriage collar.

"Canela."

She started at Tristan's voice, grew indifferent, and nodded. "I will tell the others what you desire."

She'd answered in heavily accented English rather than French.

As she padded down the hall, Diana pulled her wrist free and strode away. Tristan followed. At last, she stopped but kept her back to him. "You best take care."

"Why? What have you planned for me now?"

With those careless words, she forgot her wounded pride and indulged in righteous fury. How casually men treated women's feelings. They seduced or wooed and once they'd won a woman over they made the other rules in their own favor. Well, not here or with her. "It's what Adamo has planned. He hates you because he's in love with Canela, isn't he? He wants her but finds it impossible as she belongs to you."

"You belong to me, and your bath is waiting."

As if that made everything better.

Diana told herself she shouldn't mind if Tristan loved another woman or two hundred, yet she cared greatly. Already she wanted him for her own and hated herself for such weakness. "You forced me to wed you, and will soon force me to lie with you, and—"

"Keep behaving in this manner, and I'll wonder why I forced you at all."

"Do what you must, but hear this. You had better not use Canela or any other island woman for your pleasure from this moment forward."

He looked at her innocently. "Why Diana, are you jealous?"

She lifted her chin. "Civilized. At least until you betray me. The moment you allow another woman to so much as kiss you or you kiss her, I'll find another man. I'll lie with him and bear his children."

The feigned innocence evaporated, Tristan's features now dark and dangerous. "You had better think long and hard before you consider such a thing. Any man who dares touch as much as your little finger won't be long for this earth."

"Then I'll have to make quite certain my lover is very careful."

Tristan advanced so quickly Diana had to step back and ran into the wall.

He pulled her close. "You shan't have time for a lover. I intend to keep you quite busy."

His mouth was on hers, his kiss possessive and hard. Not even a moan could have escaped her. He used her fully, with a husband's right, and pressed his lean hips into hers, making certain she knew his arousal, her duty to satisfy him for as long as he desired.

She yielded. Not from fear but the feelings he stirred. She didn't want to wound him, nor did she want him to hurt her.

At last, he seemed to understand. His kiss grew tender and exploring, then finally torrid. Their tongues battled to see which one would fill the other's mouth. She won a few times and so did he, the bawdy sounds they made proving satisfaction.

When they'd finished, he looked sheepish.

Not knowing what to say, she stroked his cheek, careful not to touch the scratches she'd given him.

Smiling, he captured her hand, led her down the hall past numerous rooms, and stopped at the last. He pushed the door open and escorted her inside.

Polished white marble covered the floor, the same as in the hall, the ceilings high, windows large, facing trees and a clearing to show the distant water. It sparkled blue-green, matching the silk sheets on the large mahogany bed.

Never had she witnessed anything as imposing or as inviting. Given what had transpired between her and Tristan in the hall, she had no doubt what would soon happen in here. Their bedchamber for all time.

The room sported low tables, a large armoire, chairs, a basin, and a metal tub. Two bare-breasted young women filled the thing with steaming water and scented oil.

Tristan spoke to them in French. They padded to Diana and pulled at her clothes to remove them.

"Stop that at once." She pushed their hands away. "I can bathe myself."

Tristan cupped her chin. "They don't understand English. Please, allow them to assist you. I'll return shortly."

He gave her a quick peck on her lips, said something to the young women, and then was out the door and closing it. His footfalls faded in the hall.

The women stripped Diana, leaving only the diamond collar. They scrubbed her until she glowed pink and washed her hair twice. Once they'd dried her completely, the prettiest girl grabbed a container of reddish powder and tried to apply the tint to Diana's nipples.

Shocked, she twisted away and started.

Canela stood near the closed door, her chin lifted in challenge.

Diana's first reaction was to hide her nudity. She faced her instead. "What are you doing in here?"

Loathing shone in Canela's eyes, then insolence. "How sad it will be for Tristan when you cannot satisfy him."

So rouging a woman's nipples was Tristan's idea. Given Canela's comment, she'd gladly done so for him many times.

She wouldn't any longer, not if Tristan expected to share his wife's bed. Diana gestured for the young woman to apply the rouge.

Once she'd finished, the other girl tied violet silk around Diana's hips. The fabric fell so low it barely covered the curls between her legs, the cloth knotted in front, allowing Tristan to see her thighs and to have ready access to what he craved most.

The young women finished arranging Diana's hair. Her tresses flowed over her breasts. Her reddened nipples peeked through. The plainer girl rubbed a sticky white substance into Diana's navel and seated a large diamond inside.

She couldn't believe what they'd done to her, a reverend's daughter. Despite her bravado with Canela, Diana grew fevered at what Tristan would expect from her in his bed.

His feet slapped the hall floor.

Both women hurried Canela to a passage hidden behind the armoire. The furniture creaked into place and snapped shut.

Blood pounded in Diana's ears.

Tristan came inside and bolted the door.

His skin glowed from his bath, hair was freshly washed, face shaved, his silk robe scarlet, the color of passion. A fragrant breeze flowed through the windows, parting the cloth, revealing his arousal.

Heat flooded Diana, though not from shame...excitement. She took him in hungrily. His chest was as marvelous as she'd recalled. Brown hair trickled in a thin line past his navel and flat belly to his groin where it flowered thick and curly above the root of his shaft and sac.

Or rather, his balls and cock. Words the men on the Lady Lark had used when referring to a man's sex, not caring whether she'd heard them or not.

What shameful, decadent terms.

She liked them.

Tristan's cock was turgid with want, hard from lust. Prominent veins snaked up its impressive length. The smooth head was ruddy, his balls the same color, lightly furred and plump, his powerful legs roughened with hair.

Unbearable need tore through her, leaving her breathless and weak, helpless to deny whatever he willed.

"Diana."

She nodded, transfixed. His shaft had grown harder and longer within the last seconds.

"Diana."

"Yes?"

"Show me your breasts."

Her thighs tensed. A pulse beat deep within her sheath. She brushed her hair off her shoulders and folded her arms over her head to expose herself fully.

Her nipples constricted.

His shaft thickened.

Rather than experiencing shame as a reverend's daughter should, Diana had never known such wonderful vulnerability, stripped of everything separating her from him. She ached for his touch.

Tristan extended his hand for her to go to him.

Only a few steps separated them, but she understood their significance, her joining him willingly.

She crossed the space and slid her hand over his. Male desire scented his clean skin. His hair fell in soft waves on his forehead, past his ears and neck. She longed to drive her fingers through his locks to see if they were as silky as they looked, but awaited his next command.

He pressed his lips to her palm. His breath tickled, mouth warmed. "Take off my robe."

The world shifted. Lightheaded, she slid the garment over his shoulders. The silk fluttered past his hands and floated to the floor. An overwhelming urge coaxed her to kneel, cup his weighty sac in her palm, and take his stiffened rod into her mouth. A notion she'd never had until now.

Tristan swept her into his arms.

She molded to him, stroked his shoulder, then down his back.

He tensed.

Diana froze. She'd touched scar upon scar, surprised and anguished by what he'd gone through. What she'd refused to believe until now. "You were flogged. Oh Tristan, when did this happen? How? Why?"

"We won't speak of it." He avoided her gaze.

She cradled his cheek. "Why not? I want to know what happened."

"Never. I forbid it, do you understand?" He settled her on the bed.

She took his hand, needing to comfort, to know all she could about his hard life.

Embarrassment flooded his features. He pulled away from her hold and made lazy circles over her belly.

Heat burst wherever he touched her. She wiggled closer, wanting more.

Wearing a delighted look, he untied the silk around her hips and pushed the cloth away. A faint breeze licked the moisture between her legs, proving her desire. He combed her delicate curls, then sought her slick folds.

Pleasure coursed through her ruthlessly.

"Lift your hips."

The moment she had, he pulled the cloth away. Holding on to the silk, he straddled her, his cock and meaty balls resting on her belly, warming it. He lifted her arms above her head.

She tilted her face. "What are you doing?"

"Making certain you yield." He wound the silk around her wrists, then secured the cloth to the bedpost and looked down at her as a god or a pirate captain might. "I'm also making sure your obedience leads to pleasure."

Diana had no desire to defy or flee him. Even if she had, she couldn't. The cloth trapped her wrists, his weight her legs, his gaze her will. His shameless need said he would have her now and enjoy her at his leisure while she submitted.

Fighting him was the furthest thing from her mind.

His kiss thrilled, scent intoxicated, his strength and warmth a comfort she'd never known. She tugged on her bonds, needing to touch him. He grabbed her wrists to keep her still and obedient. Once she'd yielded, he pulled his mouth from hers before she was ready.

He lifted a small bowl from the table and drizzled warm, scented oil over her breasts, the act wonderfully depraved.

She closed her eyes.

"No." He cupped her mound. "I want you to watch what I do."

A daunting prospect. However, she did as he wanted.

He swirled the fragrant balm on her tightened nipples and breasts, fondling her with a husband's right and as a male demands.

There couldn't possibly be a more delightful pastime.

He suckled her nipples.

Desire thrummed through her, settling between her legs. Lust engorged her folds.

Oiling her slowly, maddeningly, he paid particular attention to her sensitive nub, grazing it.

She came alive as she never had and strained for his touch.

He stroked her folds rather than her most sensitive part, frustrating her. She lifted her hips, desperate for him to arouse her fully.

He tongued her there.

Heat and pleasure filled her to near bursting. She needed to peak, desperate for relief.

Tristan stopped. "Open your eyes. Spread your legs farther."

She barely found the strength to do either.

He rubbed her harder, faster too. God help her, she needed more and pushed closer to chase release.

He stopped.

She wanted to growl oath after oath but finally understood his intent. Obedience to his will was her only recourse if she wanted pleasure. She gave herself to him freely and fully.

He teased her sex, but wouldn't bring her to completion. Her climax barreled close and faded away, the process repeating endlessly. Damp from tension, she couldn't breathe or think.

Miraculously, the unbearable heaviness grew, then overwhelmed so unexpectedly, she shuddered in climax. Her sheath pulsed hard.

With one hand on her bound wrists, he captured her mouth, plunged his tongue inside, and stroked her nub lightly. She bucked, scarcely able to withstand his touch. Her flesh was far too sensitive. This newest climax arrived faster than the last and with such force she tore her mouth from his and gulped air.

He kissed her cheek. "Well done."

She laughed.

He settled between her legs and bathed his thick crown in her moisture. "This may hurt at first, but the discomfort will pass."

"I'm not afraid." Never had she been as ready for anything as she was for him. She pulled back her legs and invited her husband to take her virginity.

His broad grin confirmed his delight. He ran his crown down her cleft, then eased inside and pierced her barrier.

A sharp, painful sting surprised her.

His smile faded. "You all right?"

Better than he could know. His concern meant everything. "Yes. Please continue."

He eased into her with care and buried his shaft until Diana feared she couldn't take much more inside. Tristan worked her skillfully, proving her wrong. Their curls finally touched.

She'd never witnessed a lovelier sight and gave him a soft smile. The pain had already passed, replaced by longing and wonder.

He looked happier than she'd ever seen him, then concentrated on pleasure, pulling back until his cock was nearly free before thrusting inside, driving into her repeatedly. His balls tapped her buttocks.

She tightened her sheath around his length to add to the wonderful friction between them. With each stroke on her nub, extraordinary heat and delight built, coiling within her, surging to a point Diana could barely contain herself.

Her lids glided down. She lost control and dashed toward release, unmindful of anything except what happened in this bed with him.

Tristan held back on his own climax and rode her to another peak before he lost himself to pleasure. He pumped fast and hard, at last spilling his seed, his bellow uncivilized and deliciously male.

They panted in time. Her channel throbbed around his spent flesh.

He sank down, his cheek to hers.

The bed smelled of sex. Desire.

She yearned for love.

Chapter 5

Chadwick Vincent had joined Tristan and Diana's crews on the main deck of the Lady Lark. The men faced each other, though not to battle. They'd called a council and had already voted Miles Montgomery captain. An honor granted due to his excessive girth and the valuable information he claimed to have concerning Benedict Bishop.

Vincent had yet to hear anything meaningful from Montgomery. Every mariner knew Bishop was old, sour, and quite rich. "What other details do you have on him, if anything?"

Montgomery gingerly touched his blackened eye and shot Vincent a look of pure hatred for having punched him.

The swine was lucky to be alive. After Vincent's escape from the hold, he'd been eager to send Montgomery straight to the devil, but Tristan hadn't wanted a slaughter.

Vincent seethed at how Tristan had betrayed the men and him. His head pounded with agonizing pain. His yellow scarf was dirty from blood where someone hit him seconds before he'd reached Diana. "I'm still not hearing anything from you."

Montgomery dropped his hand. "Bishop's waiting for Miss Fletcher in Mozambique. He means to have her as his personal whore. Show her off to those around him as his prize. It ain't just her beauty he craves, but her innocence."

Vincent snorted. "He ain't likely to get that now."

Others made crude remarks concerning her purity. Some grumbled about not getting their share of Diana who'd surely been beneath Tristan by now.

"Bishop ain't aware of it, is he?" Montgomery scanned the group. "Nor will he be to my way of thinking. We give him what he wants and take what he's got. It's been said he powders his wigs with gold dust and eats from silver plates with diamonds in them. He'll pay dearly for the woman. After we take her from Kent and get our fair share, we'll still ransom her as though she's pure."

Vincent crossed his arms. "After she's been beneath me, she ain't likely to remember what any other man has done to her."

"The girl will be well used by each of us. As for Tristan Kent, he'll surely beg for death once I'm through with him."

The men cheered, then boasted about what they'd do to Diana and Tristan once they found the pair.

* * * *

Tristan leaned over Diana.

His heat warmed her and his scent aroused.

He pressed closer. "Open them."

After a moment of playful defiance, she parted her lids. He was so bed-mussed and virile her blood raced.

"Dear girl, I was speaking of your legs."

Of course he was. His seed and her passion dampened her cleft, her channel slightly sore from his use but craving more. She gave herself to him easily, yielding and receptive to the kisses he trailed past her cheek to her ear.

He brushed his lips over her temple. "In a few moments I want you again."

As she did him, in all ways, not only in his bed. She was hungry for information about him, how he came to be in this place, what monster had flogged him. Too many questions were poised on her lips that she couldn't give voice to. He didn't want to speak about the past. He hadn't offered her love in the future. Even though she'd always hope for his heart, she worried he'd never give her anything except momentary pleasure. For him, their coupling might be enough. For her it marked only the beginning and might sadly be the end.

She shoved those worries aside to become the dutiful wife. "Then do take me. It's surely your right."

He stopped kissing her neck. "Take you?"

His bewilderment undid her. She wanted to stroke his lashes, smooth back his hair, hold him, and promise she'd ease whatever loneliness and sorrow he'd ever known.

Not certain he'd ever want her to do so she simply nodded.

"No, Diana. You're wrong. I had you."

"You took me, Tristan."

"No. You desired this."

She had but wouldn't admit it, the same as him when she'd asked about his back. He'd refused to ease her worry then or encourage her pressing need to be close as if she had no right to know anything about him, including whatever pain he'd endured. Now that she'd shut off her innermost feelings to him, he didn't like it.

His frown went from confused to determined. "Very well. It would appear I'll have to take you and take you and take you until you do desire this."

Or he grew bored with her.

If only he'd talk, or at least listen. A lasting bond between a man and a woman wasn't forged by sex alone but with love to enrich the connection. An obvious reality men didn't appear to understand or perhaps they didn't care. When their lust for one woman ended, they too easily transferred their desire to another.

On this island, Tristan could sate his carnal needs with little effort. The women weren't only lovely but plentiful. He'd never needed her or any other Englishwoman. Paradise was at his fingertips, especially with Canela always around.

Diana looked away. "To take me is surely your right."

He muttered beneath his breath and eased her face to his.

Something rattled. He looked over.

The door groaned the way it would when someone leaned hard against it.

Diana went hot at what had transpired in this chamber and bed. "Someone's listening."

He rolled off her and yanked on his robe. She fetched her mariner's clothing. Tristan pulled the garments from her and tossed them aside.

She tried to get past him but he wouldn't let her. "Move."

"No. I'll handle this. You'll remain in my bed, waiting for me. I want no argument, understand?"

She showed him her back.

"Have it your way. At least for the moment." He padded to the door. "When I return, you'd better be on the mattress with your body and heart opened and willing to your husband."

Before she could retort, he left the room.

* * * *

Tristan prayed Diana wouldn't follow him.

The shadowed hall to the left proved empty. To the right, Canela stood in the doorway to another chamber, not trying to hide her presence or what she'd been up to. He strode to her.

She fell to her knees, opened his robe, and cradled his cock.

He stepped back. His bedchamber door still hadn't opened. For once, Diana hadn't defied him. Fearing she might, he closed his robe and frowned at Canela.

On her feet, she slipped her arms around his neck.

He bit back a curse, grabbed her wrist, and pulled her down the hall to the courtyard.

Naked children dashed about the common area, giggling in delight at their games. Nearby, their mothers worked the looms or potter's wheels.

If not for the others here, Tristan would have raged at Canela for interrupting his pleasure, him schooling Diana in how she should obey and desire him. At this point, he might need years to bring her to his side and didn't need anyone making matters worse.

"I heard you outside the door to my bedchamber." He spoke quietly so only she could hear. "You were listening to what transpired within. Do it again and I'll banish you from the house and the luxury it affords you." He released her wrist to go back to Diana.

"I heard no pleasure."

Tristan looked over.

Canela advanced. "The Englishwoman tells you to take her because it is your right, not because she desires you."

His face warmed.

"You should beat her for her cruel words. You should turn her away from this house and its luxuries. You should—"

"Diana's my wife." He faced Canela. "Which makes her my business, not yours."

Her lovely features grew hateful. "She does not love you."

Canela didn't, either. She was one of the most beautiful women he'd ever known, but also the most ruthless. No matter what Diana had thought when she'd first met him, that he was a worthless pirate, a barbarian, or a coward, her judgement of him as a man was far better than Canela's would ever be. To her, he was a means to an end to control the island riches. Nothing more.

He stared her down. "I'm warning you."

"Aye, you warn me, a woman who bends to your will. Yet you make one who defies you the mistress of this house and land. Even though she will have the finest in silks and jewels, she will not obey you. You will never have her respect or—"

"Damnation, enough."

James joined them. "Is there a problem?"

Peter and Gavra, the woman James loved, were with him.

"No problem at all." Tristan tamped down his fury, then spoke to Gavra in French, asking her to make certain Canela remained outside the mansion, away from his bedchamber.

She stole a look at Canela and nodded.

"How can you do this to me?" Canela reached for him.

He stepped away.

She moaned. "I wish only to protect you."

"Why?" Peter frowned. "From what?"

"Nothing," Tristan said. "She's mistaken."

Canela smacked her fist against her palm. "My heart and my ears heard her words. The Englishwoman wishes you harm. The moment you are no longer awake, she will injure you."

"Hurt him as he sleeps?" James scratched his freckled neck. "I hardly think Tristan's going to slumber much today or tonight with Diana in his bed."

Canela glared at him.

"Gavra." Tristan inclined his head to Canela. "Please see to her."

Canela dashed outside the courtyard walls. Gavra followed close behind.

James shook his head. "It appears she's not taking kindly to you wedding another woman and making her mistress of the house that she believes should be hers."

"Until I met Diana I had no intention of wedding anyone or siring children. Canela always knew how I felt."

"Aye, but like most women she thought she could change your mind. From the moment you took over this island, she's had her eye on ruling with you."

Over his dead body. Hers too. "I hardly wish to rule, James."

"Maybe so, but we both know Canela does."

Tristan pushed his windblown hair off his face. "Isn't it enough she already has all the riches any woman could possibly want and most of the island men desiring her? In particular Adamo?"

"He may love the girl, but he's not a pirate who returns from a voyage with silks and jewels to give her."

"Neither am I. Not any longer. Though if this continues, I may have to escape for a little while to preserve my sanity from female hysterics."

Peter sniffed. "Women."

Tristan smiled at the boy's eagerness to join a man's conversation. "Aye, women." He stepped back, eager to return to Diana. "Such lovely creatures when they're of a mind to be soft and yielding as God surely intended."

"The reason beds were created." James wiggled his eyebrows. "No better way to get a woman to do your bidding than to pleasure her greatly when she's beneath you."

Peter's cheeks darkened. Although the boy was still a virgin, Gavra's two younger sisters kept making advances toward him. "Tristan, wait a moment."

Reluctantly, he retraced his steps, sensing what the boy wanted to ask. "When it comes to women be exceedingly patient, gentle as can be, make certain her pleasure comes afore your own, tell her she's surely the prettiest thing on God's earth, and you'll have no problems whatsoever."

The truth. At least until he'd met Diana.

Peter's face flushed redder than his neck and chest. "I hardly want to know about such things. Will Diana harm you as you sleep? Are you in great danger?"

Indeed, he was. He craved her as he'd never had a woman before and proved it with his ardent attention to her pleasure. Yet, she refused to concede that he'd done more than take her, wounding him badly. Unwilling to admit the truth, he shrugged. "Not from your sister."

"What of our shipmates? Do you think they might find us here?"

Tristan and James exchanged a glance and a wink. "Well now." Tristan eyed Peter. "Not unless you told them about this island."

"I did not. I kept the secret same as you."

Tristan slung his arm around the boy's shoulders. "Then we're safe. This island's not near any harbor, and it's far too hard to reach by sloop. Remember, I only found it by accident." He directed the boy toward the mansion.

"What are you doing?" Peter looked behind them. "I was about to take a ride when I heard Canela's stupid fit."

"You must never call a woman's fit stupid. And you may ride only after you've finished your lessons."

Peter drooped. "There's no sense in learning things I'll never use."

"I want you educated as a gentleman, and so does your sister."

"But she fancies books as you do. I don't. I want to take me ride."

"My ride. Say it."

"Very well, my ride."

"Try to remember it for the next time."

"I never forgot. I don't like getting beat up."

"You won't here." Once in the structure, Tristan led the boy to the library. "No riding until you've finished your lessons, understood?"

Peter nodded but dragged his feet. "I hope you know, books will never tell me how to keep this island safe from our—Diana." He halted.

So did Tristan.

His bride was in the hall dressed in her mariner's clothing.

She stopped in front of Peter. "What did you mean when you mentioned keeping the island safe?"

Tina Donahue

Tristan pushed the boy toward the library. "Do your studies."

"Aye, Captain." Peter fled.

Diana was immune to Tristan's mood, intent on following Peter.

Tristan swept her into his arms, put her on her feet in the bedchamber, and bolted the door. "Your vows said you'd obey me, and you will."

"The vows were in a language I hardly understood, and you left me in here without your protection."

"You have it now, so take off your clothes and get into my bed."

She edged back. "Canela was listening at the door, wasn't she?"

"The matter's been settled." He shrugged out of his robe. "Take off your clothes."

"You were gone quite a while. Does it take so much time to soothe Canela's feelings?"

"It takes far longer to see you naked, but I have a solution." He undressed her, since it appeared she would never get to the task, and brought her to his bed.

The moment he was between her legs, she planted her hands on his chest. "Tristan, wait."

"What for? I want to have you now."

"As is your right, but a matter concerns me greatly."

He stroked her jawline. "Never fear, you'll enjoy this act as you did the last. Probably far more as you're no longer a timid virgin."

Diana gave him a cool look. "You would know, but my former or present state isn't what concerns me." She grew quite somber. "Peter spoke of this island's safety. What did he mean?"

"Nothing. You have absolutely no need for concern. In fact, I forbid it. I want to see you smiling constantly and laughing gaily."

"Like one who's feeble-minded or insane?"

"Like my wife who's drunk with pleasure and trusts her husband will protect her. Now lift your legs. I want you to take all of my cock inside."

"Be serious, please." She cupped his face. "Are you in danger from your old crew and mine? Will they be able to find you here?"

His bluster fell away. Her worry for him surprised Tristan. "No need to fret, please don't."

"I can't help it. You beat and betrayed them to save me."

He'd do so repeatedly, endlessly, to have another moment like this. More intimate than he'd hoped, stoking his hunger for her, his need to be close. "Do you mind lifting your legs for your husband?"

"Are we through talking about this?"

He was, but feared she'd never be. "For the moment."

"I need to speak of this again at length, please. I want your word."

She would. "You have it."

Smiling, she lifted her legs.

He drove his shaft into her silken heat, lost in comfort and wonder. Her channel sheltered him, making him feel wanted, giving him peace.

Grateful and humbled, he rested his forehead on her shoulder and fought his emotions. It was time for pleasure, not talk.

She stroked his hair. "Are you all right?"

No. Since meeting her, everything had changed for him and he couldn't bring things back. Wasn't certain he even wanted to. "I have something to say."

She stilled. "What?"

He lifted his face, pained by her dread. "No matter what your men and mine may want, there is no way in hell they'll ever locate this island or me."

* * * *

Montgomery called out, "Did you find it?"

"No." Wiping sweat off his face, Vincent slogged down the beach from the Quest and stopped short of the man. "No skiff's been hid in any of them trees or mangroves. Tristan's charts are still in the cabin. He and the others must have rowed to a different beach than this."

Montgomery made a face. "Do you think they drowned?"

"Not with Tristan and James being such skilled swimmers. Even young Peter can hold his own." He faced the sea. Beneath the setting sun, the water seemed to catch fire, shining as brightly as the gold Bishop used to powder his wigs. Vincent wanted that for himself and eating off silver plates with diamond-encrusted edges. Items he'd never have if they couldn't find and ransom Diana.

Montgomery looked north. "Where else was the Quest careened?"

Vincent named the spots. Every one would have taken Tristan over a week to reach. Unlikely he would have rowed to them.

Montgomery sighed loudly. "What islands are nearest to where the Lady Lark is anchored?"

There were several, but Vincent didn't name them. "Are you thinking Tristan and the others might have gone to one of them?"

"If you're convinced they haven't perished, then they're surely somewhere, and we'll not rest until they're found."

* * * *

Given his hunger for Diana, Tristan was surprised to have slept the night. Come morning, he reached for his bride but felt cool silk and emptiness instead.

His pulse leaped. He pushed up but didn't leave the bed.

She stood at the closest window, her attention on the outside. A mild breeze stirred her hair and the fresh sheet she held tight to her throat. Her diamond collar twinkled. Two lemurs darted past, scattering brilliantly colored butterflies. She raised her face to watch their flight before regarding the sea.

Slumped against the pillows, Tristan tried to gauge her mood. Yesterday, she'd been worried about him. Now, he sensed she might be thinking about England, her true home. His belly knotted at her craving her old life, not this place or him. He should have asked outright, but wasn't brave enough to face her answer. Skirting the issue was all he had the courage to do. "England's to the left."

She looked over at him, then back at the sea.

Her response did little to dispel his doubt. "Were you very happy there?"

She laughed softly. "Quite miserable I would say."

He grinned, then killed his joy, lest she see.

Diana faced him. "Were you happy there?"

Hungry would have been a better word. Frustrated too, at least during the times when he wasn't afraid or close to having his spirit broken. "Quite miserable I would say."

"Then you miss it too."

He laughed. "Aye. At times I fear I do."

She smiled.

Her tenderness touched Tristan's soul and quickened his pulse, making him want her as he had no other woman.

She dropped the sheet. Sunlight caressed her smooth skin and made her diamonds sparkle wildly. Her rosy nipples had pebbled, telling him what she refused to admit. She desired him.

He simply had to coax those words from her and ease his uncertainty. However, first he needed to know something else. "Turn around and lift your hair."

She gave him a questioning look but obeyed.

Her shoulders were narrow, back slender, legs long. A small mole graced her buttocks, the only thing interrupting her flawless flesh. Satisfied, he relaxed. "Lower your hair and face me."

"Were you looking for marks?"

He hid his surprise and nodded.

"Why?"

"I know what a man's touch can do to a woman's flesh. Too many times my mother's face and body bore evidence of a lover's rage."

"Your mother?"

"Aye. She was a doxy. I never learned who my father might be, other than someone named Rhys Kent. I'm quite certain he also left his mark on her."

Diana looked aghast. "You left no marks on me. That's not the kind of man you are, no matter your upbringing. What happened with your parents wasn't your fault."

He already knew that and didn't much like her sympathetic words. They weren't what he wanted to hear and cursed himself for being too forthright. "You and I have better things to do than to speak of times past." He put out his hand for her to come to him. In fact, he demanded it.

She knelt on the mattress just out of reach. "Why does compassion frighten you?"

"Pity has always disgusted me."

"Compassion isn't pity."

"You honestly believe such a thing?" He looked down his nose as a schoolmaster might. "You're wrong. Both words have the same meaning. A woman your age should know so, or didn't you take lessons as a girl?"

Her brow wrinkled, but she didn't give into anger or hurt at his unkind words. "The truth is I did, though I can see it was quite unnecessary as my husband insists on instructing me in other matters. Ones that hardly come from books."

"How right you are. There's still the matter of you admitting your desire for me."

She lowered her face.

Her silence cut deep, but he cast off his feelings, leery of opening himself to additional grief. "Very well, see to my pleasure. Do it now."

"Is that what you truly want?"

His face got hot. He refused to look at her. "It is."

"All that you want?"

He couldn't think of anything else except her consistent obedience, her confession that she desired him, and her respect rather than condolences for his horrid past. Not hoping for such a miracle, he shrugged.

On a heavy sigh, she rested her hands on his chest and pressed her lips to his throat in a gentle, promising kiss that tightened his balls and curled his toes. She glided her tongue over his jaw, then licked the cleft in his chin.

Her mouth's wet heat registered deep within Tristan, feeding his passion. She traced his nipples and suckled his neck.

He pushed into her. "Bloody hell."

She pulled in her tongue. "Is that the proper language to use around a reverend's daughter?"

He laughed. "Surely is when the girl's my wife."

"Woman, not girl. Not any longer." She licked his tiny nipples quite well, swirled her tongue around his navel, then flicked it over the hairs arrowing to his groin, tickling, warming, arousing. At length, she buried her face in the thick curls above his cock.

He'd reached the doorway to heaven.

* * * *

Diana inhaled deeply of his musk, adoring the provocative scent. Shamelessly, she glided her tongue down his beefy rod and cupped his balls. Their weight and warmth were dizzying.

He squeezed his fists and muttered lewd comments that excited her.

She explored his thick, long column and gently fondled his sac. Lovingly, she licked his velvety crown, dipped her tongue into the small slit, and tasted the clear fluid beaded there. Its saltiness surprised her, as did her wanton hunger for him. She desired everything Tristan was, her actions proving what she couldn't say. Someday perhaps. Right now, her zealous attention to his pleasure would have to do.

Determined to give him the only sanctuary he'd allow, she slipped his shaft into her mouth.

He gasped. "I said pleasure me, woman, not kill me."

She released him. "Are you complaining?"

"Demanding." He pulled in another shuddering breath. "Enough of what you're doing. I want your cunt."

Another word she'd learned since taking to sea to find him. The term thrilled rather than disgusted. In this bed and room, she'd forbid no pleasure, nor deny any delight.

She had to banish Canela from his mind forever. More importantly, Diana wanted to prove what a loving wife could do. She swirled her tongue over the uneven skin at the back of his crown. He grunted quite crudely, verifying his sensitivity.

She eased his member from her lips. "Despite what you want, I still fancy your cock. Be still."

"What?"

She took him into her mouth.

"Damnation."

His pleasure delighted her. She opened her throat to slip his entire length inside. Wasn't easy. His shaft was wonderfully long, delightfully thick. Not pausing or tiring, she soon had her nose buried in the pelt above his rod.

He groaned lustily.

Diana eased his shaft from her mouth until only his crown remained between her lips, and then she guided him back inside. His balls plumped within her gentle hold. He tugged the sheets, his face maroon, shoulders strained, his intent clear. He planned to fight her.

That wouldn't do. She wanted him to shatter, soar, and float down, so she could catch him in a tender embrace.

She flicked her tongue on his most sensitive area and ran her thumb over his furred sac. He squirmed. She followed. Nothing would break her hold or concentration.

Primitive noises poured from him, more animal than human. Sweat shone on his face and chest. He gritted his teeth and squeezed his eyes.

She'd never seen anyone as beautiful.

Patiently, she brought him close to the edge, then let him drift away before she resumed her wanton teasing. He battled her throughout but finally stilled and roared. His seed spurted into her mouth.

She welcomed his offering, enthralled at its creaminess and unique flavor. Faint saltiness, along with what seemed to her life, the future. He struggled to breathe. She licked his cock clean, then lapped his balls.

"No—enough." He trembled. "It's too much."

"I think not."

He gulped air. "Only because you desire this. You desire me. Admit it."

She couldn't.

His breathing quieted and their silence grew.

He pushed up, no longer a contented husband but a pirate. Hard and dangerous, unwilling to accept anyone's disobedience, especially his wife's. "On your knees. Turn your back to me and bend over."

She did not.

He narrowed his eyes. "Now."

Desire and disquiet flooded her. Passion won out. She eased away and did as he'd ordered.

"Lower your head to the mattress. Spread your legs widely and lift your arse."

If any other man had told her to do such a thing, Diana would have staunchly refused, unless threatened with death or harm to Peter. With Tristan, she obeyed readily. His commanding manner not only thrilled, he'd never hurt her. He wanted to prove her desire for him.

She needed to convince him how respect and love also mattered. For now, though, there was this. Her position was submissive, vulnerability complete.

He shifted, making the mattress shake. "Remain as you are."

Easy for him to say. "For how long?"

"Until I tell you otherwise."

"What will you be doing?"

"Looking at you."

Her skin burned and her sex grew wet, the familiar ache growing within her.

He pushed his foot against her ankles. "Spread yourself wider. Display yourself for your husband."

This was too much.

"Diana."

She slid her knees over the sheet.

"Arch your back."

Her buttocks lifted, the position daunting yet thrilling, dooming her to Hell for such outrageous desire. She didn't care. Only satisfaction mattered.

He crawled behind her, cupped her mound, and explored her damp folds glutted with need.

She started at his intimate touch.

"You desire this."

She cleared her throat. "I'm simply being obedient."

He stroked, then gently probed her anus.

She stilled, shocked to her core. Despite what they'd shared, she was still a reverend's daughter...and Tristan's wife.

"I want all of you, every opening." He circled her tight ring. "And your full obedience. Do I have it?"

Too shy to speak, she nodded.

He took great care in preparing her for the act, oiling her anus, slipping his finger inside, stretching her passage to accommodate his cock.

At his brazen moves, warmth filled her, the delight he generated unmatched by anything she'd experienced.

He washed oil from his hands, eased his crown inside her narrowest opening, and stroked her nub.

Heat shot through her, along with too many feelings to deny. Excitement, yearning, pleasure, lust. The pressure from his cock was unbelievably intense yet welcomed. Indulgence made her reckless with need.

He pressed toward her, she toward him. They touched at last, his rod fully inside. He paused to catch his breath. She struggled for air.

His slow, easy slide in and out of her, his relentless strokes on her sex, riveted her to the moment. The act was too much and everything she wanted, pushing her past restraint. Her ragged breaths filled the chamber, followed by Tristan's booming shout that blocked animal noises and the rustling sea.

A moment like no other.

With his cock still inside, he pulled her up and into him. Holding her wrists to her chest with one hand, he breathed hard and brushed her damp folds.

Acute pleasure shot in countless directions, overcoming her. "No, don't. It's too much too soon."

"I think not." He pushed his knees into hers so she couldn't close her legs and deny him what he demanded. With her confined, he stroked her lazily.

She squirmed.

He held on and took her past intense sensitivity to incomparable delight.

She wilted against him, letting him do what he willed.

Tristan brought her near the edge and stopped. "You desire this."

Of course, she did. Any woman would unless she was an utter fool. Even so, Diana refused to say so.

He played with her flesh, making her mad with longing, but still wouldn't allow her release. "You desire this. Admit it."

She could barely catch another breath and lacked strength for a lie or the truth.

"Very well." He rested his damp fingers on her hip. "I'll never do anything that you don't desire."

She pushed against him. "What are you saying? You must finish this."

"Why must I?"

She struggled for an acceptable answer, unwilling to admit her true feelings. She'd offered him compassion and he accused her of pity. She'd worried about his safety, and he came close to opening up but then shut down. Wasn't fair for him to expect everything yet give nothing. "Because you must."

He gave her nub a few precious strokes. The moment she shivered, he stopped touching her. "Why must I?"

"It's your duty as my husband."

"Allowing you to climax wasn't in the vows." He stroked her and stopped.

She argued, peppering her demands with oaths she'd heard.

Didn't change Tristan's mind in the least.

He rubbed and stopped, stroked and paused.

She broke. "Very well—all right. I desire this. My God, how I desire this."

He rested his hand on her hip.

Her head fell forward. "Go on. Continue."

He did not.

"Tristan, please."

"Why? Tell me. Say what's in your heart."

She dug her nails into her palms, resisting.

So did he.

Unable to bear this any longer, she relented. "I desire you, Tristan...only you."

* * * *

He brought Diana to completion and embraced her tenderly for the loveliest declaration he'd ever heard. She desired him. Wanted him. Couldn't live without him.

He released himself from her and lowered them to the bed. She lay limp beneath him, breathing shallowly.

He kissed her satiny cheek. "Tell me again how you desire me."

She looked pleasantly weary. "I do."

He grinned. "I've finally had you. You fought well and long, but you couldn't win against my determination. I told you I was never discouraged, and I'm not. Repeat the words. I want to hear them. I may never grow tired of doing so." He was behaving stupidly but couldn't help himself or his soaring happiness. "Go on."

"I desire you and you had me."

"I did. Why?"

"You're a skilled lover."

His smile faltered. He already knew his prowess in bed and waited for the words he wanted to hear. There weren't any. "You desire me for no other reason?"

"Do you mean adoration or love?"

"What else?"

"Those feelings come only with friendship and respect."

Which he didn't have from her. Not only did her words sting, they crushed. "Then you're saying your desire for me is only in this bed."

A bird flew into the chamber. She watched its disoriented flight around the room before it found its way back outside. "I would think for most men a woman's satisfaction in bed is inconsequential. For those who worry about such things, her physical release should be enough and surely all they could handle."

"I'm not most men."

Diana looked at him. "No, you're not. You're my husband. I was wrong to say you haven't marked me. You have, and for all time it would seem."

More riddles. He wished she'd simply speak her mind. "How have I accomplished such a miracle?"

"With the collar you demand I wear."

He'd given the thing willingly and had hoped she'd accepted it in the same spirit. Apparently not, bruising his feelings further. "Perhaps I demand you wear it as I'm not assured of your love, adoration, or whatever else you want to call it. I barely have your desire. And only because I'm such a skilled lover." He rolled off her and left the bed. "Maybe the day I'm certain you've given me your all, I'll allow you to remove the collar."

She didn't retort.

He looked over.

She stared at his back, scars from a flogging that nearly cost him his life.

He faced her, hiding them. "Do you want to remove your collar?"

"Canela would surely like that. Perhaps you should have wed her."

"I wed you."

She opened her mouth, then sighed and kept quiet.

"Go on." He planted his hands on his hips. "Say what's on your mind."

"I need to ask you something."

Of course she did and her question would most likely wound. "I'm listening."

"Am I mistress of this house?"

Surprised, he nodded.

She pushed up. "Then I have a demand."

"You have a what?"

"From this moment forward I want the women to cover themselves properly whenever they're in public."

Tristan smiled. "No. Even though you're jealous—"

"Civilized."

"Have it your way, but they're accustomed to their manner of dress."

"They're hardly dressed. Peter's far too young to see a woman's flesh."

"Peter's not the one who's bothered. You are. No matter what you say or how much you complain, I won't order the women to change their ways or their culture."

"Because you're not wed to them. You're not their master."

He rubbed his chin. "Delightful word, master."

"Not as delightful as friend, one who's accorded respect rather than blind submission, a willing and free love, not mindless obedience."

He dropped his hand. "Do you have another request? If you do, I may listen to it before I say no."

She gave him a chilly look.

Tristan ignored it. "I'm famished. Get yourself in order. Breakfast awaits." He washed at the basin, then pulled a fresh shirt from the armoire.

After Diana tidied up, she tied the violet cloth around her hips and unbolted the door.

He stopped her before she opened it. "What do you think you're doing?"

"Leaving the room. I presume the food won't be brought here as it was last night."

"Your presumption is correct. Today we eat with the others." He took her in, lingering on her tightened nipples as any sane man would. "You're hardly ready to present yourself to the world."

"I'm not presenting myself to the world, only to the people who live on this island, the women as well as the men."

"You're not going about as you are, Diana."

"The other women do."

"They aren't wed to me. You are."

"Surely your collar will tell them my place."

He kept in an oath at how skillfully she'd led him into this argument. One she fully intended to win when she was the one who'd been born to yield and should willingly obey as she'd done in his bed. Apparently, it was the only place she would do so. Weary of battle, he opted for a softer stance. "No matter Canela's manner of dress or undress I'll never share her bed. I'm quite aware you doubt my fidelity, but there's no need. You have it."

Surprise crossed her face. "And you have mine."

He had better or he'd kill any man who dared touch her. Now probably wasn't the time to remind her of that. He kissed her fingers. "Thank you."

She smiled, then became serious. "About my getting dressed, should I wear my mariner clothing or will I be wrapping myself in sheets?"

"Neither." He led her to the armoire.

"My." Diana touched the satin, silk, and lace gowns inside, the fabrics bearing more colors than a rainbow. "These are lovely. To whom did they belong?"

The woman who lived with the pirate who once owned the island until Tristan won the land and everything on it during a night of wagering. For his good luck, the pirate tried to kill him. During the battle, Tristan's luck held. As he and James buried the man, his mistress ran off. A week later, the islanders found her in a ravine, the fall having broken her neck. Clutched within her hand was a sack of jewels, including the diamond marriage collar.

Tristan wasn't about to share the story with Diana. "We took the gowns off a prize. From the looks of it, the woman who commissioned them had a form similar to yours. I'm quite certain they'll fit."

She eased into him. "What made you go on the account? Who lashed you? Who lashed Peter? What—"

"Enough." He held firm. "I've already told you I'll not answer those questions."

"A friend would. Please." She touched his chest. "I want to know."

"I need to forget."

She curled her fingers into a loose fist and stopped touching him.

A lash from a whip couldn't have hurt more. "Someday I'll tell you."

"Would it be when we become friends?"

"It will be the day you give me your all. So, I suppose the answer to your question is yes." He swatted her ass playfully. "Now hurry and get ready. I'm famished."

Chapter 6

Once dressed, Diana understood why the island women didn't bother with this civilized nonsense. The silk gown laced in front, the cut so tight her breasts squeezed together, the scandalously low neckline barely covering her nipples. The pleated back and voluminous skirt had as much yardage as bedsheets, the high-quality fabric in a deep rose shade.

Given the heat in her cheeks, her blush was surely as dark.

Tristan smiled roguishly. "Oh, I do like your gown."

"It's hardly mine, and it's far too disgraceful. Give me one of your shirts to wear."

He closed the armoire doors. "No, you're wearing that. My God."

She crossed her arms. Her breasts plumped, nearly falling out. Tristan's grin widened. She dropped her hands to her sides. "Do you really want the other men to see me exposed like this?"

"I'd murder the first one who looked and everyone who followed." He stroked the neckline, touching more skin than fabric.

Her head fell back. She moved into his touch. "To avoid bloodshed, I shan't be wearing this or the others."

"Pity." He traced the swells of her breasts.

Tingles rippled through her. "No need to waste them, though. Perhaps the island women would care to wear a few."

"I think not. They're accustomed to their manner of dress." He pressed his lips to her neck briefly and eased back.

Diana sagged into him, not wanting them separated yet. "I'm merely suggesting they use the fabric for the cloths they tie about their hips. Unless they'd prefer to use the gowns for something else. I'm quite good with thread and a needle. I could show them any number of designs they might like. It would be up to them, of course, to wear the new clothing, but until they realize what else is available, how could they possibly know they won't like it?"

He held her chin. "No."

"You won't even allow me to offer?"

"I don't want you giving away all the gowns. The one you have on now remains here. You're wearing it when we retire tonight. I'm going to bend you over a table, lift the skirt, and take you from behind."

Her belly fluttered. She smiled.

"Ah… Would that be your desire I see?"

"It would."

Pleasure radiated from him. He opened the armoire, chose a shirt, and tossed it to her. "We'll have to see about getting you something proper to wear. I'll also speak to the women about the gowns."

* * * *

In the dining room, James and Peter sat at a massive mahogany table large enough to accommodate thirty. Air whispered through the long windows, and the sun streamed in from an opening in the roof. Amazed, Diana drank in the scene. A soft breeze stirred the fronds of numerous potted plants and delivered the sweet morning scent along with a clean ocean fragrance.

Bananas, pineapples, and grapes overflowed large bowls. Next to them were trays heaped with dark bread, bacon, and cooked fish. Her mouth watered at the bounty and splendid aromas.

Tristan ushered her to a seat across from the others. "Glad to see you two left us some food."

James glanced up from the banana he peeled and took in Tristan's shirt on Diana. The garment was so large the hem hung below her knees, covering a good deal of her canvas trousers. James's reddish eyebrows lifted but he didn't comment.

Peter snickered. "Ain't you never going to dress like a girl anymore?"

"Tonight." Tristan smiled.

She elbowed him.

James lowered his face to hide his grin and blush.

Peter took in everyone. "What?"

"Never mind." Tristan pointed at the boy. "And the word you should have used would be aren't, not ain't."

He slumped in his seat.

Tristan helped Diana into a mahogany chair boasting cushions in dark blue silk, then took his spot at the head of the table. A casual observer might have believed he wanted to prove he was lord and master. She knew better. Seated where he was, she couldn't get a good look at his scarred back. Sorrow for his brutal past and tenderness for their future overwhelmed her.

He took a slice of bread. "So, Peter, have you done your lessons?"

"Already? I just got up. I haven't even had nothing to eat."

"You haven't had anything. We've had this discussion before. In fact, just a few seconds ago. From here on out, it's proper English, as you were taught as a young boy, do you hear me?"

"Aye, Captain, but I don't rightly understand why. This ain't— isn't England."

Diana gave him a stiff smile. "We'll pretend it is."

Outside the windows, several native girls passed, speaking French, their youthful voices sweet and animated, their naked breasts bouncing with each step.

Peter craned his neck to follow them once they stepped away. "I never saw anything like that in England."

Diana turned to Tristan for help. He ran his fingers over his mouth, trying not to laugh. James did the same.

A young woman carried a silver tea service into the room. She seemed familiar. Of course. James had kissed her upon arriving.

"Bonjour." She smiled sweetly at Peter, Tristan, and Diana, then winked at James.

His face flushed pink.

She poured his tea last. Her naked breast brushed his arm. His face colored so badly his freckles were lost in the deepening red.

Grinning like a fool, Peter faced the window. Framed within the space were the young women who'd called him Pierre, both winking and smiling.

This was too much. Even though Diana had engaged in wanton pleasures with Tristan, for Peter to entertain the same with those young women wasn't something she could abide. Of course he was heading for manhood, but there wasn't any reason to hurry him along.

She leaned toward Tristan. "Why not mention the gowns now?"

He stopped cutting his fish. "To whom?"

She inclined her head to the young woman who exchanged soulful gazes with James.

"That's Gavra, James's woman." Tristan shook his head. "Not my place to mention her clothing. James likes her as she is."

The man practically frothed at the mouth every time she was near. "You could ask her to mention the frocks to the others. Perhaps they'd like to try something new."

Tristan finished his tea and stared at his cup.

"Please?"

On a sigh, he spoke to Gavra in French. She listened without comment, glanced at James, then nodded to Tristan and left the room.

James shook his head. "Canela's surely going to love this."

Diana's belly cramped. She didn't understand why he'd specifically mentioned Canela. She was hardly the sole woman here, simply the only one actively and deliberately pursuing Tristan despite his marriage. Though that was horrid enough, she wasn't ever going to leave. She belonged on the isle, always would. Diana was merely an interloper brought here by Tristan, who was trapped here for life. Given his piracy, if he dared sail from this place, he risked capture and hanging. What she'd prayed for a short while ago.

So much had changed these last days, including her feelings. Her heart already belonged to him. For her to come into his home and demand anything was unconscionable. He knew the islanders far better than she did. Her designs for the clothing might upset the men, especially if the women displayed themselves to honor a native tradition. They might revolt against Tristan because of her.

What an idiot she'd been. She was supposed to support her husband in his decisions, not cause him grief.

She rested her hand on his. "Perhaps I spoke too rashly before. If these women are comfortable dressed, or rather undressed as they are, I have no right to suggest any new designs for their clothing." She spoke to James. "Please tell Gavra she's not required to wear anything over her... What I mean is she doesn't have to cover herself any more than she already does."

Confusion swept over his face.

Peter snickered.

She frowned at him. "Stop behaving so abominably. Pay attention to your food, not adult conversation."

"I'm not laughing about her breasts, Diana."

Good Lord. She gripped her cup, her face and chest burning. "You will not speak about such matters in polite company."

"What are you going on about? It's just Tristan and James here. Nothing polite about them. We discuss these matters all the time."

Tristan cleared his throat.

Diana looked from him to her brother. "Not any longer. Confine your interest to your lessons."

Peter crossed his arms over his skinny chest. "You might learn some French yourself."

James chuckled.

She threw up her hands. "Will someone please tell me what is going on?"

James didn't say a word.

Peter smiled smugly. "As I said, you should learn some French yourself. Then you'd know what Tristan said to Gavra."

"Peter." Tristan gave him a hard stare.

The boy lifted his shoulders. "What? Diana won't quit until she gets the truth out of you."

Tristan shot him a harsher frown, then spoke to her. "I merely asked Gavra to tell Canela she has to change her manner of dress."

Heat prickled Diana's cheeks and throat. "Just Canela, not the others?"

He leaned in, his mouth on her ear. "I knew she was the one making you uncomfortable, so I thought if she covered up, everything would be all right."

Canela ran into the room, her tinkling laughter filling the air. "Oh, Tristan, how generous of you."

The gowns hung over her arm, the deep rose one on top. His favorite.

Diana couldn't believe it. The only way Canela could have known Tristan's preference was if she'd resumed eavesdropping or had looked into their windows.

Canela threw her arms around his neck and showered him with kisses. He jerked his face before she could capture his mouth. Undaunted, she kissed his cheek and ear. Her fragrance surrounded them, a combination of the wind's fresh scent and the musky odor of sex.

Of all the things Diana had feared when Tristan had broken free on the ship, she hadn't considered this. Unable to stomach the scene any longer, she pushed to her feet.

He pried Canela from him. "Leave. Now." He grabbed Diana's wrist. "Sit down."

She didn't want to but wasn't about to make a spectacle, and sat.

He spoke to Canela. "I told you to leave."

Hurt welled in her eyes. "Before I eat? I can no longer take my meals in this room? Do you want me to sleep in the courtyard now, too, on the dirt rather than my mattress? Have you ordered me to wear these gowns so they might protect me from the night when I sleep outside?"

Tristan slouched. "You can keep your bedchamber but take your meals with the other women, not here."

"Today?"

"Ever."

She ran from the room.

James lifted his eyebrows. "That went well."

Peter looked bewildered. "Are you serious? I thought it went quite badly."

A loud crash sounded down the hall.

"Bloody hell." Tristan left the room.

"Diana." James gestured her back into her chair. "It'd be best if you stayed here."

She flushed at his interference, her embarrassment complete. "Why? I'm already aware he's going to Canela."

James elbowed Peter. He shoved his bacon into his mouth, then fled the room and coming trouble.

James smiled sweetly at her. "Tristan wed you."

Indeed, he had and had promised his fidelity, proving he was a good man. However, even a saint couldn't avoid temptation forever, especially with someone as persistent and cunning as Canela. She'd lure and bewitch, playing to Tristan's honor, his need to be fair. She'd pretend hurt, encourage his pity, and would seek comfort.

Diana didn't want to consider what would happen then. She'd never been more disheartened or afraid and had no idea how to fight the woman. "Yes, I know he wed me. I wear his marriage collar so I can hardly forget my place. If you'll excuse me."

She left the room in the opposite direction Tristan had gone.

* * * *

By the time Tristan reached Canela's bedchamber, she'd already broken a large vase and had taken her dagger to the gold-colored gown.

Breathing hard, she stopped slashing the fabric and glanced over.

He focused on her blade. "Lower your weapon."

"As you wish." She lifted the dagger above her chest, the point directly over her heart. "Should I bring it down now?"

He strode into the room and caught her wrist. "Stop it."

"No. I want to die."

He was tempted to challenge her lie but took the weapon and threw it into the hall. The thing clattered across the floor. "Quit behaving so foolishly, understand?"

She yanked her wrist from him. "I understand nothing. I am no more than a servant now. I must dress in these gowns. Very well, I shall." She untied her bright red cloth and tossed it aside.

He backed into the hall.

Diana hadn't followed him. Yet.

He had to end this before she did show up. "Put the cloth back on."

Canela held her hands behind herself, flaunting her nudity. Youth made her skin smooth and plump, its color flawless. The delicate curls between her legs were as dark as her hair. Although breathtaking, she wasn't Diana.

He fought his rising temper. "Cover yourself."

"Why?" Her eyes widened. "Will the gowns protect me from the night's cold wind when you make me sleep on the dirt outside?"

"I've already said you can remain here. That hasn't changed, nor will it as long as you behave yourself."

"How?"

She wanted to play. He wouldn't with her. Ever. "By keeping your hands off me. I'm wed now and it's time you thought of doing so yourself. Adamo adores you. He'll be a good husband."

She curled her upper lip. "He is a fool who does not live in this house. He is nothing. He has nothing. Not the diamond marriage collar, nor silks and jewels."

Tristan couldn't hide his surprise. It wasn't like Canela to speak the truth or lose control.

Her color drained. "I did not mean what I said. I was hurt. You hurt me."

"I'll give you silks and jewels as a dowry when you wed Adamo. You can also have one of the larger rooms in the other wing as a wedding gift. There's no reason for you and Adamo to live elsewhere on the island."

Canela stepped back. "He would never agree to live here."

"Then we'll build a house for you and him when you're wed."

"A house of mud, not stone."

"Damnation, be grateful for what's being offered to you."

Contempt turned her beautiful features ugly. "I am most grateful you offer me what the Englishwoman does not want."

"There's enough for all. None of this luxury matters to Diana, only to you. Now, get dressed and don't force my hand. If you do, I'll put you out of this house." He left.

"You will regret choosing her."

He looked over. "Are you threatening me?"

"I speak only the truth. You have chosen the wrong woman to rule beside you."

"No one rules here."

"Then why did you order me to wear the gowns? Why do you keep threatening to turn me away from this house?"

He had no ready answer.

Canela smiled, her manner seductive and assured. "Do not worry. I know the Englishwoman is jealous of my beauty, so I will wear the gowns, but I will not wed Adamo. I will save myself for you. Only you. I will wait until my time comes to be at your side where I belong."

"In that case, you'll have to wait an eternity."

Her smile faded and her eyes grew cold. "My people wanted me, one of their own, to rule beside you. For the moment, you have denied them." She advanced a step. "Think of what they will say if you do turn me away from this house. Do you want them to know how you treat me? How you wound me?"

He strode away.

She shouted, "Do you?"

He stopped. For the first time he considered what the other islanders would think if he denied her this luxury. Would they accuse him of merely using her until an Englishwoman arrived, then hate Diana for his sins, and demand he choose Canela instead?

A chill raced through him.

He'd never discard Diana for Canela, and worried what the islanders would do at that point. This was their land by birth, not his. There were nearly two hundred adults. They could easily force him, Diana, Peter, and James to leave with nowhere on God's earth for them to go. England was completely out of the question. Islands reachable by the skiff might not have enough fresh water, game, or arable soil.

Days ago, bringing Diana here had seemed perfect. Not once had he considered these complications.

At last, he looked over.

Canela's smile was icier than her eyes.

If she did anything to harm Diana, he'd kill her no matter the consequences to him. For the moment, though, he had no choice except to allow her in the house. At least while she was here, he could keep an eye on her. "I'm warning you, stay away from my wife."

He left the hall before she could respond.

Chapter 7

As the new quartermaster, Vincent stood next to Captain Montgomery on the main deck. They and the crew waited for Roger Beemer to speak.

Like the other pirates, Beemer was a young man who looked older than his years. "We've been at this fool task for days. We ain't getting nowhere. I say we forget Miss Fletcher and Tristan. Surely, they're at the bottom of the sea by now or in the belly of a fish. We need to set sail and take another prize."

The crew exchanged glances.

The men had now checked two uninhabited islands and had grown reluctant to waste their efforts on a third, increasingly convinced it was a lost cause.

Vincent knew better. Although he hated Tristan for escaping with Diana, he also respected the man's determination and intelligence. Tristan understood the sea as no other mariner did. He wasn't likely to have taken a route where he might have starved or drowned.

No, he was still out there, and they had to find him. A moment Vincent coveted. Last night, he and Montgomery had made a pact to split the ransom between them and to take Diana in the same manner. To hell with the other men. Vincent needed them to run the ship and to fight Tristan wherever he may be. Afterward, they wouldn't share in any prize.

The other pirates grew increasingly animated and shouted "Aye!" to Beemer's newest complaints about how they'd worked for nothing.

Beemer put up his hands for silence. "I say we now take a vote on where we should—"

Vincent's shot tore away the man's forehead, his blood spraying the main deck, the report lingering in the muggy air. Oddly enough, Beemer remained standing, seemingly frozen in place.

The ship rose on a gentle swell.

Beemer dropped like a rock.

With his other pistol in hand, Vincent pointed its muzzle at the crew. "The next fool that suggests giving up the search receives the same."

Although the men were armed, they were still like sheep, waiting for someone to lead them. They voiced no opposition to the original plan. If they had, Vincent would have executed them without pause until they cut him down. He had no desire to be evenhanded and fair as Tristan had always been, which only wasted precious time. Hard violence always worked faster with complete obedience the reward.

He kept his weapon trained on them. "We sail for the third island."

* * * *

In the last moments before waking, Tristan had an overwhelming sense of Diana watching him.

Days before, he would have pulled her into his arms and kissed her savagely, enjoying her surprise and desire. Now the promise of her quiet scrutiny annoyed rather than aroused. Here of late, Diana did little except look at him, her expression neutral, thoughts unknown. During their lovemaking, she searched his face to the point where he wanted to shout, 'What?' but was afraid her answer would hurt. The times he'd smiled to coax out her playful side, she'd answered with the saddest looks he'd ever known.

When he spoke to her, which was necessary, as she never initiated converse, she answered politely and succinctly. No wasted words. No sweet teasing. Her behavior drove Tristan quite mad. This had to be about the incident with Canela and the gowns. How dare Diana refuse the closeness he wanted and needed when he'd tried to mend the situation. After he'd promised Diana his fidelity, she had no reason to be jealous of anyone or to wonder if he lied. She couldn't have believed he'd ever enjoyed a woman as he had her, or had the desire, not to mention the stamina, to make love hour after hour with anyone else as they had.

He'd never been as exhausted, pleased, happy, frustrated, angry, and damned tired of her blasted civility. He wanted her fire, passion, even her rage. At least, she'd give him something to work with.

This had to end now.

He opened his eyes and froze, a razor inches from his face. The steel glinted murderously in the morning light. Alarmed, he grabbed Canela's wrist.

She gasped.

He squeezed, forcing her to release the weapon. The moment the blade hit the mattress, he was on his feet and pushed her against the wall. "What do you think you're doing? *Answer me.*"

She blinked wildly. "I came to shave you as I always have."

Tristan opened his mouth, then shut it. Since Diana's arrival, he'd forgotten about his and Canela's morning ritual. Diana hadn't known about it. She wasn't in their bed or anywhere in the chamber.

He shook Canela. "Where's Diana? Tell me."

"I do not know. I found the door open and came inside."

He tore through the room for his robe but couldn't find the blasted thing. Finally, he tied a silk sheet around his hips.

If his sudden modesty surprised Canela, she hid her feelings well. Her provocative smile said she'd also forgotten these last seconds, the gowns, and his marriage, *again.*

"I will shave you now." She padded to the razor.

He stood in her way. "There's no need to."

"It has been so long since I have." She stroked his bristly cheek.

He pulled away.

Anger flashed in her eyes, but she recovered effortlessly and gestured to a chair. "Please sit so I can begin."

"No. You'll not shave—wait, the gown you have on." She wore the rose-colored one he'd loved so much on Diana.

Canela ran her palms over her breasts barely contained by the silk. "You gave it to me with the others."

"I did not. It belongs to my wife, and I want it returned to her."

Fury flickered across Canela's face, followed by seduction. "Then I will remove it."

"Not here."

She undid the laces.

He clenched his jaw. "Go to your own room."

"It is so far away. Too far." She bared her breasts.

He tore the sheet from his hips, yanked on his breeches, and left the room before Diana saw this. That is, if she came back.

She wasn't in the dining area.

He bolted to the stables, praying she hadn't taken a mare in a futile attempt to ride to the beach and the skiff to escape.

No horses were missing.

Mist hovered over parts of the island where the sun hadn't burned it away. She wasn't racing through the filmy whiteness or darting around trees.

She had to be in the mansion.

Short of it, island children spotted him.

"*Capitaine!*" Three-year-old Henri ran into Tristan's legs.

Tristan staggered, pretending he might fall.

The child shrieked in delight and wrapped his chubby arms around Tristan's legs. "*Donnez-moi un tour.*" Give me a ride.

The other children squealed the same request.

Tristan loved the little ones but wanted to find Diana so he could rail at her for worrying him, after which she'd probably nod politely, give him nothing else, and behave as a stranger, not his besotted wife. He had to settle this to his satisfaction today. Tempering his eagerness to leave, he swung each child over his head and in a full circle, then returned to the mansion.

Diana wasn't in their bedchamber, but at least Canela had left. The rose-colored gown lay crumpled next to the razor. He tossed both into the armoire, padded to Peter's room, and rapped hard on the door.

"Whu?" Sleep thickened Peter's voice.

"Is your sister in there?"

"Uh... I don't know. Let me check under the bed."

"Never mind."

She wasn't in the other rooms. Finally, he stopped in the doorway to the library.

Diana was inside, wearing his robe, her back to him. She struggled to reach a volume on an upper shelf.

He closed the door gently and came up behind her.

She flinched.

"Easy, it's only me." Lightheaded at her sweet-musky scent, he pressed his length into her and reached for the book she wanted. After reading the spine, he slipped his hand beneath the silk robe and cradled her naked breast. Its weight and warmth stole coherent thought. His cock stiffened and his lids slipped down. "Is this the book you wanted?" He lowered his mouth to her ear. "It's in French."

"Yes, I know, but thank you for pointing that out."

Her good manners were going to kill him. He leaned over to see her face. She turned away. Disappointed, he straightened. "Then you're also aware you aren't skilled in reading it."

"Thank you, I know that too." She took the volume and tried to sidle away.

Tristan stepped back. When she reached the door, he couldn't let her go. "Diana, wait. Please."

She stopped lowering the handle, but she didn't face him.

Never had he met such a willful woman, one he couldn't live without. "I only meant to remedy the situation with Canela, not anger or humiliate you. I know you're concerned about Peter being around bare-breasted women. However, I haven't the right to tell them what to wear. The only reason I tried with Canela was because of our past. And it is in the past. But you must understand, what the women do is up to them and their husbands or lovers. Not me. Not you."

She looked over. "I do understand the situation you were in, which was of my own making. I take full responsibility, and you have my sincerest apology."

Stunned, he gestured helplessly. "Then why have you been so somber and polite with me like you are now? You're not to leave the room until you tell me what's on your mind."

She gave him one of her sad looks.

"None of that, either. I can't guess what you're thinking. Out with it."

"Very well." She leaned against the door, the volume to her chest. "When you told me your mother was a doxy and your father was unknown, you said pity disgusted you."

He tensed. "It does. I'll not abide it, especially from you."

"You honestly believe it's pity I feel, and for you of all people? Are you completely unaware of what you've accomplished despite your humble beginnings? How many languages do you speak? Five?"

"What does it matter how many?"

"I want to know. Tell me."

"Seven."

She shook her head and regarded his volumes. The bookcases stretched from floor to ceiling. Other works were stacked on the long table and chairs. "From the looks of what you have in here, you also know history, geography, science, literature, so many subjects I can hardly remember them all. Can't you see how brilliantly you've survived and how educated you are? Far more than most nobles."

"But I'm hardly noble, am I?"

"How dare you make light of this. You live like a veritable king."

That meant nothing. Although Diana's hair was sleep-mussed and her attire just a shade away from wanton, she was the most elegant woman he'd ever known. If anyone had a claim to nobility, she did. Without meaning to, she'd made him feel so unworthy of her.

"I live this way because I won the island in a night of wagering, after which I had to kill the man who lost it before he put a bullet in my head.

Now you know how truly noble I am. Have you forgotten I'm a pirate? A common criminal?"

Insults she'd once used.

Her face flushed. "Surely you had good cause to go on the account."

Ah, now he understood her true intent. She wanted to learn the bleakest part of his past. However, they had a deal. He would only tell her everything when he had her respect and heart. "You speak as if we were friends. Are you saying you're finally prepared to give me your all?"

"You have that from Canela."

"To hell with her, I want it from you."

"She's quite beautiful, and you've had relations with her."

He crossed the room and placed his hands on her shoulders. "Is it impossible for you to believe the only reason I had relations with her is because I'd yet to come upon you?"

"You didn't come upon me. I came upon you."

He threw back his head and laughed. "So you did. With a kick to my leg and your first demand that I get to my feet. You seemed quite intent on it." His smile faded. "And calling me coward."

Embarrassment flooded her features. "At the time I thought you were."

"No more?"

Her gaze softened briefly before she grew distant. "You've been brave enough to repeatedly request I give you my all."

"Request?"

"No one, not even you, can demand such a thing. One can only hope. Most men in your position would have settled for a wife's simple compliance in their bed."

"I've already told you I'm not most men." He ran his hands down her arms. "I demand all you have to give. Do I have that from you?"

She lowered her face. "I can't offer so much as yet."

"Why not? Do you expect me to say the words first? Very well, I shall."

"No." She rested her fingertips on his lips. "Remember, words have power, they should be used with great care, not simply parroted."

He kissed her fingers. "What makes you think they would be?"

She sagged. "I can hardly keep up."

"With what?"

"You, of course."

"Me?" He shook his head, not understanding and then he did. "Well, dear girl, as a man, my hunger's far greater when it comes to carnal desire."

"I'm well aware of your sexual appetite, which isn't any greater than mine."

He leaned into her. "Are you quite certain?"

She pushed him back. "Quite. Lust is hardly what this is about." She lifted the book, a history of France. "I must understand this."

"Why? I hardly expect you to do so."

"Your expectations aren't what drive me. I require this. Diana, the woman. Not Diana your wife or mother of your children. You won't leave me behind. I intend to learn French to keep up with you, to share your interests, and to communicate with the islanders. I'll also learn their customs. If this is going to be my home, then—"

"Not if, this *is* your home. Your place will always be beside me till your last breath, understand?"

"Then I want to belong. I won't have the islanders pitying me. Nor will you do such a thing, do you understand?"

"Pity you? Surely you can't be serious."

"At the moment you hardly consider me at all except for the pleasure I can bring you. I intend to change the situation." She slapped the volume against his chest.

He caught the book before it fell to the floor.

"You'll use these works to teach me French. After French we'll tackle the other languages, then history, geography, and whatever else remains."

Tristan shoved the volume under his arm fearing the lessons would take the remainder of their days. "And what's my reward for this?"

"My gratitude. It's what makes a friendship. Doing kind acts for each other."

"I see." He rested his palm on the door near her head. "Gratitude is hardly an act. So, what kind act do you intend to do for me?"

A smile played across her lush lips. "I'll be as wanton as you want in our bed."

If she were any wilder, she'd kill him. "I already have your passion. I need something else."

She traced his nipple. His skin tingled. "Name whatever you want and it's yours."

What she did right now was nice, but he should choose something new. A task he'd definitely enjoy. "From this day forward you'll shave me."

Her slender eyebrows lifted. "Is that why you've neglected your beard these last days?" She ran her thumb over his whiskered chin. "You don't know how to shave yourself? I thought you were a grown man. Perhaps I was wrong. So, little boy, how old are you?"

He liked her saucy tone. "Old enough to have my needs taken care of by others." He backed away. "However, if you refuse to shave me, I'll have to find someone else to do so."

"You will not." She advanced until she was toe-to-toe with him. Hand on his chest, she combed the short hairs. "No other woman has the right to shave you. Shall we proceed?"

Tristan could hardly wait. He opened the door. "Tell me, have you ever shaved a man before?"

"Never. But I'll learn."

* * * *

If her father had been alive to see this, Diana was certain the shock would have killed him.

Tristan sat in a chair in their bedchamber, her straddling him. Male flesh effortlessly touched female flesh because he wore naught except the healed scratches on his cheek. She was equally nude, clothed only in diamonds to show how he possessed her.

Despite his masculine privilege, she held a deadly razor, while being very close to offering him her heart.

Days ago, she wouldn't have believed this possible. After the dining room scene with Canela, Diana had despaired that she and Tristan's relationship would ever work out but couldn't deny her feelings for him. That left one choice. Fighting for his love and friendship in the only way she knew, by becoming a full part of his life and this island.

Shaving him in the nude was a fine start. She dissolved into giggles.

"You find this amusing?"

"No. I'm quite certain every man is shaved in the same manner."

He palmed her breasts. "Pity the poor bastards who haven't been."

She nestled closer, incomplete without his touch. "Haven't been what?"

"Shaved in this manner."

His cock thickened beneath her. Unspeakably lovely. "I'd have to include my father in your comment. Shall I proceed with my task?"

"Please do."

She lathered the soap and applied the bubbles to Tristan's cheeks, upper lip, chin, and throat.

He played with her nipples.

Her aim was so unsteady much of the froth wound up in his hair. She pressed her mouth to his ear. "You must quit arousing me or I'll never be able to keep my hand firm, especially when I'm holding the blade."

He wrapped his arms about her waist. His long fingers dangled over her buttocks. "When you mentioned your father, were you saying what we're doing now wouldn't have met with his approval?"

"The man was determined to resist all pleasure."

Tristan shook his head.

"Careful or I may miss my mark and cut your throat."

He was as still as a corpse. "What of your mother?"

"She never would have cut your throat as she was—"

Tristan tickled her.

"Very well, very well!" Diana squirmed and laughed. "I give you my word to be far more serious. I'll even outdo my father."

"A simple answer is what I ask."

"My mother was a lovely woman, and I miss her greatly." Diana brought the razor to his face. "I'm about to begin on your cheek. *Menton* in French, correct?"

"Not unless you mean chin."

She hung her head. "I did study the language, though I wasn't at all good at it. I shall be now. How do you say cheek in French?"

"*Joue.*"

"I'm about to begin on your joue. Keep still."

"You have my complete obedience. How old were you when your mother died?"

Diana eased the razor down Tristan's cheek. "*Huit.*"

"Eight?"

She nodded.

He sighed. "So young. When did your father pass?"

"When I was seventeen. I forget, how do you say that in French?"

"*Dix-sept.*"

She drew the blade down his cheek in short, careful strokes.

"Were you just seventeen when you met Benedict Bis—"

Her hand jerked. The blade cut Tristan.

He yelped. "Damnation, that stings."

"Do forgive me." She washed the cut and daubed it with linen. "You must keep still."

"And not ask questions about your benefactor?"

She recalled Tristan's anger when she'd told him she belonged to Bishop. It seemed a lifetime ago, yet his fury then was the same as her jealousy over Canela and not soon forgotten. "There's something you must understand. When I learned pirates took Peter, Bishop was the only one who offered to help with my rescue plan."

"You went to him then? His offices?"

She rinsed soap and whiskers off the razor. "No. I had known him before."

"Through your father?"

"No. I met him upon my father's death. Bishop said he was a friend from long ago."

"Was that true?"

"I have no idea. My father never confided his past or present to me. Why? Are you saying Bishop wasn't my father's friend?"

Tristan touched the cut and regarded the blood on his fingertips. "Before he came into your life, did Peter ever have a desire to go to sea?"

"Why?"

"Did he?"

"No, but he was a child. In many ways he still is. Quite impressionable. Surely, Peter overheard Bishop speaking of a mariner's life and took it upon himself to run away, thinking it would be more exciting than doing lessons and becoming a reverend. Besides, when we were on the Lady Lark, Peter said he'd taken off to spare me the expense of housing and feeding him."

"Where did he get the idea? From something you'd said?"

"Never." She slapped Tristan's shoulder lightly.

"What was that for?"

"Your offensive question. Peter's my brother. I would have starved before he had to. When I told him Bishop was concerned for his safety, Peter seemed surprised. He asked how I could be certain it wasn't Bishop who put him in harm's way." She shook her head. "Peter said he'd heard things about the man. What things? Please, you must tell me. Aren't we almost friends?"

Tristan's face flooded with what looked to be love, but he didn't answer.

She stroked his newly shaved cheek. "Please tell me."

"Very well. But keep the razor from me while I do."

Her stomach rolled. If he worried about her reaction, what he had to say must be dreadful. "What did the bloody bastard do to my brother?"

"Diana, I insist you remain calm."

She squeezed the razor handle, nails digging into her palm. "I shall. But give me the truth on Bishop. Tell me everything."

Tristan watched the blade. "Most mariners know he coaxes or kidnaps young boys to his side, then supplies them to captains who command his ships."

"He coaxes? He kidnaps? Why? To avoid paying the boys' wages?"

Tristan glanced past.

"Tell me."

"What he does involves more than money. Voyages are long, wives and lovers missed, women aren't allowed to work on ships so captains seek to ease their needs with—"

"My God. Are you saying Peter was—"

"No, I'm not saying anything of the kind. Although it was Bishop's plan, Peter refused to let anyone use him in such a vile manner, even after the captain had him lashed, then held in irons. He was lucky. Many boys don't survive."

She tried to comprehend such an evil scheme, her and Peter falling into Bishop's hands. They would still be there if not for Tristan. "Peter survived because you saved him."

"I took the ship he was on. The boy chose to come with me."

"Damn you, Tristan, you saved my brother, admit it."

"It's best you be careful with that." The razor nearly touched his chest. She laughed, then cried. "Admit it."

"Yes, I saved Peter and would do it again, for him or any other boy."

Diana threw her arms around him. "Thank you." She kissed his ear, temple, cheek. "You're a wonder and a true man, my dangerous angel."

"Your what?"

She blinked back tears and eased away. The lather she'd put on his chin and throat now clung to her neck and shoulder. "My dangerous angel." She wiped her nose with her finger. "You're quite beautiful, you know."

Tristan pushed back in the chair. "I hardly know such a thing."

"You are. Was your captain's foul plan the reason he lashed you? You received those injuries when you were a boy because you also resisted?"

"No. Peter's story isn't mine, and you've surely had enough history for one day. Come now, shave me. I have work to do teaching you French along with seeing to the animals and land."

"Can I embrace you before I continue?"

He smiled. "I believe I can allow that."

She held him tenderly. Not only had he rescued Peter, he'd saved her too. Diana loved him so much she couldn't keep her feelings hidden any longer and needed to tell him what was in her heart.

Something blue flashed near the window.

Startled, she regarded the heavy foliage and the sea.

The same blue fluttered. Canela wore the silk gown, her face stony, filled with unmasked hatred.

"What is it?" Tristan rubbed her back. "You've gone quite stiff."

She tried to relax but couldn't.

"Diana, what is it?"

"Nothing."

If she told him about Canela, matters would only escalate. Embracing him, Diana let Canela know Tristan was no longer free.

* * * *

James's face flushed deep red. He seemed ready to burst.

Tristan wished he hadn't asked the man to accompany him to check on the crops and animals. "I know you want to laugh. Get on with it."

James howled so loudly, his and Tristan's geldings crab-walked at the unexpected noise.

Tristan prodded his mount to the rise. An impressive head of cattle grazed below. Farmland stretched to the cliffs. Scores of rice paddies lay to the right. This season they'd have an excellent yield. Coupled with the fruit and other crops grown here, there would be plenty to eat. Come this time next year he hoped to have another mouth to feed. A son or perhaps a daughter. He beamed at the thought of a little girl who might look like Diana.

James couldn't stop laughing. "Tell me, are you going to allow your wife to shave you again?"

There were cuts on both cheeks and his chin, not to mention several bristly spots Diana had missed completely. She'd promised to be better at the task tomorrow, and to shave him every day.

Even the thought gave Tristan pause. Still, he adored her eagerness and new warmth. "Shaving me is Diana's task, no one else's. It's what friends do."

"Draw blood from each other's faces?"

Tristan suppressed a smile. "Hardly. They do kind acts for each other. Diana wants to be my friend, so—"

"Wait. Why would she want to do that? Good Lord, man, she's your wife. Surely she must be aware of it by now."

"She also wants to be friends along with everything else, even learning all the languages I know and the other subjects I've studied so we have shared interests."

"Odd notion. Think you can live with it?"

"Actually, her idea strikes me as quite brilliant. It's far easier to converse with a woman who knows what you're going on about than one who doesn't."

"I suppose. Though I've never thought of a woman as someone I needed to converse with, at least about things other than making me happy in my bed. However, if that's what you want, just make certain Diana doesn't learn everything. She could become a shrew. It's happened with other women."

"I have nothing to fear with her. She's quite taken with me. Calls me her dangerous angel."

James threw back his head and laughed heartily.

Tristan smacked his freckled chest. "You should be so lucky."

"I should wonder why she calls you such a thing."

"I told her about Peter."

James's laughter bubbled for a moment before fading away. "You did? What did she say?"

"She thanked me for saving him." Tristan gave James a knowing look. "She truly thanked me."

He nodded and wheeled his horse around to follow Tristan's mount. "Did you tell her how you came to be lashed?"

"No."

"Why not? I would think that tale would have her worshipping you."

Perhaps, but he wanted her love for who he was now not because he'd suffered. Besides, he and Diana had a pact. He'd tell her his history when she gave him her all. Until he heard her declaration, he'd forget his past. "I have other ways to woo my wife."

"You never mean to tell her?"

"The time will come. So keep your big mouth shut, do you hear? You and Peter nearly did me in with the incident concerning the gowns."

"It was hardly our intent. You should have told us your plan to have Canela cover herself. We would have stood by you. We always have."

They surely had. He smiled until James looked past, his manner cautious. Tristan twisted around.

Canela was nearby, wearing the blue silk gown. The skirt flared in the breeze. Her dark hair whipped around her shoulders.

To his surprise, she and Adamo faced each other and held hands.

Tristan slapped James's arm and pointed behind himself. They directed their horses to the new path to avoid disturbing the couple.

When they were far enough away not to be overheard, James reined in his gelding. "Do you think Canela's finally decided on Adamo as a husband?"

"I offered her a large dowry and one of the nicest bedchambers as an incentive."

"It appears she's accepted."

"She said she intends to wait for me." Unease gnawed at him. "She said the island people wanted to see her, one of their own, ruling next to me. Do you believe her?"

"This is the first I've heard of it. Are you worried she's going to cause a revolt?"

"They outnumber us, James."

"True, but you're a good man. You share whatever crops we have, much of which you developed. I believe you're worrying over something that's never going to be. Canela's interests are finally where they should have been all along. If you want to make matters right, tell her she doesn't have to wear those gowns. They look quite ridiculous."

"I fully agree. Diana said as much this morning concerning the other woman. Once she agrees about Canela, the matter will be settled once and for all."

"Oh, you are wed."

"Enough or I'll be forced to run you through."

James laughed.

So did Tristan. "Come on, we have work to do."

* * * *

Although Tristan and James were some distance away, the wind delivered clopping noises from their horses' hurried retreat.

Outrage punched through Canela. Her shoulders burned. Tristan had seen her with Adamo and hadn't been jealous. Instead, he'd wheeled his mount around to allow her a moment alone with her new lover.

"Canela." Adamo squeezed her fingers gently. "Are you hearing me?"

She nodded.

His mouth moved with more words she didn't care about. His eyes and hair were as dark as hers, skin as richly brown, features decidedly handsome.

None of it mattered. Not his youth, virility, and his obvious love for her when he'd never own colorful silks, sparkling jewels, or the fine stone house. Only Tristan did, and he'd taken it from her to give to his English wife.

Canela fumed at Diana shaving him, a task that belonged to her. Diana had nicked his face repeatedly. Tristan merely laughed. He'd taken the razor and helped her into the rose gown. After working the laces, he ordered her to bend over the table. The moment she had, he lifted the silk, bared her, and then he'd mounted.

Diana's lewd moan said she no longer remembered or cared that Canela watched. He'd never known. Finished with his passion, he'd leaned over Diana, his face flooded with love. Never had he looked at Canela that way. Never had she required it. She wanted his riches, not his heart.

"Become my wife." Adamo kissed her palm. "I will make you happy."

Repelled, she wanted to pull away but considered his usefulness to her. "What if the Englishwoman tries to stop us?"

"How could she?"

Canela gestured to her gown. "She demanded I wear this. Who knows what else she has in store for me?"

"Wed me and I shall rule you."

She pushed back her annoyance and feigned worry. "If I tell you something, will you keep my words close to your heart and not reveal them to the others on this isle?"

"I promise. Tell me what troubles you."

She lowered her face. "I heard the Englishwoman say she wants our people to stay out of the courtyard and to never come near the stone house."

Adamo pressed her hands to his chest. "When did you hear this? Who was she speaking to?"

"Her brother. She told him this morning. As Tristan's woman, she has the right to put me out of my bedchamber. But to deny our people use of the courtyard in a house they built goes too far. I fear she and Peter will try to convince Tristan to do so."

"Then we must speak to him first."

"No, that would be madness."

"Why?" Adamo looked puzzled. "You know I have no friendship for Tristan, but after he won this land, he promised we could use the courtyard. He will listen to us."

Canela held back a frustrated shout, wanting to call Adamo a fool. "He will listen to his wife. Why else would I be in this gown? What else will she convince him of in order to harm us?"

"Then we must do something."

She agreed and snuggled close, reveling in the moment they murdered Diana. Tristan and his wealth would then belong to Canela alone.

Chapter 8

As Diana bathed, the shuttered windows commanded her full attention. Although she missed the sunlight and soft breeze spilling inside the bedchamber, anyone might come in while she was alone. She'd never considered such a thing until Canela spied. Equally unsettling was Diana's response, her desire not suffering a whit during her and Tristan's impassioned lovemaking.

She didn't want to consider how many other intimate moments the girl had witnessed or if she'd ever leave them in peace. Not that Canela's future moves mattered. Despite what anyone here did or didn't do, Diana would enjoy Tristan.

She was becoming more uncivilized by the day but did trouble over what to wear when she finished her bath. Her mariner's clothing wouldn't do. She wanted these people to accept her as one of them and had to dress the part except for baring her breasts. She tied a silk cloth around them, discarded that as obscene, and wrapped a sheet about herself, draping the end over one shoulder and arm like a Roman toga. An acceptable solution and almost civilized.

She padded to the library and stopped at the closed door. Loud sighs came from inside, most definitely Peter's.

Tristan must have given him quite a lesson to do. Good. At least he was getting a gentleman's education. Pleased, Diana opened the door.

The young woman in Peter's arms flinched. She mumbled something in French and fled the room.

Peter sank to his chair and yawned.

Diana slammed the door.

He jumped, then frowned. "Don't bother lecturing me. We're not in England any longer."

"Quite right, but we are still civilized. Look at me when I speak to you."

He laughed. "Are you wearing a bedsheet?"

Diana crossed her arms over the ivory silk. "We're speaking about you, not me."

"No reason to discuss me at all."

"Have you gone mad? You were kissing a girl."

He colored. "So? It's not a crime."

"You're just a boy."

"The hell I am."

"Watch your language and quit behaving like a sullen child, which proves you're not yet a man."

"I am too."

"Not until you can make your own way in the world. Look around you, Peter. Do you truly believe Tristan accomplished this by amusing himself with women every waking hour?"

"Of course not. He became a pirate." The boy shrugged. "It's what I'll be."

She sank to a chair, her legs no longer able to hold her. "You are aware piracy is morally wrong and does carry risks such as you being hanged or dying during battle."

"Tristan did all right for himself."

She wanted to trounce him. "Has he ever bragged about going on the account? Did he tell you he always wanted to be a pirate? I think not. It's my guess he was forced into the life like many other men. He also saved your silly neck from the vile captain you served. He wants you to have better than he did, and this is how you repay him?"

Peter pressed into his chair. "He told you what happened to me?"

"He did. And you're lucky he saved you. So let me tell you this, little brother. Until you're a man and can make your own way in this world, you will do your lessons just as your benefactor demands. If you refuse, I'll ask Tristan to put you to work in the fields or tending the cattle and pigs. Trust me, the labor will be hard, the pleasures few."

"None of that's going to happen. He's my friend, not yours."

She nearly laughed. "You can't possibly believe that. Tristan's my husband, or have you forgotten?"

He crossed his arms. "Say whatever you want. I'll never be a gentleman, no matter what you threaten me with."

"I'm doing no such thing. I'm advising you as to your options. You may become whatever you wish as long as you try."

"Is that what you think?" He regarded her as if she'd lost her mind. "What if I want to become a merchant? How would I do so here? How am I to do anything on this isle except farm or engage in piracy?"

"You'll leave this island of course." The words had spilled out before she could stop them. Although the prospect pained her, someday Peter had to return to civilization and his own future.

"You think so? What about my time with Tristan and his crew? You said he and the other men would hang so I could go free. Clearly they won't, which makes me as wanted as them. I have to stay here like him and you. Far as I can tell, there aren't any cities or towns here. They're back in England where these stupid lessons are required. Here, they're quite useless." He grabbed a volume and slammed it open. "But as you have Tristan's ear and I do not, I'll learn these bloody things." He slouched.

Diana's first reaction was to tell him to sit erect as a gentleman should. Her second was to forego the instruction, his words haunting her.

He was right about being marked. Even if his former shipmates didn't point the finger at him, Bishop would. The bloody coward would make her pay for reneging on their bargain.

She went queasy. A few minutes before, Peter's future had seemed so bright. Now, she couldn't bear to consider what would become of him. She also feared for her and Tristan. They'd have children surely. Those precious little souls would be stuck on this island. She'd never stop worrying about their safety, whether they'd have enough to eat, or what might happen to them if Tristan's former crew arrived one day and...

No, she didn't want to consider such an outcome. He'd insisted there wasn't anything to fear from the other pirates. She hoped that were true and not just his boundless confidence speaking.

The library door swung open.

Tristan smiled. "Working hard?"

Peter huffed. "What choice do I have?"

Tristan winked at her.

Tears filled her eyes.

He glanced at her French lessons. "Did I make the work too difficult?"

"Indeed, you did." Peter flipped a page so forcefully he ripped the paper.

"I wasn't speaking of your lessons." Tristan regarded her. "Are you having difficulty?"

The greatest. On the day they'd met, she thought her only challenge would be lying with Tristan, allowing him to rule her future. Now, she understood how quickly her world would end if she were to lose him or their children.

"Diana?"

She ached to say what was in her heart; only now wasn't the time. Perhaps tonight when they were in their bedchamber. "I'm managing."

He nodded slowly. "Good to hear. However, if you could spare a moment I need to have a word with you."

Peter looked up and gaped at Tristan. "Have you been in a fight? Your face has cuts all over it."

"Worry about your work, not my face."

"Why do I have to keep at this when she gets to stop?"

"She's my wife."

Peter sighed loudly but resumed his work.

In the hall, Tristan regarded her toga. "Quite unusual and fetching." He rested his hands on her upper arms. "Tell you what, I'll have the women make several gowns in the same design. Would that please you?"

She wanted his and their children's safety. She required their future. "It's very thoughtful of you."

He gave her an odd look. "Are you feeling all right?"

She lied with a nod. "You wanted to have a word?"

"Right. Earlier, when James and I were out riding, we saw Canela sharing a tender moment with Adamo."

Diana couldn't believe it. "Are you quite certain?"

Something passed over his face.

"You aren't certain."

He shrugged. "All I can say is they seemed quite intent on each other, so I thought now would be a good time for her to go back to her usual attire. It suits this climate far better than those foolish English gowns." He stroked the swell of Diana's breasts. "If your overwhelming jealousy has passed."

"I doubt that moment will ever happen when it comes to you. As I recall, you've repeatedly threatened to murder any man who fancied me."

"The threat holds. You are in agreement concerning Canela, right?"

Diana could hardly relax about any decision concerning the girl. However, insisting she cover her breasts would only increase the tension and make Canela more headstrong, possibly dangerous. "I am."

"Splendid. I'll have Gavra tell her."

"No, wait. I will."

He shook his head.

"Please." She rested her palm on his chest. "As long as we're here I want to belong."

"What do you mean, as long as we're here? Where else would we be?"

She couldn't get into her concerns now. "Nowhere. We'll be here, of course. And I must belong, so this can be my first step in doing so."

"I'd prefer you avoid the first step and go straight to the second."

"I can't hide from her forever. Do you want her to think I'm afraid and she has the upper hand?"

"Of course not."

"Then we agree. By telling her, I can prove I respect the islanders' customs. I'm certain it's important to the other women and men."

"It is."

"Well then, where can I find her?"

He rubbed his neck. "As I came in here, I saw her in the courtyard feeding the fowl."

"I should get on with it then."

"I'll go with you."

"No." She kissed him softly, then backed away. "Allow me to do this on my own. Go back to your work. I'll be fine."

* * * *

In the courtyard, traveler's trees and other types of palms rustled in the light wind, Canela nowhere around. Squealing and giggling children ran past Diana. Affection filled her, reminding her of the babes she might have, and if they'd be happy and safe here.

As Peter's comments dogged her, children of all ages engaged in play. Infants nursed at their mothers' breasts. Needing to be a part of this, no matter her concerns, she smiled in greeting to the new mothers and gestured to their infants. "*Beau bébés.*" Beautiful babies.

They beamed.

Pleased, Diana approached the women who worked the potter's wheels and looms. When they noticed her watching, she tried to relax and look friendly. "Bonjour."

They returned her greeting, expressions expectant.

She struggled to put together a proper French sentence to convey how happy she was on the isle and hoped to stay forever. Sadly, she had to settle for something far less. "*Beau jour.*" Beautiful day.

Despite her poor pronunciation and the difference in dialect, the women's faces brightened. One after the other spoke, the words coming so fast Diana had no idea what they said.

At last, they fell silent and waited for her response. She offered a wobbly smile and a nod, hoping that would do. Surprisingly, they seemed pleased.

She stopped holding her breath. "If you'll excuse me."

They exchanged glances.

She turned and started. Canela was only a few feet away, dressed in the crimson gown, flinging feed to the fowl. Their wings fluttered wildly. Their cackles filled the sticky air along with the children's excited shrieks.

Steeling herself, she approached Canela. The other women fell silent. Diana was tempted to check if they watched, but didn't.

Striving to be civil, she inclined her head. "Good day."

Canela stopped tossing the feed and stared at Diana's diamond collar.

The thing seemed too tight, like someone's hands around her neck. "I want you to know, it's my sincere intent to make everyone's life on this island as pleasant as possible. Therefore, my husband and I have decided—"

"Tristan."

"Yes, Tristan. My husband."

Jaw clenched, Canela regarded the collar.

Diana cleared her throat. "He and I discussed the matter of your attire. We've agreed you should wear what the other women do as it's far more comfortable in this climate. However, please keep the gowns. You can use the silk for the cloth you tie about your hips."

A chicken cackled. Canela kicked the creature and faced Diana, her mouth a hard line, hands gripped on the feed bowl.

Diana wanted to flee, but recalled what she'd said to Tristan about being afraid, allowing Canela to have the upper hand. Diana leaned in so the others wouldn't overhear. "About you looking into the bedchamber when my husband and I are in there."

Rage burned in Canela's eyes, her hatred even deeper than before.

Diana's skin crawled but she couldn't let the girl cow her. "This is your first and last warning. Never look into our room again." She left.

* * * *

Tristan didn't see Diana until the evening meal. When he asked if she'd handled Canela to her satisfaction, she claimed the matter was settled and offered nothing else. She picked at her food, followed none of the converse, offered no comments, but chose instead to stare at Peter.

Peter noticed and frowned.

She retreated further into herself, keeping her thoughts from everyone.

When the islanders brought out their musical instruments, she declined the entertainment and went to the library.

Tristan had business to conduct at the stables and entered their bedchamber hours later. The room was so stuffy he threw open the shutters to let in the cooling night air.

Diana immediately extinguished the lamps, save for one that offered scant illumination.

"What are you doing?" He squinted, scarcely able to see her in the gloom. "There's no moon tonight. Light the lamps at once. When I have you, I intend to see what's going on."

"Close the shutters first."

"It's too warm in here to do so. Light the lamps now."

"No. Someone might see."

"What? You mean someone might watch us?"

"It's possible. All one has to do is come up to the windows and look inside."

"Here?" He chuckled at the preposterous notion. "The islanders are proud people. They're hardly concerned with our activities. I would think they find our pale flesh and features quite repulsive. Go on. Light those lamps and quit behaving like a silly virgin. You're hardly one anymore."

"I am well aware of that."

He'd meant to tease, not irritate her, and offered a smile.

She didn't soften. "My purity or lack of it has nothing to do with this. I'm simply trying to be civilized and retain some measure of decency."

"Very well, but since when?"

She made an annoyed sound, held a sheet to herself, and lit the lamps.

He glanced at the windows. "This is about Canela, isn't it? Have you seen her out there, looking in?"

Diana drew the sheet to her throat.

"You have. When? This morning? While we were—"

"While I was shaving you."

Rage shot through him. "Why didn't you tell me this before?"

She lit the last lamp and sat on the mattress. The sheet covered her from throat to toes. "I handled the matter."

"Are you quite sure? Given your current modesty, it would appear you're hardly convinced of her obedience."

"She's determined."

"So am I."

"Where are you going?"

He stopped at the door. "To turn her away from this house. I told her what I'd do if she didn't respect our privacy."

"Tristan, wait." Diana pulled her legs under her. "I need to have a word with you on another matter. Please. Hear me out."

He closed the door and leaned against it. "What's wrong?"

She looked at the opened window, the inky night beyond. "Earlier today I came upon Peter kissing one of the young women."

Tristan grinned. "Well done."

"What?"

"Not you seeing it. Him doing it."

"What?"

Tristan tempered his approval. "Peter is of an age when those things happen. You should have expected it."

"I hardly expected any of this."

"What do you mean?"

"I thought Peter was going to be educated as a gentleman."

"You think I'm not accomplishing that?" Tristan held up his hand. "Wait a moment. This is about the tutor I promised, isn't it? I meant myself, Diana. I didn't tell you at the time as you wouldn't have believed me capable, but I fully intend to tutor Peter until he knows everything he should and more."

"Why bother?"

Tristan frowned. "It's hardly a bother."

"It's hardly necessary as Peter will never have an opportunity to use his skills."

"If he applies himself, he will."

"How can he do so here? He can only use the knowledge in England with no likelihood to return there, since he'd face the gallows, the same as you and James. You're here for life, as I am. For myself, I can accept it. But for Peter? He's only a boy. He could have been anything in England, though here his only options are farming or engaging in piracy, as he so aptly explained. What of the children yet to be, our sons and daughters?"

As warm as he'd been before, Tristan was now as chilled. "What about them?"

"Will there always be enough here for them to eat? What if a storm destroys the crops and cattle? What will our children survive on then? What will they become? Once they're grown, whom will they wed? The islanders?"

Until she'd entered his life, he'd never considered marriage for himself or having a family. His past had been too bleak. Only now, she spoke of the future, needing to know what it held for them.

"Will our children be safe here?" Her eyes glistened in the lamp light. "Will you? Will your former crew—"

"I've already told you, they'll never be able to locate the island as they're unaware of its existence. I happened upon it quite by accident. You're safe here, and I would never allow anyone to harm my children. They and you will never starve, nor want, nor be in any danger. I give you my word on it."

Before she could ask anything else, Tristan left the room.

He ran down the hall to the courtyard, then outside the walls. The breeze whipped his hair. Blood pounded in his ears. At a hilltop, he stopped and rested his forearm against a traveler's tree. What a damn fool he was. Worse, a bloody bastard for not having considered how selfish he'd been.

He'd captured Diana, thinking only of the pleasures he might have with her. She was such a delicious challenge he'd been determined to win and have her desire, love, and respect. To make certain she blessed him with many children.

Not once had he considered the real future.

He rammed his fist into the trunk, pounding his knuckles, drawing blood. A cry caught in his throat, though not at the pain in his hand. The agony lay deep in his heart at Diana's questions about the crops failing, her and their children having nothing to eat, a storm striking the island destroying everything.

Even if none of those events happened and his children grew to adulthood that hardly settled things.

He slammed his fist into the trunk repeatedly and bellowed his torment.

There were no Englishmen on this island for his daughters to wed. His sons would have no commerce. His children would face a future as bleak as their father's, unless he brought Diana back to civilization before any babes were born.

He was here for life, but she wasn't. She'd done nothing wrong, nor had Peter. It would be easy to explain how the boy had no choice except to join a pirate crew. If words didn't suffice, then gold would convince the authorities of his innocence. Peter and Diana could easily escape, provided Tristan released them.

He shivered, cold seeping into his soul. The ceaseless surf mocked him. The salty air did the same, reminding him of the only solution.

He had to provide Diana and Peter safe passage to England. With the gold and jewels he'd give them they would do well. The marriage collar alone could support Diana for decades. The gems would also be a fitting dowry and might possibly capture a noble for her, the aristocratic husband she deserved.

He sank to the ground, drew his knees to his chest, and rested his head on them. Wind washed over him, no longer balmy and caressing, but raw and wretched. As his future would be when Diana was in another man's arms. Even if she were already with child, her new husband could raise the babe as his own. The boy or girl would call him father.

Tristan squeezed his eyes, despair defeating him. "I love you, Diana. My God, I adore you."

He'd wanted to tell her, but hadn't. She'd asked if they were almost friends.

Tina Donahue

They were, but what she'd said tonight convinced him they could go no further. She had to return to England where she'd be truly safe and could thrive under another man's protection and love.

Away from Tristan Kent. A coward and pirate.

Chapter 9

Vincent's rage built at the endless, unproductive search, Tristan and Diana still out of reach. He'd been so certain they'd be on this isle, he had the men comb the remaining vegetation in the dark. One had fallen into a pit, the tumble breaking his spine. Careless fool. Served him right that the crew left him there for the animals and birds to finish off.

As to Tristan, this had been the last location he might have rowed to and survived. Yet, they'd found nothing. Vincent ground the heel of his hand into his forehead.

The crew gave him wide berth at the fire. A short distance away, Montgomery sprawled over the sand, having enjoyed too much rumfustian. His hearty snores matched his overwhelming girth.

Filthy pig. Vincent had a new plan for the captain, which didn't include Diana or the ransom. He'd have those prizes for himself. All he had to do was find his damned quarry.

Fury flared. He drew his pistol and fired.

Someone let out a startled cry. Others looked over. A lemur fell from a tree behind them.

Vincent shoved his pistol back into the brace across his chest. "Cook it."

Two men fetched the animal.

The sea was a great black mass rolling and licking the beach. Even when Vincent squinted, the Lady Lark was invisible to him, the night too dark, though the ship was out there waiting.

Here, firelight danced over the longboats the crew had used to reach shore.

The men threw the lemur to the cook, who proceeded to skin the animal. The promise of warm food brought a festive air to the crew. Some played their fiddles and reeds. Others traded tales. Vincent made no move to stop them or join in, his attention on the longboats. They were much larger than the skiff Tristan had used in his escape.

Damp wind trailed over Vincent's unshaven jaw. His yellow scarf fluttered. The younger men danced. The older ones drank.

Vincent's pulse beat hard. There were islands in these parts few vessels could get near, which meant a man had to use the smallest craft possible. No wonder Tristan had taken the skiff.

Vincent laughed heartily, startling many in the crew. Knowing what his next move would be, he ignored their fearful looks. Come morning, he would implement his plan.

* * * *

Diana waited for Tristan in their bedchamber. He never came back. She worried herself into a fitful sleep and a nightmare in which his crew was on the island stalking them.

She awakened with a start, heartsick at the empty space next to her. Morning light spilled into the room. Dressed in her canvas trousers and Tristan's shirt, she left the bedchamber and ran from room to room. He wasn't in any of them. She rushed to Canela's chamber but didn't enter. He couldn't be inside. No matter his anger or whatever else he'd felt when they last spoke, he wouldn't betray her.

She hurried to Peter's room, rapped once on the door, and opened it.

His arm hid his face. His upper lip fluttered with soft snores.

She shook his shoulder.

He pulled away.

"Peter, wake up. Have you seen Tristan?"

He ran his tongue around his mouth. "How could I? I've been asleep."

"Where would he be at this time of morning?"

"How should I know?"

"Think. You know his duties."

He finished his yawn and rolled onto his belly. "Perhaps he's with the cattle."

"Can I get to the pastures on foot?"

"No. You need a horse. Now leave me be."

"Gladly."

She dashed to the stables. Using her poor French and hand gestures, she convinced an island man to saddle a bay mare for her. After he helped her mount, she smiled. *"Merci. Pâtures?"*

He nodded.

When he didn't indicate their location, Diana warned herself to be patient. She repeated the word, pointed right and left, then lifted her eyebrows in a questioning expression.

He gestured to the right.

Deliberately, she kept the mare at a slow, steady pace. Life as a reverend's daughter had prepared her for endless household and church tasks, not horsemanship on this island. Once in the forest, she rode up a hill and topped the crest, this one different from the one she and Tristan had been on. No farmland lay below, only an impressive amount of cattle grazing. A sprinkling of island men stood to their left, Tristan among them. His blond hair danced in the wind.

Relief washed over Diana.

She ached to join him, but held back, reluctant to discuss their personal problems in front of anyone. She'd wait until after the midday meal to tell him last night's questions and her concerns didn't mean she'd given up on their future. She simply wanted to make certain they were secure, and to work with her husband to ensure happiness, especially for their children.

She rode back to the mansion.

* * * *

Tristan didn't arrive for the midday meal.

When Peter finally came to the table, Diana jumped from her chair. "Where is he? Please, you must tell me."

Peter dropped into his seat. "Tell you what? Who are you going on about?"

"Tristan, of course. Have you seen him?"

The boy shoved two pineapple slices into his mouth. His cheeks puffed with the fruit. "Last I saw he was headed for the fields."

Hours passed.

He entered the dining room during the evening meal.

She pushed to her feet, barely able to contain her emotions.

Tristan leaned down to James. "I need to have a word with you."

"Tristan, wait." She rounded the table.

"Not now." He spoke to James. "Come on."

They left the dining room.

* * * *

The following day was a repeat of the last. In the evening, Diana remained alone in her and Tristan's chamber. The bed was horribly empty without his large body taking up most of the space. The silk sheets were never warm without his heat.

She worried well into the night. When the oil lamps finally burned out, she refilled and lit them so Tristan might see her waiting for him. She made certain the shutters were open as he liked.

He never came.

Sleep overtook her.

* * * *

Tristan lay on the grass, face tilted to the stars, gut churning. After he finally broke down and confided his worries to James, the man was absolutely no help.

James hugged his knees to his chest and rocked like a schoolboy, unable to stay still for a second. "We must be going."

"Not yet."

"Very well, I must be going." He pushed to his feet.

Tristan kicked James's leg, bringing him back down. "I thought you were going to help me."

"I have bloody well tried these last hours but you refuse to listen. Diana is yours. Haven't I said that any number of times? I have. She's required to take the good with the bad. It's in the wedding vows."

"I never heard of any vows that mentioned piracy or hanging. And what of my children, if I'm foolish enough to have them? I have to think of their future."

"That's a long way off, my friend." He punched Tristan's arm. "Tell you what, when your daughters are of an age to wed, I say you and me set sail and drag several Englishmen back here for the little beauties to choose from. How's that sound?"

So outrageous, Tristan finally smiled. "Lovely way to begin a union."

"'Twas the way you and Diana began yours."

He sobered. "Look what it did. How trapped she is."

"You have gone mad. Trapped?" James threw up his hands. "She has all she wants to eat, a beautiful place to live, no real work to be done, and you, her dangerous angel."

Tristan rolled his eyes. "What about our children not being raised in a civilized world?"

"Like England, you mean."

"Where else?"

"Let me think. How about a place where no one hangs? When's the last time we did so here or beat a man till his blood flowed? Or threw him into prison where he died from lack of food and a broken spirit? Or forced a woman to lay with any number of men so she could feed her little ones? Or made some man king by virtue of his birth when all other people are considered less majestic than him, not worthy enough to have shelter, enough food and drink, a future for their children? What makes you think England's so civilized?"

Tristan couldn't have been more stunned. "Have you been reading my volumes on Aristotle?"

"On what?"

"You mean who. Never mind. Where did you come up with those notions?"

"Just looking at what we got here." His gesture took in the land. "My father was a shoemaker and could barely feed my seven siblings, our mother, and me. This is by far the nicest home I've ever had. Isn't it the same for you?"

It was. Still... "It has no cities. No commerce. Not like England. Here, my children would know none of that."

"Then how would they miss it? This would be their home, England simply a word. As far as them getting wed, what would be wrong if they chose one of the island people? Perhaps the sons Gavra might give me." James pointed. "You saying my boys ain't going to be good enough for your girls?"

As far as Tristan was concerned no man on earth would be good enough for his daughters. Though he wasn't about to tell James. "Even if our children fancied each other, it's hardly a solution. What if the crops fail? What if a storm hits and destroys everything?"

"Then we move to another island. We begin again if we must. Besides, what makes you think living in England's so safe? Diana's mother died from the pox and her father got the fever. You see any of them sicknesses here?"

He did not.

James slapped Tristan's arm. "Keep Diana. It's your right as her husband. Go to her and let me go to my woman." He rolled away and escaped at a run.

Tristan bypassed the other side of the compound, where he'd spent last night, and approached his bedchamber from the outside. Uncertain what to do, he finally sat on the windowsill.

Diana's left arm circled her head. Her right rested on his side of the mattress, slender fingers splayed over the sheets seeming to search for him.

Unless she reached out in her dreams for England. Home.

In this barbaric land, he'd insisted she lie naked and willing in his bed each night. A small mole graced her right shoulder, another her left breast. He'd licked both so many times he'd never been able to keep count and had suckled her flesh shamelessly, always ending with a hungry kiss. Her nipples puckered at her wanton dreams or the cooling breeze. He didn't want to consider which.

No matter how long he stayed away, his love and desire for her remained. He needed her more than life.

If James had been here, he would have said to take her.

Tristan swung his legs over the sill and shed his clothes before crossing the room. Dizzy with longing, he draped himself over Diana and entwined his fingers with hers.

Her eyes flew open. She searched his gaze, her worry turning to relief and finally arousal. "Fill me." She pressed into him, her nipples hard against his chest, skin moist, her scent holding the promise of sex.

Surprise and pleasure raced through him. Given their last conversation, he'd feared she'd spurn his love. "Are you certain? The shutters are open, the lamps lit."

"I don't care who watches. I want you. I've missed you terribly."

Her sweet confession touched his soul. "What of my having to remain here? I can never go back to England, though you—"

"Hush." She brushed her mouth over his. "My place is at your side."

Her warmth and scent did wicked things to him, yet his caution remained. "For how long?"

"Till my last breath." She meant it. The truth shone in her exquisite eyes.

"What of our children? Are we to deny them their chance?"

"You said you'd never allow them to starve or be in danger. I believe you."

"I said the same where you're concerned."

"I thank you." She ground her hips into his.

Blood pooled in his groin, thickening his cock. "I hope you know I would never allow any men but the very best to wed my daughters."

"Spill no blood, that's all I ask." She kissed his neck.

Desperate to be inside her, he trembled at her wet heat. However, he had to be certain there were no barriers between them this night or any other. "I shan't spill blood. What about Peter's future?"

Her head fell back to the pillow. "Can you turn him into a farmer?"

Tristan laughed.

"I'm serious."

Hence, the problem. "I'll convince the boy piracy isn't for him. Past that, I make no promises especially when it comes to women. He's fast becoming a man. No way to stop it."

"Very well. Where have you been? You need a shave. Were you deliberately avoiding me until your cuts healed?" She squeezed his fingers.

Pain shot up his arm. He winced.

Diana lifted their hands and gasped. "Good heavens, what have you done to yourself?"

His knuckles were swollen, skin scabbed. "Beat up a tree."

"What—why?"

"I was picturing you with another man."

She gaped. "Why?"

"Don't worry, it won't happen again." His mouth fit perfectly to hers, his kiss rich with raw lust, pure possession, and aching need to prove she'd always be his. He drove his cock into her sheath.

She moaned throatily.

He imprisoned her arms above her head, same as the first time he'd had her. Then, she'd been a virgin and he'd taken care with her untried flesh. Not tonight. His actions imprisoned and tamed, aroused and satisfied.

Her breasts shook from his relentless thrusts.

He stroked her nub.

Her mouth fell open on a strangled gasp. Her channel tightened around his rigid cock.

The pressure stole his breath. He took what was his.

When he'd finished, he remained inside, suckled her throat and each nipple, loving how her cunt pulsed around him with her climax.

The first of many.

He took Diana vaginally, orally, and anally, to prove she'd never be free from his touch.

* * * *

The following morning, Canela joined the other woman in Tristan's bedchamber where they presented the new gowns to Diana. The Englishwoman's lids were puffy from lack of sleep, cheeks and chin reddened, lips swollen slightly. Tangled sheets lay in a heap on the bed. The room stunk of sex.

Canela bristled.

Diana smiled at the other women. "These are lovely. I—wait a moment, let me say that properly." She chewed her lip, frowned, then nodded. "*Elles sont si belles.*"

The women giggled and smiled.

Diana hugged them, then pressed the first gown to herself, unconcerned with her nudity.

Tristan wore his scarlet robe. He lifted the violet gown. "Same color as your eyes. I like this one best. Did they make enough for you?"

Gowns covered both chairs. He'd never given Canela so much.

Diana laughed. "I think these will do for quite some time."

"Until they don't fit any longer." He caressed her belly.

Cheeks burning, Canela faced the window. Adamo waited for her near a stand, still offering his heart and endless love, but no plan to get rid of Diana. Not even after Canela had shown him the bruise on her arm and shoulder, injuries she'd given herself but blamed on the Englishwoman. She'd told him Diana had pushed her when she hadn't moved quickly enough, and had caused her to fall against the wall.

Fury had burned in Adamo's eyes, but his only suggestion was that she wed him so he'd be the one to rule her.

She'd argued, coaxed, pleaded, tempted. He'd finally lifted his fist and promised to kill Diana if she ever did such a thing again.

Canela wanted him to do so today.

"Gavra, Veronique." Tristan gestured them closer and spoke French. "Please help my wife dress."

They hurried to her.

He thanked the other women and gave each a gold bracelet for their work. When they left the chamber, he looked over. "Canela."

The Englishwoman seemed unconcerned at Tristan speaking to her. Canela wasn't certain whether to be outraged or hopeful that he'd give her a gift, even though she hadn't worked on the gowns.

He inclined his head to the window. "Adamo's waiting for you."

She wanted to scream at Tristan for ignoring and humiliating her. With no other choice, she left quietly, but he wouldn't put her out for long. The stone house belonged to her, along with the lovely jewels and island. She'd settle for nothing less.

* * * *

Despite Diana's desire to belong, which included strutting about nude, the new gowns did give her pause. The design bared her arms and shoulders, except for thin straps, and had a slit up the left seam that showed a great deal of her leg when she walked or sat.

"Was the opening in the skirt your idea, Tristan?"

He scratched the healing cuts on his jaw. "Makes it easier for you to walk and sit I would think."

"After last night, I can't do, either."

"If it makes you feel any better, I'm sore too."

"Then I'll have to be especially attentive to you tonight."

He gathered her to him for a hungry kiss. When Diana was breathless, he tore his mouth free and playfully swatted her ass. "Do your lessons. I have to see to my own work with the geldings."

"Will you be joining us for the midday meal?"

"Aye. See you in a bit."

Given the lovely morning, Diana chose to tackle her French lessons in the courtyard. A woman worked the loom, one was at a potter's wheel, several sewed, and another plucked chickens. All were competent and lovely. They radiated good health, the promise of a future. Two women were heavy with their coming infants, most likely their second or third pregnancies considering how they repeatedly scolded the same children. The small boys and girls behaved for a while, then tore through the courtyard unmindful of their piercing shrieks and bare skin.

Diana smiled at their reckless joy. If her father or his kind had been here, the nudity would have horrified them. Shouts of "heathens" and "savages" would have frightened the little ones, filling them with unnecessary fear and shame.

How right Tristan had been about words having power, to use them with care.

These children were perfect. Why would any creator be ashamed of them? Stroking her belly, she found it far too flat, new life not yet stirring within her. Perhaps in a few weeks.

She looked over.

Canela slipped behind a stand of palms.

The other women hadn't noticed the girl. Diana figured she should follow their lead. She put her lesson aside and pointed at the potter's wheel, then herself. "May I try?"

The young woman gave her a blank stare.

Diana struggled with her imperfect French. *"Puis-je essayer?"*

The girl's eyes lit up. Smiling shyly, she scooted aside to give Diana the wheel.

She made a mess quickly. Clay had flown on her new gown, shoulders, and onto little girls who'd come close to watch.

The women laughed.

Diana brushed hair from her cheek. "Make fun now, but I'll show you how skilled I am on a loom."

The islanders exchanged quick looks.

Diana pointed to the loom closest to them.

They all spoke at once, impossibly fast, their words blending. Having no idea what they'd said, Diana pointed to her gown, then the loom. She hoped her gestures would explain how competent she was in weaving cloth.

The women conversed briefly, pushed to their feet, and hurried inside, leaving Diana alone in the courtyard.

Her face burned at having run them off, possibly having offended them. Perhaps custom allowed only certain women to use the looms. She stood to follow and apologize, but didn't, remembering her poor French. Anything else she said might make it worse.

Hopelessly torn, she stayed at the looms. The one nearest her wasn't like any she'd seen in England. Its construction was quite primitive, the heddles little more than crude hooks used to separate the threads. The shuttle was fashioned from materials that belonged on a ship. Her immediate guess was Tristan or James had built this.

Wanting a closer look, she kept her hands behind her so no one could say she'd touched or harmed the thing. She bent at the waist, on the same level as the heddles. A chicken cackled loudly behind her. Startled, she spun around.

Feed flew in her face.

She blinked wildly and coughed at the dust.

Another volley of feed stung her shoulder and arm.

She flinched and looked up.

Her smile pure evil, Canela threw more feed, hitting Diana's chest. The children giggled. Diana grabbed Canela's arm.

She screamed. "Adamo!"

Diana expected him to come running. He didn't. "Why are you calling him?"

She yanked her arm away. "How dare you hurt me."

"Hurt you? You deliberately threw feed in my face. Stop it." Diana frowned at a little boy who tossed dirt at her and laughed as he had at play.

Canela growled. "Would you harm him too?"

Diana gripped Canela's wrist. "I've had enough of you. I'm going to tell Tristan what you—"

"How dare you try to harm me." She pulled away and shoved Diana.

Her arms windmilled. She stumbled over a child and fell against a loom. A hook cut into her neck. She cried out and tried to right herself. Another hook caught on her marriage collar, the diamonds tightening on her throat.

"No." She held up her hand to keep the children back. "Stay away."

They laughed the way children do when playing a new game. Their excited shrieks filled the warm air. They mimicked their mothers and pressed the loom's treadles, putting the tool into motion. Two boys swung the batten back and forth.

Diana struggled to take off the collar but each time the loom moved it jerked the band into her throat. She couldn't swallow or breathe. Frantic, she tried to work her fingers beneath the necklace but wasn't able to. She opened her mouth to scream. No sounds escaped. She flailed her arm in a desperate attempt to get the children to stop.

Squealing and laughing, they played harder at their game.

Terrified, Diana looked for Canela to help.

The girl had already left the scene.

* * * *

Canela hid behind the palms. The little girls jumped on the treadles. The boys shoved the batten repeatedly.

Diana's eyes were wild, features twisted in pain and panic. She clawed her neck to free herself. The harder she struggled, the deeper the collar dug into her throat, strangling her.

Canela kept her voice low. "Play little ones. Continue your silly game. Do not leave. Do not stop."

They jumped and shouted.

Canela smiled. Soon, the Englishwoman would be dead. The innocent children to blame.

* * * *

A piercing scream reached Tristan and James in the stables. Before another one sounded, they bolted toward the mansion.

Gavra ran down the path to them. "Come quickly. Capitaine's woman needs help."

Tristan's heart slammed into his throat. "What happened? Where is she?"

"The courtyard."

He tore through the mansion and raced to the outside.

Women and children surrounded Diana. Several of the sturdier females tried to lift and tug her from a loom.

He shouted for them to get away. They scattered.

The marriage collar dug into Diana's throat. Eyes closed, she didn't seem to breathe. He shoved her hair away and hit a hook trapped beneath her collar. Blinking sweat out of his eyes, he yanked on the hook. Bloody thing wouldn't budge. With all his might, he pulled. Wood splintered. The hook released and slipped from the necklace.

She slumped to the ground.

He found the collar's clasp, opened it, and threw the blasted diamonds aside. "Breathe." He shook her. "*Breathe.*"

An eternity seemed to pass before she finally inhaled. She struggled for another breath and touched her throat. A mean red line marred her perfect flesh. Blood from the wound dirtied her shoulder.

He scooped her into his arms.

James followed him into the mansion. "Do you want me to get Simone?" The healer.

"Not now. Maybe later, if Diana needs her."

"The women said they only left Diana for a moment to fetch the gowns she wanted. How did her collar get caught in so short a time?"

He had no idea, but if this were Canela's work, he'd kill her. "Find Canela." He carried Diana to their bedchamber. "Bring her to the library and keep her there."

"Do you think she's responsible for this?"

"Do as I say, James." Tristan kicked the door closed, brought Diana to their bed, and gently touched her throat.

"No." Her voice rasped as it would after not speaking for a long time. "Hurts."

He dropped his hand. "Can you breathe freely now?"

She made a face.

"Diana?"

She trembled. Tears followed, then wrenching sobs.

Tristan gathered her close and brushed her hair aside.

She gasped.

He'd accidentally touched her wound. "Forgive me. One of the hooks cut you. Were you injured anywhere else?"

Weeping, she shook her head.

"Do you want Simone to tend your wound?"

"Don't leave." She clutched him.

He held her as tightly. "Who did this to you?"

Diana pressed her face to his neck.

"Was it Canela?"

Another sob escaped her but she shook her head.

Tristan wasn't certain how to react. "Are you sure?"

"I am." Her voice cracked. "It was an accident."

"Diana!" The door flew open. Peter hurried inside. "I was out riding. I just heard. Is she all right?"

"She's fine." Tristan cradled her to him. "But she and I need to be alone."

Peter flushed pink. "Oh...right." He fled the room, slamming the door on his way out.

Diana giggled.

Tristan smiled softly. "What's so amusing?"

She wrapped her arms around him and shivered badly. "I have no idea."

"How did this happen? You have to tell me."

"What I have to do is learn French."

"Your inability to speak the language caused this?"

She rested her forehead against his shoulder. "I was using hand gestures to tell the women I wanted to work on the loom, but I must have insulted them because they left." She swallowed and winced. "After they were gone, I stumbled over a child and fell against the loom. They thought it was a game so they played with the treadles and batten, even though I cried for them to stay back. The poor things couldn't understand me. They kept playing. The collar tightened about my throat. I must have swooned. There you have it."

He stroked her back. "I'm still confused. Why did you stumble over a child?"

She held him more closely.

"Did Canela push you?"

"It was an accident. I hardly think she meant—"

"Then she did do this to you." He muttered an oath and eased Diana away so she had to look at him. "Why are you protecting her? She deliberately pushed you into the loom."

"It didn't happen that way. She was throwing feed to the fowl, some hit me, we had words, and I grabbed her arm. I was wrong to have done so. She was only trying to get away."

"She's about to get her wish because I'm making certain she leaves our home today."

"You can't." Diana clutched his arm. "I don't want you to upset the islanders by taking my side over any of them, especially if no harm was meant. What will they think?"

"I'll explain to them as I'm explaining to you. Canela did mean harm because she's a menace."

"Where will she go? How will she live?"

"With Adamo. It's high time she wed the man and shared his home and future. Perhaps having a child will tame her, but whether it does or not, she's no longer welcome in our home. No one who tries to harm you is. Nothing's going to change my mind on the matter."

Diana touched her throat and frowned. "Where is it?"

"What?"

"My marriage collar." She patted her gown and even looked inside her top for the thing. "What happened to it?"

"After I took it off you at the loom I threw it aside."

"Why?"

"It nearly killed you."

"It was an accident. I want it back."

"No. If it's diamonds you like, I have others."

"I want the marriage collar. Please. It proves I belong to you and I'm at your side willingly. I love you, Tristan. My God, I adore you."

Chapter 10

After a lengthy search, James hadn't found Canela in the mansion or courtyard. He questioned the other women. None had seen her, nor had the men. Daunted, he finally trudged to Adamo's house, close enough to reach by foot. With the last of the path angling to a high point, James was sweaty and breathing hard upon reaching the structure.

Adamo waited, eyes narrowed, jaw set. He'd certainly prepared for the worst with a brace of pistols across his chest. An obvious display of force when James had stupidly arrived unarmed, not having considered he'd need a weapon. He recalled telling Tristan how peaceful this land was, nothing like England. It appeared the blissful state had ended. "Bonjour."

A muscle jumped in Adamo's jaw.

James tried a smile. "Tristan wants to speak to Canela. Have you seen her?"

"She is my concern. Not his."

James guessed she was in Adamo's house. The mud building was of sound construction and lovingly tended, but smaller than Canela's chamber at the mansion. He figured she hated it. Too bad Adamo couldn't see how grasping she was.

James held up his hands. "I want no trouble, nor does Tristan. He's been more than fair about sharing everything. You recall the last pirate who ruled this land. He never allowed the islanders near the stone house. He took the best for himself and his woman. All Tristan requests is your cooperation in finding—"

"Canela has done nothing wrong. When I wed her tonight, I will rule her, no one else. Tell that to the Englishman."

James tried like bloody hell to be nice. "Tristan would appreciate it if you and Canela gave him and Diana the good news at the stone house."

"How can she be alive?" Canela asked in English. She lifted the cowhide over the entryway and came out warily, her hair in disarray.

"Diana's quite well." James spoke French, wanting Adamo to understand the conversation. If Canela persisted with English, he'd translate for the man. "Why wouldn't she be?"

Canela frowned. "I do not believe you. Tristan sent you here to blame me for what the children did."

"What are you talking about? What would they have to do with Diana?"

"Go into my house." Adamo gestured her there. "I will handle this."

She ignored him. "Tell Tristan her death is not my fault. I was here, not in the courtyard."

Yet she was certain Diana had died. James got a sickening feeling about what Canela had done. "If you refuse to go to the stone house, Tristan will come here."

Adamo advanced a step. "This is my land. She is my woman."

Canela shot him a disgusted look.

James was wary of both, focusing at last on her. "I give you my word Tristan won't harm you. He's never hurt a woman in his life. He simply wants to speak to you."

Raw fury flared in her eyes. "This is not about his love for me, but the collar."

"The marriage collar?"

She smiled.

James had seen the same on pirates before they killed someone.

"The collar belongs to me now." She lifted her chin. "The diamonds should have always been mine."

Adamo stared. "You have the Englishwoman's marriage collar?"

"It. Is. Mine."

"Where is it?"

She pressed her lips together.

He pushed past into the house. She followed. Pottery clinked. Items slapped and rustled. Canela wailed. "No! Give it to me. It is mine."

Adamo stormed outside, the diamonds in his fist. She tried to snatch them. He held them away from her.

"Take it." Adamo tossed the collar to James, then grabbed Canela's arm to keep her at his side.

She pummeled his hand and shouted.

He held tight and glared at James. "Tell the Englishman I am not a thief, and that no one comes onto this land without my permission. If he tries, I will shoot him."

* * * *

Tristan cupped Diana's face. "What did you say?"

"I adore you. Not only are you my husband, but also my friend. One I love and respect. Now, I want my blasted collar. Fetch it for me at once. Please."

He laughed and pulled her into him. "That's not the pact we made."

"Pact?"

"I said I would release you from the collar when I knew I had your all."

"Rubbish. Freedom isn't what I want, at least not the kind to take me from your side. I want to wear the collar. I'm proud to do so."

Tristan smiled briefly. Although her voice had already improved, she wouldn't speak normally for a while and the marks on her throat pained him. "You could have died because of the collar."

"I didn't. It was a stupid accident, nothing more. Make me yours. Allow me to wear the symbol of our love for the rest of our days."

After a hearty embrace, he pushed off the mattress. "I'll fetch it." He'd reached the door, stopped, and came back.

She left the bed. "What is it?"

As happy as he'd been a moment ago, he was now uncertain. "I have to tell you something. I beat up the tree because I was angry with myself for bringing you here and restricting your future. I thought I should give you your freedom so you could sail to England."

"How could you ever think—"

"Let me finish." He didn't want to tell her this, but had to. "I was willing to give you gold and jewels, including the marriage collar, to use as a dowry for another husband. Preferably a noble."

She laughed.

He stepped back. "You find my confession amusing?"

"I find your reasoning downright mad." She gestured to him. "Who could be nobler than you?"

He smiled self-consciously. "You do keep saying so. I want you to know how much I adore you. You also have my deepest respect and friendship."

She glowed, her embrace straight from paradise. "Then it's time for me to hear about your past. When you return with my collar, I want you to tell me every detail. You gave me your word you'd do so when we became friends."

He could curse himself for promising such a thing. "Every detail? If you want me to put you to sleep, I can think of a more pleasant way to do so."

"I won't be sleeping. Will you tell me your story, please?"

"When I come back."

* * * *

Vincent strode past his men to an islander.

The native flinched.

As well he should. Vincent was now ship's captain as Miles Montgomery had met with an unfortunate accident last night. The man's body lay at the bottom of the ocean, his ability to deal with Bishop no longer required. Vincent had enough information about the wealthy merchant to ask for Diana's ransom himself. He simply needed to find her and Tristan.

Vincent gestured for Storley, who held a tightened cord in his fists. Storley knew a smattering of the Malagasy language used in Madagascar. "Ask the savage how many islands can be neared only by skiffs, possibly longboats, not sloops."

Storley presented the question.

The islander trembled.

"Wrap the cord around his head." Vincent spoke to his crew. "Bring the others forward. Make certain they see this."

The pirates hauled the natives close to witness what happened when a man refused to answer a direct question. The term for this particular torture was woolding, quite effective in loosening a victim's tongue. After securing the cord to a piece of wood and putting the device around the man's head, Storley turned the wood, tightening the cord. Eventually, the man's eyes would burst from his skull.

Well before that happened, the native screamed and told Vincent what he needed to know.

"Very good. Now ask the fool if he's seen a white man who has light hair and eyes. A tall man who sometimes carries a book."

The islander nodded even before Storley had finished relating Tristan's description.

Vincent could scarcely contain his excitement. "Ask him where the man is."

Storley did. The native shook his head and babbled something. Storley looked over at Vincent. "Says he don't know."

"Twist the cord."

The native screeched, but offered no answer.

When the man was dead, the other natives were openly terrified but said nothing.

Vincent refused to believe they didn't have the information he needed. He pointed to a man who trembled uncontrollably. "Bring him forward. Do the same to him as was done to his friend. Then to the rest until they tell us where Tristan is."

* * * *

Tristan didn't find the marriage collar in the courtyard. "Eduard." He gestured the little boy over.

Eduard ran up and bumped into Tristan's legs. After Tristan had given him a good swing, he asked the giggling child if he'd seen the collar.

Eduard stuck his finger in his ear. "Canela *a pris*." Canela took it.

Curbing his anger, Tristan patted the child's head. "Merci, Eduard."

Once he'd given rides to the other children, he stormed to the library to confront Canela, but found Peter inside.

The boy looked up from his book and shot to his feet. "Is Diana still all right? I thought doing these lessons would bring her around. She's not ill again, is she?"

"No."

Peter grinned. "Good. Then there's no need to do the lessons."

"There is unless you want me to put you to work in the fields, stables, or pig pens. Do you honestly want to labor there?"

The boy sank to his chair. "I'll do the lessons, all right?"

"Has Canela been in here?"

"No."

Tristan frowned. "Where's James?"

Peter lifted his shoulders.

Tristan checked James's room and the mansion. His friend wasn't about. Tristan hurried to Adamo's house, guessing Canela had hidden the collar there. Halfway to the spot, he came upon James. The man was deep in thought. When he looked up and saw Tristan, he flinched.

"Are you all right?"

"Fine. Here." James tossed the collar. "Canela had it."

Tristan gripped the diamonds. "Did she put up much of a fight?"

"Only with Adamo." James dragged his hair off his shoulders. "He didn't know she took the thing. When he found it, he handed it right over and said he ain't no thief, and you best not come onto his property without his permission because if you do, he'll shoot you."

That didn't sound like Adamo. Despite his overwhelming jealousy for Canela, he was a good man. "He actually said those words?"

"I think he's only trying to protect her. Claimed they were getting wed tonight."

"She didn't dispute it?"

"She was inside his house at the time. Told me she was there, not the courtyard when Diana was hurt, yet she asked how Diana could be alive. To me, she seemed surprised Diana hadn't perished. She also said what happened was the children's fault."

Fury tightened Tristan's chest to the point he could barely breathe. "It was hers."

"Wait." James grabbed Tristan's arm, keeping him from going to Adamo's house. "If you confront her now, there's no telling what might happen. Diana's not going to like it if you're shot dead. Let Adamo wed the girl; then she'll be his problem. He'll keep her away from the mansion and Diana."

"He better."

"How is your lovely bride?"

Tristan breathed deeply, trying to calm himself. "On the mend, thank God, with only a small cut on her neck and scratches on her throat from the collar."

"Looks as if that's not going around her neck anytime soon."

"Actually, the moment I get back. She insists upon it."

James smiled. "And here you were going to give her up."

"It would be easier for me to stop living."

Back at the mansion, he worked on the collar's clasp, a special design by the previous pirate so the wearer couldn't remove the diamonds once they were on. Finished, Tristan returned to his bedchamber.

Diana sat on the mattress wearing a smile and the diamond in her navel. "Did you bring it?" She cleared the catch from her throat.

He held up the collar in one hand and bolted the door with the other. "Are you certain you want to wear it now? You could wait and give your neck a chance to heal."

"I want it immediately." She lifted her hair. "Come on."

Tristan loved her order, but did take a moment to check the cut on her neck. With the blood washed away, the wound wasn't as awful as he'd feared. Joining her on the mattress, he slipped the piece around her throat and fastened it. "I worked on the clasp. If the collar catches on anything, tug hard and it will come right off."

"Quite brilliant." She scooted around until they were eye-to-eye, her face sad. "Please turn and keep still. I want to see your back."

She would. Despite his reservations, Tristan did as she wanted.

Diana mewled.

He closed his eyes. Until this moment, he'd taken great pains to ensure she hadn't fully seen his injuries. If the weather was too warm for him to wear a shirt, he never turned his back to her. When they slept, he always laid a certain way to keep her from what she looked at now.

She stroked his scarred skin carefully. "Who did this to you?"

"My captain."

"Bloody bastard."

He laughed softly. "Is that any way for a reverend's daughter to speak?"

"It's the proper way for your wife to vent her rage. How dare he do this to you." Diana leaned over his shoulder to see his face. "Why did you allow it?"

"I was hardly given a choice."

"Was your ship one of Bishop's?"

Tristan nodded.

"That's why you went after his ships as a pirate?"

"Partly. They also carried valuable cargo I didn't want the bloody bastard to have."

"Good for you. Was your captain the one who lashed Peter?"

"No, though both took great delight in being cruel." He shrugged. "Ignorant men often do. I suppose brutality makes them feel superior."

"Face me."

He did gladly. She'd seen enough of his back.

Diana searched his face. "Was your captain envious of what you know and how well read you are?"

"I was sixteen before I managed to read one word. The following year, I was finally able to write my own name, far later than most."

"But you did and so much more."

There wasn't a trace of pity in her voice. If anything, she'd spoken with fierce pride, the kind a mother has for a precious child or a wife for a beloved husband. If Tristan hadn't already loved her, he would for this moment. He brushed his lips over hers.

"Why the sweet kiss?"

Heat rushed to his face. "For believing in me."

"Always. Now back to your story."

"If we must."

Diana grew somber. "When did you first go to sea?"

"I'd just turned ten."

"Oh no." She looked pained. "You were only a child."

"A hungry child."

She embraced him fiercely. "No one will ever harm you again, I swear."

"You intend to protect me?"

"With my life if need be."

"I have seen your skill with a rapier."

Laughing, she released him. "I nearly swooned when you deliberately cut your thumb on the blade."

"I was trying to impress you."

"You accomplished your goal. Why were you lashed?"

Tristan shrugged, a childish response but he couldn't help himself. It was best to forget those days.

Diana regarded him patiently and unwaveringly.

Any man who thought women were the weaker sex was a damned fool. "I was given an order and refused to carry it out. Quite simple. I was willful and promptly flogged."

"What was the order?"

"What does it matter?"

"What was the order?"

He fiddled with the sheet, face lowered. "The captain told me to whip James. I refused."

"James Sullivan, your friend?"

"At the time I barely knew him." He looked at her. "Our friendship came later."

"Because you saved his life by refusing to whip him?"

"Because we genuinely like each other."

"Yes, of course. But what had he done for the captain to order him whipped?"

"It's quite horrid. Are you certain you want to hear this?"

She made a face but still nodded. "What was his crime?"

"He fell ill."

"What?"

Tristan smiled, enjoying how easily he could shock her.

She regarded him coolly. "If it pains you to tell me the truth, then—"

"It is the truth, my love. James fell so ill he could barely stand. Despite his condition, our captain ordered him to take his turn at the wheel. Any fool could see those four hours were likely to do him in, so I offered to take his place. I was strong and able to do the work."

"Your captain refused the gesture?"

"The bastard laughed. Then he told his quartermaster to bring James on deck. After he did, the captain told me to tie James to the mast and give him a hundred lashes."

Diana gasped. "My God. That would have killed any man."

"It nearly did."

She whimpered and slipped her arms around his neck. "He ordered you to take the flogging instead?"

Tristan held her closely. She was so warm and soft he lost his breath. "That kind of choice usually convinces a man to do as he's told."

"But you still refused to obey and the captain lashed you."

Tristan nodded. "He was a fair ways into it when James found the right moment to grab the quartermaster's pistol and put a bullet in the captain's head."

A shiver tore through her. She held him even tighter. "That's how he saved your life and you saved his by keeping him from the whip."

"It's what friends do for each other."

Diana pressed her face to his neck. "Is that why you went on the account, because James shot the captain?"

"It was more or less required if we wanted to avoid being hanged."

"But you never would have gone into piracy otherwise, would you?"

"To survive, I fear I would. To eat, I would do anything. To protect you, our children, Peter, and James, I would kill without pause."

"You aren't a violent man by nature."

"You're right. I would rather lie with you than fight."

She laughed. "Good."

"But fight I will, if I must."

"There's no need. You'll never return to piracy and everyone here is peaceful, right?"

They had been until Adamo's threat. "I didn't banish Canela from here if that's what you mean. She never gave me the chance. Tonight she's wedding Adamo and moving into his house."

Diana leaned back. "Are you quite certain?"

When it came to Canela, he wasn't sure of anything. However, before the day ended he'd have her things and dowry delivered to Adamo along with a message stating she was no longer welcome in the mansion.

* * * *

At sunset, Canela faced the priest with Adamo. There was no other choice. She could either live in his house as the mistress or beg her people to let her stay with them. Gavra and Laure had already delivered her things from the stone house. When Canela protested, they told her she'd brought this on herself by pushing Diana into the loom and taking the diamond collar. The children had seen her.

Adamo looked ashamed at what the others had said, then stunned when James and Peter delivered cattle, chickens, pigs, and horses as her dowry, gifts from Tristan, Diana, and the islanders. For Canela there were also silks, jewels, a looking glass, and a music box. Gavra and Laure put those items in Adamo's house, built from mud, not stone. With a dirt floor, not cool marble.

The priest finished saying the words over them. Adamo slipped his marriage collar around her throat, one made of leather, not silver. Instead of diamonds, its beads were fashioned from glass.

He kissed her reverently. "*Je vous aime.*"

His words barely registered. She recalled the lacy fan Tristan had brought her after his last voyage. Before that, he'd come back with combs for her hair, velvet coverings for her bed, but never the offer to make her mistress of this isle. She'd always promised herself a place at his side. She, alone, deserved his power and wealth.

Adamo led her into his home, eager to create a child.

She convinced him she'd be in too much pain because of her monthly cycle. Seducing him was easy. On her knees, she lowered his breeches, took his rigid shaft into her mouth, and brought him to climax. When he wanted more, she worked him with her tongue and lips, then removed her silk cloth. On her hands and knees, Canela invited him to take her tightest opening as Tristan always had, so there would be no infant.

After Adamo was finally sated, they lay together on his simple bed. Wind rustled the leaves on the thatched roof. In the stone house, the air was sweetly scented. Here, she smelled defeat.

Adamo rolled into her. "You are so beautiful." He stroked her jaw. "I will protect you well and see to your every need. With the cattle, pigs, and horses we now have, our future is bright. When you birth our first child, I will build you an even larger house."

Of mud, not stone. Filled with trifles, not marble and jewels.

In the light of the solitary oil lamp, his dark eyes flooded with love, his handsome features content.

Hatred and disgust filled her, but she pretended to be meek. "This home is enough. It would be wrong for us to desire anything else."

He looked at her questioningly. "Why? I want to give you everything I can."

"No. I was wrong to take the diamond collar. When Tristan threw it aside, I thought he no longer wanted it. I hoped you might slip it about my throat when we…" She shook her head, feigning too much distress to go on. "What does it matter? I allowed Tristan to seduce and use me. Can you ever forgive me for doing so?"

He cradled her breast. "We will never speak of it again. It remains in the past and forgotten."

"How can I deserve you or anything good?" She kissed his knuckles. "I will never be English. My skin will never be pale."

He frowned. "You deserve the best because you belong to me. You deserve what the English have and far more."

"May I ask you something?"

"Whatever you want."

"Why must the English rule?"

He stared, then yawned.

She wasn't about to let him put her off. "Why are the English allowed to be the masters of this isle where our ancestors have always lived? They and the French hurt our people. Have you forgotten the last pirate killed your parents and mine, murdering everyone who was old or lame and unable to work? Did you like how he used us as if we were his slaves?" She pointed to where the stone house stood. "The pirate's home, now Tristan's, was built by our people. You and I should be living there along with the other islanders. Everything here is ours. Why do we let him or the others have any of it?"

Adamo looked away. "It would be best not to speak of such things."

She squeezed her fists but kept her manner patient and coaxing. "Then you do believe Tristan and the Englishwoman deserve what we do not."

"I never said that. Tristan had no right to seduce or use you." He punched his pillow. "I will always hate him for doing so. But he has also made life better for our people. Our crops yield more than they ever did because of what he taught us. His knowledge of cattle saved the animals when they fell ill. Now the herds are twice what they used to be. He has never denied us anything. He shares the food, water, and clothing."

"Water taken from our land. Food sown and harvested by our people. Cloth woven by our women."

"That may be, but what does it matter if Tristan uses the stone house? He helped our people. The other pirate was cruel, or have you forgotten what you just said and what it was like to live here when he ruled?"

Although she'd feared and hated the pirate, she'd tried to seduce him the moment he'd arrived with a white woman as his mistress. Canela had only been thirteen at the time. Even at that tender age, she'd wanted the jewels, silks, and finally the stone house. She'd had it with Tristan until he gave Diana his name. For doing so, he would pay. She'd see him lose everything, especially his wife.

"Tristan is fair." Adamo drew lazy circles around her nipple. "We should be grateful he is."

She wanted to scream at him, but tempered her fury. "Tristan is fair until we need something his children want. Then the land, cattle, or water will go to them, not our sons and daughters. One day our children will labor for his."

"No!" He lowered his voice. "Our children will never work for anyone but themselves."

"Then they will starve, unless this island is in our people's hands again. Only islanders should live here."

He exhaled noisily. "You speak of something that will never happen. We cannot force Tristan to leave. Too many of our people love him and accept his rule."

"What of his people?"

"What do you mean?"

"James Sullivan told Gavra how Tristan deceived his crew to bring the Englishwoman here. He tied up his men and left them aboard her ship to die. What if they seek revenge for his actions? What if they come to this island searching for him and slaughter our people while he escapes?"

"How could they? No ship can use the shallow waters around here. Few come close. Even so, we watch the sea to make certain no one approaches in a skiff or longboat. If they did, we have pistols. We will never allow them on our shores."

"You may stop the first and then the next, but you cannot stop them all. His men are certain to find and destroy us unless you strike first."

"What?" Adamo pushed to his elbow. "How can one man fight—"

"Not fight, control the outcome of the encounter." Excitement raced through her, a plan forming. "Use the glass to search for Tristan's old ship or the one the Englishwoman was on. Before it passes, row out and make a deal to deliver Tristan. You have my silks and jewels to show his men and hers what riches are here. After they kill Tristan, we can kill them. The land will be ours again."

Adamo sagged back to the mattress.

She leaned over him. "Do you want them to destroy us?"

"No, but perhaps they will never come here."

They had to. She would settle for nothing less. Once Tristan was gone and his crew took over the island, she'd rule beside the new pirate captain.

Chapter 11

With Canela wed, a relaxed mood settled over the mansion. Diana found the days peaceful and perfect, especially when Follie was about to birth her first child.

At breakfast, Tristan pointed his fork at Peter. "We need to prepare for a celebration."

The boy stopped slouching over his meal. His eyes glittered. "We'll have lots of food, music, and drink."

"Not you." Diana peeled a boiled egg. "You're far too young to drink."

He rolled his eyes.

She spoke to Tristan. "Shouldn't we wait to celebrate until the infant's born? Follie's just begun the birthing process."

"All the more reason to hurry and prepare. These things are usually over before one knows it."

Spoken like a man who knew none of the pain. "Do what you must then. I'll be needed with the other women in the birthing room."

"Watch everything carefully and learn all you can." He played with her fingers. "I want you well-prepared when your time comes."

Peter straightened. "You going to have an infant too?"

She stopped eating her egg and shot him a look.

"I suppose I'm to leave now?"

Tristan took another helping of bread and bacon. "You'd be well-advised to do so."

"I'll see to the meat we need for the celebration." With a banana stuck in his mouth, Peter hurried from the dining room.

Tristan leaned in. "We'll make a farmer or cook of him yet."

"One can only hope. Not a word to anyone about my condition, please. It's simply a feeling I have. There's no proof yet."

"Nine months from now we'll have indisputable evidence. However, you have my word to keep your condition to myself. Now go to Follie before you miss anything."

* * * *

The chart wasn't yet finished, the thing drawn crudely, its scale hardly accurate. To Vincent the map was priceless because it showed the location of Tristan's island. Only a few savages knew of its existence, the secret finally revealed after days of questioning and torture.

Even as the native drew the chart, Vincent worried the man might be making things up to spare himself additional woolding or death. To ensure against it, Vincent had ordered his men to capture the savage's youngest child. Once the boy sat on the ground in front of him, Vincent gestured to Storley. "Tell the child's father his son's coming with us. If we find Tristan using the chart, the child will live. If not, well, who's going to mourn the murder of a native boy?"

Storley delivered the threat.

The islander's face went slack. He revised the chart yet again.

To show his gratitude, Vincent spared the boy, then ordered his crew to kill the father and the other men. And to be quick about it, so the pirates could put the boats to sea.

* * * *

"Canela! Canela!"

Despite her husband's excited shouts, she remained on the mattress, eyes closed.

Adamo ran inside his home, breathing hard. "Why are you still in bed? Are you ill?"

She willed him to leave.

He fell to his knees by her side. "Answer me."

"I was only resting. Why are you here? You should be watching the sea."

He tried to catch his breath. "Follie's infant is coming. You must go to her."

"No. Though our people built the stone house, I am not allowed within its walls."

"The courtyard is opened to all. So is the birthing room. You must go there and join the other women. Today we celebrate with our people for this blessing of new life."

Resentment pulsed through her, but she remained quiet and meek. "If you go to the festivities, who will watch the sea?"

"One day will hardly matter."

She clenched her jaw.

"It is only one day."

"During which other men might rape and kill me." She covered her face with her hands. "I thought I had your love, but now I know the future you truly want for me."

"No. Canela, please. I will forego the celebration and keep watch. But you must attend. This is our home. We are not outcasts. We must show Tristan we belong here."

"Far more than he."

"That is why you must attend." Adamo stood.

She pushed up and swung her legs over the mattress. "During your watch, will you promise to use the glass to see if any boats approach?"

"I will do exactly as you asked."

"Have you buried the jewels and other items I gave you? You need them on the beach so you can take them with you when you see the pirates."

He shifted nervously.

She stood. "Have you done it?"

"I have but there must be another solution."

"There is. I will go to the edge of the sea and wait until a skiff comes near. As I lack pale skin, my future can hold nothing but grief. I cannot fight it. I bow to—"

"I will do as you ask." He let out a low growl, then a pained moan. "I will do whatever you ask. All I want is your love."

She slipped into his arms. "You have it. With you taking control of the encounter, I know I will be safe and this isle will soon be in our peoples' hands."

* * * *

Follie's wails filled the birthing room. Men's laughter rang from the courtyard as they'd already begun to celebrate.

Diana shook her head. "Silly little boys."

Simone, young and quite lovely, looked at Diana questioningly. So did the other women.

Diana smiled, hoping the pleasantry would serve as an answer.

Follie writhed with renewed agony and let out a piercing shriek.

Diana wiped Follie's brow, the same as she'd done for numerous women in her father's congregation. They'd been in equal pain during childbirth, yet shame at being partially nude and screaming had compounded their distress. Worse, the coming child confirmed the passion they'd shared with their husbands when piety demanded somberness and restraint, not joy.

Here, everything was so much better and entirely natural.

Follie's nudity hardly bothered her. Supported by Simone on one side and Gavra on the other, Follie squatted rather than lay on the bed, helping the process. Quite brilliant.

How anyone could call these lovely people savages was a mystery to Diana. They had better sense and a greater appreciation of life than any Englishman.

She stroked her belly. There were no outward signs of pregnancy yet, but she had conceived. An inner peace flowed through her, a sense everything would be all right. Smiling at the promise of her own infant, she wanted to catch Tristan's eye and padded to the window.

Canela stood near the sill.

Diana stopped short.

Impassively, Canela regarded the birthing room, its marble floor, stone walls, rich bed covering. Those items didn't hold her attention long. She stared at Diana's marriage collar and promptly gripped her own. The disgust on Canela's face said she wanted to rip off the leather and beads. Only silver and diamonds would do for her.

Diana wasn't certain whether to feel disgust or pity. She would have worn rags if Tristan couldn't have provided better. As a reverend's daughter, she was hardly accustomed to life's luxuries and coveted them even less. All she wanted was Tristan's love.

Follie shrieked.

Transfixed by the diamonds, Canela smiled quite coldly.

Diana stepped back. The last time she'd seen such evil on anyone's face was when the pirate with the yellow scarf had crossed the cabin to take her.

James hurried into view. "Canela, the men could use Adamo's help. Where is he?"

She glanced past James and stiffened.

Diana guessed the girl had spotted Tristan. His laughter paused abruptly. He must have just seen Canela.

She flicked her gaze at James. "Adamo has matters to attend to at his home." She left.

James watched her, then looked into the birthing room and immediately turned away, his freckled face redder than his hair. "Ah, Diana, might I have a word?"

She joined him at the window. "Don't worry, James. One look won't kill you."

He groaned.

She smiled. "What did you want to ask?"

"How's it going?"

Follie howled, followed by what sounded like French oaths.

Diana couldn't help but tease. "I wish I knew how to answer, but I have no idea what Follie just cried out. I have it, why don't you translate?"

"If I did, Tristan would have my head. Is she nearing the end?"

Panting hard, Follie rested against the wall. The infant's head had crowned.

Apparently, Tristan had been right. On this island, birthing was over before one knew it. "It shouldn't be too much longer."

James scratched his chest. "When the babe does come, bring it out and show it to each of the men. It's what we do here."

"Of course. I'm certain Gavra or Simone will be more than willing to do so."

"Not them. You. As mistress of this house it's your duty."

"And one of Tristan's rules?"

"'Fraid it is. Go along with him, all right?"

"Certainly. James, wait."

He stopped and looked over. The sun hit him full in the face. Squinting, he shielded his eyes.

She leaned closer so the others wouldn't overhear. "Where's Canela?"

He peered over both shoulders before turning completely around.

With his sudden pause, she had her answer. The girl was near Tristan. "Please keep my husband safe."

"Till my last breath."

* * * *

Peter elbowed Tristan. "Think we need more pineapples?"

The courtyard tables literally groaned with food, the women and men still hauling out platters and baskets. Heavenly aromas of beef and pork mingled with the sweet scents of bananas, pineapples, fragrant rice bread, boiled eggs, and no end of delectable island fare. Everything seemed well in hand, but Tristan wanted Peter elsewhere. "I think the men might appreciate some spirits, especially Follie's husband."

"Last I saw he was talking to the priest in French, even though the man only knows Portuguese."

"I've already told the priest to say a special prayer so Follie delivers a son. It's all Étienne wants. Go get the spirits and give both men our very best."

Peter ran to fetch the stock.

As Canela edged closer, Tristan finally faced her. Although his fury had passed from the loom incident, his caution remained. He wanted her out of his life. "Canela."

Despite his mild tone, she recoiled and looked away as one would when embarrassed.

He wasn't certain if she was putting on an act or not and hardly cared. "Is Adamo well?"

She nodded.

The man wasn't about when he should have been.

James caught Tristan's eye, inclined his head to Canela, and lifted his reddish eyebrows in a questioning manner, possibly as to what she wanted, other than the obvious.

Not knowing, Tristan shrugged in answer and focused on her. "Is Adamo here?"

"He has matters to attend to at his home."

"Will he be joining us later?"

Her forehead furrowed. "Are you ordering him here? I thought Adamo was a free man. Should I tell him you demand he be at this celebration?"

"We having a celebration?" James joined them and slapped Tristan on the back.

Canela's attention remained on Tristan. "Soon, there will be much to celebrate."

Tristan didn't like the sound of that. He spoke to James. "Did you have a word with Diana as I requested?"

"Aye. Told her about presenting the infant. She promised she would."

"When was that?"

"Just before I came over here."

Then Diana was all right, at least for the moment. He inclined his head slightly to Canela. "Enjoy yourself.

"James, I need a word." He grabbed his friend's arm and pulled him well past her so she couldn't possibly overhear.

James broke free. "What is it?"

"Keep an eye on Canela. She's not to touch any food or drink except what she takes for herself. Keep her away from Diana."

"Your wife told me to protect you."

"Did she? Well forget what she said. I can take care of myself." He looked past James to Canela. She edged toward the birthing room. "Do you think we can trust Adamo?"

"To do what?"

"Keep his good sense and not allow Canela to involve him in something he'll regret."

"Such as?"

Tristan wasn't certain. "I wish I knew, but in order to prevent a tragedy, keep your eye on her. And if you do see Adamo, let me know."

James nodded.

* * * *

Gavra ran from the birthing room. "*L'enfant est ici!*"

Even with her poor understanding of French, Diana knew the woman had announced the child's arrival.

Follie's husband, Étienne, made the sign of the cross over himself. The priest looked concerned until Tristan said something in Portuguese that made the man breathe easier.

At their parents' scolding, the usually boisterous children fell silent. A hush fell over the courtyard. Wind snapped the silk tablecloths and rustled leaves, birds called out to their mates, a new life cried.

Moved deeply, Diana left the birthing room, the swaddled babe in her arms, the infant's face scrunched, a shock of dark hair on its head. She caught Tristan's gaze. Her smile promised that one day the child she held would be theirs.

Until then, this newcomer demanded attention.

Diana padded to Étienne. "You were blessed with a little boy."

The man stared at her. He, the priest, and the others exchanged quick, worried glances.

Peter sniggered until Diana scowled.

Tristan spoke to the priest in Portuguese and to the others in French.

Cheers broke out. Étienne threw his arms around the holy man. They bounced in place and cried out in their separate tongues.

Laughing at their joy, Diana presented the child to the men, who nodded their approval.

When Tristan's turn came to view the babe, his smile was the broadest Diana had ever seen.

He asked, "Think you might want one of these for your own?"

"I would, though ours might not be a boy. Would you be disappointed?"

"Only if our daughter didn't have your lovely eyes."

"Might be a blessing if she didn't."

He frowned slightly. "Why would you say such a thing?"

"What if the odd coloring makes it hard for her to find a husband here?"

"You mean among the islanders?"

Diana nodded. The infant's sweet warmth and weight brought tears to her eyes. "He's perfect. I've never seen anything more beautiful in my life. So what if our daughter fancies him, but he thinks her coloring strange?"

"He'd have to answer to me for the insult."

Tears ran down her cheeks as she also laughed. "Remember, you promised to spill no blood."

"You might have to keep reminding me."

Her happiness faded. "What do you mean?"

"Nothing."

"Rubbish. You sounded quite serious. Has something happened?" Her stomach twisted. "Has Canela done something?"

"Not that I know of." He glanced over.

Canela looked past the opening in the courtyard walls to the sea, her hair floating on the wind. Perhaps the girl wanted to leave this isle because of her reduced status. Given her marriage, it might not be possible.

"Where's Adamo?"

"Canela said he's attending to matters at his home."

Diana hadn't expected that. "Leaving her here with these other young men about? Adamo struck me as murderously jealous."

"He is, but she's wearing the marriage collar. Every man here honors it."

"Does she?"

Gavra ran up. "Bébé?"

Diana blushed. "Do forgive me." She placed the infant in Gavra's eager arms. The woman hurried to the birthing room and delivered the boy to Follie.

"Tristan." Peter shifted in place. "Should I light the torches now?"

"Go on."

Firelight ate away the first of the night. The musicians brought out their lutes, drums, and reeds. While they played, everyone else feasted and laughed.

Diana even tried out her awkward French. The men's chuckles evolved into loud howls.

"Stop it." She leaned against the table. "What did I just say?"

Tristan and James trembled with laughter. They shook their heads, either unable or unwilling to explain. Peter laughed so hard the bench vibrated.

Diana giggled, then finally laughed and joined in, feeling so at home she couldn't recall having lived anywhere else. She loved this island. The night was warm and fragrant, breeze gentle, food plentiful, the people good, her husband and brother as happy as she and everyone else.

Except for Canela, who stood by the opening in the courtyard walls, staring out to sea. Scarlet, plum, and gold from the setting sun streaked the sky behind Canela, making her a dark silhouette against the vivid colors.

Chapter 12

The pirates rowed toward the dark, a trace of sunset behind them. Vincent checked the first stars, matching them to the savage's crude chart.

"Go southwest." He pointed.

The man in front looked over. "Will we take them tonight?"

Vincent regarded the deepening gloom. Undefined shapes represented the hidden islands, one of them belonging to Tristan.

* * * *

While the others celebrated, Canela stood just outside the courtyard walls.

The wind changed course, blowing her hair against her face and neck. Annoyed, she clawed the strands away and cut her knuckle on a glass bead adorning her marriage collar. On an angry growl, she dug her fingers beneath the leather to rip it off.

"Canela." A man's voice rang from the forest.

She dropped her hand and stared at the darkness where the moon didn't reach.

"Canela."

Tristan's deep, rumbling voice transfixed her. Her anger receded, replaced by quick hope. Finally, he'd called, wanting her to return to her rightful place at his side, with him giving her new jewels, silks, and combs. Excited, she stepped deeper into the darkness.

Hearty and familiar laughter sounded from behind.

From this distance, Tristan's features weren't readily apparent, but his hair was unmistakable, pale as the moon, his laugh unrestrained. He hadn't called to her from the forest. He sat next to his wife.

"Canela!" Adamo called from the woods.

She glared. He should have been watching for the pirate ship. She made certain no one looked her way, then hurried into the trees and stopped before she ran into her foolish husband.

He reached for her.

She stepped back. "Why are you here?"

His eyes reflected moonlight filtering through the leaves. "Phillipe is on watch, leaving me free for pleasure." He glanced past her to the music, laughter, and conversations. "After we lay together we can join the others."

"Go back to the point. You must replace Phillipe."

Adamo frowned. "No. I intend to lay with you, then remain in the courtyard until dawn with everyone else."

She pulled away to keep him from bringing her to the ground. "What if a ship comes near while you enjoy me, the food, and drink?"

Laughter roared louder, the musicians playing a new tune. Adamo tapped his foot in time to the music. "There will be other ships. Where are you going?" He caught up and clamped his hand on her wrist. "Answer me."

She suppressed her contempt and became the dutiful wife. "Go on and enjoy yourself with your friends. Afterward, I will yield to you." She touched his chest. "Until then someone must see to our safety. I will go to the point and watch for the pirates."

"No. Phillipe is there."

"Will he see to the liberation of our island as you promised? Does he love me as you do?" She wrenched away, darted past him, and ran down the path to the vantage point.

Adamo overtook her easily.

Canela forced herself to smile. "If you send Phillipe away, you and I could keep watch." She caressed his cheek. "We can also enjoy each other."

His frown became a quick smile. "Once we do, then we will join the others." He laced his fingers through hers and led her to the point.

Phillipe pushed to his feet. "Has something happened?"

"No." Adamo squeezed her hand. "Canela and I will keep watch for now. Join the feast. Enjoy yourself."

Muted music floated on a breeze scented with roasting beef, succulent pork, burning torches, and the sea's tang.

Phillipe grinned. "I will, my friend." He bolted up the path.

"Wait." Canela lifted her hand. "Your glass."

He tossed the telescope to Adamo who promptly dropped it on a thick cushion of grass. Before Canela could reach for it, he gathered her in his arms, kissed her cheek and throat, and murmured his love.

The gentle waves caught the moonlight and glimmered like thousands of diamonds, reminding her of the ones around Diana's throat. Canela pulled away from Adamo. "Show me how to use the glass."

He frowned. "Why do you keep moving away from me?"

"I want you to show me how to use the glass."

"Why? Women have no need for such knowledge. I want you to come to me now."

Her hatred flared, but she melted into him and used her sweetest voice. "I only wished to see a star." She pressed her lips to his throat. "The most important one of all."

He slid his hands from her back to her breasts. "One star more important than the rest?" He flicked his thumbs over her nipples. "Why?"

"The star is yours and mine. Legend says it would be a good omen for our union."

"I never heard of such a thing."

"Neither had I until Follie told the other women she wished on her and Étienne's star, and today she gave him a son."

Adamo's face brightened. He fetched the instrument and instructed her on its use.

She put the glass to her eye and swept the sea for a ship or a skiff.

"Do you see our star?"

"Not yet."

"The glass is too low." He tilted it upward.

Canela tensed. "Merci." She sidled away from him and searched the sea.

"I told you the glass is too low." He took the instrument and flung it on the grass.

She bent to retrieve it.

Adamo stepped in her way.

She straightened. "What are you doing?"

"We can look for our star later, when we keep watch." He untied her silk cloth and tossed it aside. With his hands on her naked flesh, he smiled. "Now I intend to have you."

* * * *

As the musicians played a slow, seductive tune, Diana leaned into Tristan, recognizing the heat in his eyes.

When they left the table, no one paid attention, too busy with their own happiness. He led her toward the birthing room, empty now and clean, the closest hideaway for lovers. To Diana's surprise, he bypassed the chamber and padded toward a thick stand in a secluded area.

It was a distance away from the tables filled with celebrants, but not far enough to subdue their laughter and the music.

Men sang a boisterous song. Infants stirred and cried. Older children, exhausted from too much food and play, slept on the ground near their parents.

Tristan pulled her into his arms, his mouth hot and hungry on her throat.

She softened against him but still worried. "The others."

"They can't see us." His lips were to her ear. "This spot's too dark."

Shadows blanketed them, leaves blocking the moon and torchlight.

Her pulse raced at his arousal and the other's proximity. Months ago, she wouldn't have considered indulging in sex outdoors much less with a crowd nearby. She'd been too English. Far too proper. Now, she stroked his hardened cock.

He grunted lustily, then slid her gown to her waist and off, baring her to the mild night. Heat pooled between her legs, moisture dampening her soft folds.

He suckled her nipples, making her want everything he had to give, then kissed the hollow beneath her throat. "On your hands and knees. I intend to mount you from behind."

His commanding tone was the same as when he'd first captured her. Eagerly, she assumed the position, spreading her thighs widely, lifting her buttocks. The breeze licked the dampness between her legs, confirming her base desire.

Settled behind her, he gripped her hip with one hand, dipped the other to her nub, and worked her flesh.

Heat, pleasure, excitement rolled through her. She bit her lip to keep from crying out.

He plunged his rod into her snug channel, filling and arousing her.

Diana shuddered.

With his next touch, she pushed into him, desperate to get closer.

Tristan quickened his thrusts, propelling her and him past the edge. She pressed her mouth to her arm to stifle her harsh breaths. His rough growl spilled out, quieted by the other noise.

Contentment replaced passion, both of them settling down.

He leaned over her, his lips skimming her shoulder.

His tenderness was delightful, but still an interlude. She didn't want to stop playing or loving.

Wantonly, she squeezed her sheath around his cock, encouraging it to grow rigid. Approving sounds rushed from him. When he'd filled her to bursting, she pulled away.

He reached for her. "What are you doing? Come back here."

"I shall." Once she'd faced him, she held his member aside and licked his sac.

He started, then groaned quietly. "More."

Delighted by his command, she eased one ball into her mouth, savored its salty flavor, and licked his hot, hair-roughened skin.

A gruff sound escaped Tristan, proving his delight.

She suckled gently, worshipping him with her tongue, then did the same with his other ball, proving her love.

He cradled her face, keeping her at the task.

Only a pistol to her head would have made Diana stop. She released his testicle and slipped his cock into her mouth.

His legs wavered. He drove his fingers into her hair.

Concentrating on his rigid shaft, she licked the veins dashing up the column and took his full length inside. Her lips touched the root nestled in his thick, fragrant thatch.

He fought climax as he always did, wanting to draw out pleasure, but couldn't for long. He came, quietly like before, his strength weakened by what she'd done. She drank him dry and sheltered him in her tender embrace until he regained his strength and took her again.

They should have been exhausted. She'd never been alive as she was now. Given his devilish grin, neither had he.

Back on their feet and dressed, he kissed her lingeringly, then pulled back. "Nine months from now the celebration's going to be for our child."

She stroked his bristly cheek. "I wouldn't have it any other way."

* * * *

Damn near giddy, Tristan escorted Diana back to the celebration.

He'd just poured himself more ale when Phillipe laughed loudly at the table. The man's presence surprised Tristan for reasons he couldn't immediately identify. The pleasure of having been with Diana, along with the food and spirits, had blunted his senses.

James told a tall tale, but Phillipe kept drawing Tristan's attention. Something about the man nagged him.

"No." Peter waved his hands, stopping James. "You're telling it wrong. I was the one who helped you to…"

Tristan put his tankard down. Phillipe was here when he should have kept watch. Tristan swung his legs over the bench to leave the table.

Diana grabbed his arm and leaned close. "Where are you going? What's wrong?"

"Nothing." Not wanting to ruin her happiness, he lied. "I just noticed Phillipe. I want to have a word with him about a gelding. It can't wait till morning."

He reached the man and gestured for him to follow, not stopping until they were on the other side of the courtyard, out of earshot. "What are you doing here?"

Bacon hung from his mouth. He shoved it inside. "Honoring the new infant."

"*Oui.* But you were supposed to keep watch. Did you forget?"

"I was there until Adamo and Canela offered to take my place for a while."

"Adamo *and* Canela?"

Phillipe swallowed his food and nodded. "Adamo told me to enjoy myself." A number of men laughed loudly. Phillipe danced from foot to foot. "I thanked Adamo and came here. Must I return to my watch now?"

"No, of course not." He squeezed the man's shoulder. "Enjoy the celebration. I see one of Follie's sisters has her eye on you."

Phillipe laughed self-consciously and ran to the table.

Tristan held back. Although Adamo was hardly his friend, the man did have a close relationship with the others here. Given the recent events, Adamo might have found keeping watch more comfortable than attending the celebration. Canela, though, she'd never offered to do anything productive. Lazing in bed was her style.

Worried, Tristan slipped past the outer walls. Once his eyes had adjusted to the moonlight, he ran to the path that led to the point. Music and laughter grew muted, replaced by the sea's endless hiss. The sound reminded him of times past when land was only a memory and a ship his home. Never again. How he'd lived so long without a wife and the promise of his own family didn't make sense, but then he'd had to wait for Diana to come into his life, rapier in hand and an order for him to stand.

Grinning, he reached the point. Adamo sprawled on the ground, arm draped over his eyes as he slept. Unless he was dead.

Tristan stilled.

Adamo's chest finally rose and fell with quiet breaths.

Canela faced the sea, the glass to her eye, making a slow sweep of the water. Not as one would do if playing, but rather searching.

Until this moment, she'd never shown interest in anything other than jewels, silks, combs, and other spoils from his piracy. Yet, she was now eager to keep watch so Adamo could sleep. Not trusting such generosity, Tristan edged closer.

She lowered the glass and faced him.

He crossed over to her as quietly as he could to avoid waking Adamo. "What are you looking for?"

She hid the glass behind herself and lifted her chin.

A playful stance he knew well and wasn't interested in seeing. "Answer me. What are you looking for?"

She stepped back.

He advanced. They were close enough to touch. "Why are you here rather than the celebration?"

She studied his mouth, her lips parting.

Surely, she wasn't mad enough to think he'd kiss her. Quelling his frustration, he kept his voice low. "What did you see with the glass?"

Her features grew soft, seductive.

He put out his hand. "Give it to me."

She turned from side to side, coy and teasing, keeping the instrument behind herself.

Bloody hell. He reached around her for the damn thing.

"How dare you touch my wife." Adamo lifted his pistol.

Tristan backed away. "I only wanted the glass."

Hatred twisted Adamo's features, his brutal reaction saying it all. Until Tristan wed Diana, Adamo had never been a passing thought to Canela. The humiliation hadn't been forgotten or forgiven, but tonight he might possibly avenge the wrong done to him.

Tristan tensed as he always did before battle, except this time he was unarmed and had no real desire to kill Adamo. The man loved a woman who hardly deserved him. "Tell your husband I only wanted the glass."

Canela said nothing. Despite Adamo's rage and the weapon, she showed no emotion.

Tristan bared his teeth. "Tell him."

"Quiet!" Adamo's shout tore through the night. "You will not speak to my wife in that manner."

Sweat ran down Tristan's back. His pulse pumped hard. "Consider what you're about to do. I didn't dishonor your wife. Not only does she wear the marriage collar, but I love my own woman. I wouldn't disrespect Diana by touching another."

"You have had Canela before." Adamo stalked closer. "You seduced and used her."

His throat tightened at the lie Canela had surely put in Adamo's head. From the moment Tristan arrived on the island, she'd pursued him. To argue the truth now would get him shot. To admit he'd used her wouldn't be any better. "She loves you. She wed you." Tristan looked at her. "Isn't that true?"

"He never used me as you did."

Alarmed, Tristan tried to reason with Adamo. "I simply wanted the glass. Only the men are supposed to use it to watch our shores."

Canela made a derisive noise. "My people's shores, not yours. You have us do your work keeping watch. So why are you at the point tonight?"

He focused on Adamo. "I saw Phillipe at the celebration. I asked why he wasn't here. He told me you and Canela had offered to keep watch."

"So you came here to humiliate me by seeing me lie with my wife."

Tristan frowned. "No. Of course not."

"Then why are you here?" Adamo trained his pistol on Tristan's heart. "You came to watch us and to reclaim Canela. How dare you. I should have shot you long before—"

Diana shouted, "Lower your weapon!"

She stood on the path above them, gown fluttering in the wind, moonlight touching her marriage collar, the diamonds winking. With both hands, she lifted Tristan's pistol that he'd left on the table, and pointed the muzzle at Adamo.

"Diana." To Tristan, his voice seemed to come from far away, this scene a nightmare he wanted to end. "Get out of here, now."

She didn't take her eyes off Adamo. "*Vers le bas.*" Down. "*Arme.*" Weapon.

Adamo stared at her pistol but didn't lower his.

"Harm my husband in the least and I'll kill you." She inched the weapon to Adamo's head rather than his heart.

His fury drained away, fear replacing it. He looked from her to Tristan to Canela.

Diana inched closer. "Tristan, tell him to put down his weapon."

James appeared behind her, his firearm trained on Adamo. "*Abaisser votre pistolet.*"

Peter arrived next, a pistol in each hand.

Tristan spoke to Adamo. "Lower your weapon."

"No." He trembled. "You will kill me if I do."

Tristan held up his hands. "No one's going to be shot. Not if you lower your weapon and put it away. I give you my word on it. James?"

"I also give mine."

Peter said, "As do I."

Confusion swept over Diana's face. Tristan didn't have to ask why. They'd spoken in French for Adamo's benefit and she had no idea what they'd said.

James and Peter lowered their weapons.

She gaped. "No. You must stop Adamo. He's going to shoot—"

"Diana." Tristan wanted to run to her but didn't dare move with Adamo still wielding his gun. "Lower the pistol."

She frowned. "Not until Adamo lowers his."

Tristan looked at James.

She backed away from him, though not quickly enough. James took her weapon.

Tristan pleaded. "Go back to the celebration. James and I will handle this."

"No. I fully intend to remain."

His shoulders ached, his heart hammering uncontrollably. Adamo finally lowered his pistol but didn't shove it beneath his belt. He could still fire on anyone, including Diana. Fear and fury constricted Tristan's throat. "Peter, escort my wife back to the celebration, *now*."

"No!" She fought hard but couldn't win. Although younger, Peter was far taller and stronger. He slung her over his shoulder and plodded up the path.

* * * *

Diana lifted her face to see what was going on, terrified the worst would come.

Tristan spoke to Adamo. The man still hadn't put his weapon away. James edged close, his firearm raised. Either of them could shoot at any moment.

She smacked Peter's back. "Put me down."

He stomped toward the mansion.

"Please. I have to stay and make certain Tristan's all right."

"He will be." Peter breathed hard and shifted her on his shoulder. "As long as you stay out of his way and stop messing things up."

"If I hadn't arrived when I had, Adamo would have shot him."

"It's hardly likely. You'll have to walk from here. You weigh far too much for me."

Her feet hit the ground with a thud. She whirled around to go back to the point.

Peter promptly grabbed her arm and hauled her to the walls.

"Stop it." She pummeled his hand. "Let go of me."

"No."

They entered the courtyard. The others stopped talking and stared.

Peter gestured dismissively. "*Elle et Tristan a eu un combat.*"

Diana yanked her arm. Her brother held tight. She glared. "What did you just say about Tristan?"

"I told everyone you two had a fight." He released her. "Now, sit down and stay here until your husband tells you to move."

She ran past him into the mansion and raced for the bedchamber. Once there, she slammed the door and bolted it.

Feet slapped the marble, Peter catching up. He hit the door once. "Stay in there now, understand?"

She glowered. If her little brother thought he could give her orders, he was sorely mistaken.

"Oh, and Diana? Phillipe's outside your windows should you try to escape."

The moon softened the room's hard shadows and washed the outside to faint silvers and grays. Phillipe leaned against a tree, arms crossed over his chest, guarding the windows.

"I'm never speaking to you again, Peter Fletcher."

"Do what you must." He breathed heavily. "But stay put. Let the men handle the danger. It's what we were meant to do."

She wanted to scream. Trapped and helpless, she lowered her head, worried Tristan would get shot. For him to have gone to the point when Adamo and Canela were there had been sheer madness and didn't make any sense to her. After all Canela had done, Tristan couldn't be that blind to the girl's treachery. Anyone could see how easily she manipulated Adamo, possibly leading him to kill.

Frustrated tears filled Diana's eyes. She stormed to the bed and threw the pillows across the room. Outside, music played, laughter peaked, fell, then rose. The clamor drove her mad. She feared the noise would drown out a pistol's sharp crack, then worried she'd hear the sound, anyway.

She sank to the mattress, horrible scenes bombarding her: Tristan maimed, killed, dying alone without the chance for her to say good-bye.

She buried her face in her hands.

A fist rapped hard on the door.

Startled, she straightened, her stomach clenching at Peter having come back to tell her she was a widow. "Go away! I won't hear it!"

Footfalls sounded and faded.

She rocked, then rushed to the door, wanting to know what had happened, dreading the worst. As she fumbled with the bolt, the laughter and music intruded, quite loud in fact. If anything untoward had happened, the others wouldn't be celebrating.

A scraping noise sounded behind her.

Tristan swung his legs over the sill.

Relief flooded Diana, bringing her close to tears and joyous shouts. She hurried across the room, but stopped short, recalling how worried she'd been. He'd taken little care with his safety and hadn't allowed her to protect him in the least. How dare he. "Go away."

"What?"

"You heard me. Go away." She pointed past him to the forest.

"I suppose this means you're in no mood to rejoin the celebration. Very well."

He unfastened his breeches, pushed them off, and padded naked to their bed. His weight shook the mattress. By the looks of his stiffened cock, he intended to take her as though nothing had happened.

Not bloody likely tonight.

He folded his hands behind his head and regarded her. The moonlight sharpened his features, making him look seductive and dangerous.

She wasn't cowed or aroused. At least not much. She strode to the bed. "I saved your hide."

"You did. But you also put yourself in harm's way."

"I don't care about myself." She sank to the mattress. "I'd gladly die for you."

"The hell you will. I forbid it."

Diana laughed at his damned arrogance and spoke through clenched teeth. "You're impossible."

He pulled his hand from behind his head and cupped her breast. "But you still desire me, admit it."

"Not tonight." She pushed his hand away. "You treat my love too lightly."

"I do not."

"Yes, you do. You might have died. I might never have seen you again, not even to say a last good-bye."

"It wasn't as serious as you believe."

"A pistol pointed at your heart by a madman who wants you dead isn't serious?"

"Adamo misunderstood why I went to the point."

"Indeed. And how was I supposed to know when you had Peter haul me away like a sack of grain? You forced me to wait here not knowing whether you lived or died. How would you like to be in my position?"

He shrugged. "I'd make the best of the situation."

"Like bloody hell. I've yet to see a man who has the stamina to withstand childbirth, much less the death of a woman he loves, unless your feelings for me aren't that great or enduring."

"You know they are." He glared as she did. "And you've made your point. I'd hate not knowing what happened to you. But Adamo speaks French. You don't. You kept threatening him with the pistol."

"He was threatening you."

"Only because he misunderstood why I went to the point."

"Why did you?"

Tristan draped his arm over his eyes and fisted his fingers. "My God, can't we just sleep? I've never been so tired in all my days."

"Then answer me quickly, and I'll allow you whatever rest you want."

"James warned me about you becoming a shrew."

"Remind me to have a word with him in the morning. For now, I want to know why you went out there."

He inhaled deeply and sighed. "Phillipe was at the celebration when he should have kept watch."

"Then you weren't speaking to him about a horse as you said."

Tristan squirmed. "No."

"You lied. Why?"

"I didn't want to worry you."

"About what? Wait." Nausea gripped her. "You said he should have kept watch. Do you have men on our shores each night in case your former crew comes here?"

"We've always had a watch in the event anyone shows up." He slid his arm to his forehead and looked at her. "I knew if I told you about it, you'd fret when there's no need. The island is more than secure. It's hidden from the usual routes. On the outside chance someone does finds the land, I'd prefer to be advised of the matter."

"So when Phillipe shirked his duties, you decided to keep watch yourself without your pistol or the glass?"

He caressed her cheek. "I forgot my pistol because I was still feeling the effects of your overwhelming lust for me."

"Do not make light of this."

He dropped his hand. "Very well. I assumed Phillipe had given Adamo the glass when he and Canela offered to keep watch."

"Both of them? How curious. Why?"

"I went to the point to find out. When I arrived, Adamo was asleep, and Canela was using the glass."

Diana frowned. Earlier Canela had watched the sea instead of joining the celebration. "Do you think she wants to leave this island and was using the glass to view the others?"

"With her it's difficult to say. But the others nearby aren't habitable. She'd have to sail on a ship like the Lady Lark to reach one that is."

"Why did Adamo pull his pistol on you?"

"Before he awakened I had asked Canela what she was looking for. She refused to tell me. When I tried to take the glass, Adamo awakened and misunderstood my intent. Now I have a question for you. Why did you come to the point and with my pistol no less?"

She shrugged as casually as he had. "After you spoke to Phillipe and left, I noticed Canela wasn't around. I guessed the two of you were together. So, I grabbed your pistol and followed, fully intending to murder you both."

Tristan blinked.

Diana traced his jawline and smiled wickedly. "You see, my love, you betray me at your own peril."

"It would appear. Are you serious? You believed I was rendezvousing with her?"

"I thought you might be set upon by the she-devil and seriously injured because you were unarmed. As I was not, I was fully prepared to deal with her, or anyone else, and would have if you'd only allowed me to stay."

"Learn to speak French and the next time I may."

Her smile faded. "Next time? You expect more trouble from Adamo? Didn't you convince him you have no interest in Canela?"

"I think he already knows I don't. What happened in the past galls him. He wants what all men want, a woman who's never belonged to anyone else. With Canela that's impossible. Adamo's no fool, though. Nor is he evil. He's not about to murder us as we sleep."

"What about Canela?"

"I'll kill her if she tries. Now quit asking so many bloody questions."

She gave him a hard stare. "Never. I'll ask as many as I want."

"And here I thought I'd finished taming you."

"If I'd been tame tonight, you might be dead."

"Did I thank you for saving me?"

"You will." She caressed his thick cock. "But I insist you take care around Adamo."

"You've nothing to worry about."

She worked his shaft and fondled his balls. "Truly?"

His lids slid down. "James and I did our best to soothe him. He seemed mollified. For the time being, at least, there should be no more trouble."

* * * *

Ever since Tristan and James had left, Adamo had faced the sea, saying nothing. Canela sensed his fury.

When he finally looked over, hate glittered in his eyes. "This is our land, not theirs."

"It has always been ours."

He faced her. "They have no right to the stone house, crops, water, or animals on our land."

"They never have."

"Tristan and James would have killed me if you hadn't been here. They knew if I died, you would have told the others what happened."

"I love you."

He smiled, but her declaration didn't soften his rage.

Excitement ran through her. "Will you watch for the ships and row out to them so the pirates can remove Tristan from our land?"

"I long for the day. I will see you, not the Englishwoman, living in the stone house. You will have the finest jewels and the loveliest silks. You will be mistress of our land."

Canela lowered her face, pretending his words had humbled her. When Adamo turned to the sea, she grinned.

Chapter 13

By the time Tristan and Diana awakened, the sun shone high in the sky. Given the pleasant quiet, the others had yet to get up.

He left the bed and stretched, trying to shake off fatigue. "I shouldn't have slept so long. I have far too much to do today."

Diana finished her yawn. "I don't hear the other men moving about."

"Most drank well into the night." He washed his face at the basin. "They'll surely need help in finishing their tasks."

She rolled onto her belly and propped her face in her hands. "Do you ever overindulge in drink, my love?"

He smiled at her question and endearment. "Never. I far prefer to read. At least I did before I had you to take in my bed."

"You have me to have." She grew thoughtful and shook her head. "Does that make sense?"

"Very little you say does. You will not throw the pillow."

She scowled playfully, then rested her elbows on it. "Go on. Finish your work so you can come back to me for indecent pleasure and a shave."

After washing, he pulled on his breeches and gave her a peck on the cheek. "Unfortunately, I won't be home till sundown."

She grabbed his hair and held him to her. "If I promise not to shave you, will you arrive sooner?"

"'Fraid not."

"Not even to join me for the midday meal?"

"It's nearly time for it now." He pulled his hair from her and straightened. "While I'm away you can perfect your French."

"Should I also have a pistol at the ready?"

He lost his smile. Adamo wouldn't harm her, but Tristan wasn't as certain about Canela. "A weapon's hardly necessary." He'd tell Peter to remain close and protect her. "As I told you last night, I've settled matters with Adamo."

"And as I asked last night, what about Canela? I saw how she looked at you at the point. She hates you now nearly as much as she does me. Promise you'll be armed today."

"I always am when I'm away from here. As long as you stay within these walls you're well-protected."

She made a face. "Please don't tell me you're going to have Peter guarding me."

"He's your brother. I thought you liked him."

"After last night I'm never speaking to him. How dare he order me about, telling me where I can and cannot go."

"Very well, I'll tell you. Don't go past the courtyard. And do not, under any circumstances, go into the forest, to the point, or the beach."

Her mouth turned down. "Life on this island will never be the same, will it?"

"No, it won't. It will be far better. I give you my word."

* * * *

Vincent trudged up the beach to the island's southernmost point. Turned into the wind, he lifted the glass to his eye. Tristan's island was hidden from sloops unable to traverse its shallow waters. However, a skiff or longboat could easily manage the journey.

He inched the glass to the right, gauging which area served best for a surprise attack. With the right not to his liking, he shifted his instrument to the left and stilled at a bare-breasted young woman, a beautiful native girl. She wore a scarlet cloth about her hips and an odd leather collar around her throat.

She lifted a glass to her eye.

For one horrible moment, Vincent couldn't move. When his hesitation broke, he brought down his instrument and ran to a stand of palms. Hiding behind them, he breathed hard and tried to slow his racing heart, mystified as to who she was and what she was doing on the beach with a glass.

Tristan's island was so concealed Vincent had foolishly thought the beach would be deserted and unprotected. Since it wasn't, he and his men would have to approach at night and find their way through the blasted forest to wherever Tristan slept.

Muttering an oath, Vincent brought the glass to his eye. His crew was in the distance, sleeping off last night's rum. He feared going back to them, worried the native girl might see and warn Tristan.

Vincent sank to the ground, rested his back against a palm, and then yanked off his yellow scarf before its color gave away his hiding place. Swearing repeatedly, he didn't want to consider when movement would be safe.

* * * *

Shocked, Canela kept the glass to her eye. The man with the yellow scarf had seen her and now hid in a stand. She pulled in a ragged breath and finally trained the glass on the sea, not wanting him to know she'd seen him.

He had to be from Tristan's old crew or Diana's. No one else would have been so cautious or would have traveled this far.

At last, she lowered the instrument and left the beach. She kept her pace unhurried and natural until she reached the point. With the trees protecting her from view, she broke into a run.

She was breathless, skin damp, hair tangled when she reached Adamo outside his house.

Seeing her, he stopped grooming his horse and reached for his pistol. "What is it?" He looked behind her to the forest. "Has someone touched you?"

"No." She pushed Adamo's hand from his weapon. "The pirates are here."

He glanced past her. "Are you certain?"

"Lower your voice. I saw one just now, a man from Tristan's crew or the Englishwoman's."

"On the beach?"

"Not ours. The next one over." She lifted the glass. "I was using this and spotted him."

Adamo grabbed her arm. "Did he see you?"

Canela pulled in more air, stalling for the best answer. "No. I was hiding behind the trees. As I watched him with my glass, his swept our beach." She pulled her arm from Adamo. "This is your chance to take back what belongs to us. Row out to show him the jewels and silks you have. Tell him how we protect the island so he can avoid discovery and capture Tristan. Then you and I will have the stone house for our children."

Adamo breathed hard but didn't move.

She grabbed his arm. "Why are you waiting?"

He pulled away and resumed grooming his horse.

"What are you doing? You must row out to him."

"What of our people? How will they protect themselves? Once the pirates are on our land and have Tristan, how can we be certain they will treat us fairly and not use us as slaves?"

"I will warn our people in time. No one will be a slave."

He regarded her, then drew the brush over his horse's flank.

She held back a scream. "Would you like for me to row out to him, risking my safety and life for our island? Very well. Where did you hide my jewels? Tell me, I will go and do what you will not."

He threw the brush. "I will go, but make certain you warn the others in time. These are our people."

"They will come to no harm."

"Nor will you. Stay hidden in the forest. You are not to go to the beach or the stone house and let the pirates see you."

She nodded.

The moment the men arrived, she'd approach them and their leader, perhaps the one with the yellow scarf. If so, she'd seduce him, then take what was rightfully hers.

* * * *

Although Diana couldn't leave the mansion, Peter behaved like the prisoner. He slammed volume after volume on the library table. She picked up the largest book she could find and pushed to her feet. "Make any more noise and I'll bring this down on your head."

He glared at her.

She glared right back. "What's the matter with you?"

"What else?" He pushed his chair against the table, jostling it.

A stack of books tottered and fell to the floor.

She banged her volume. "Do you intend to tear this entire room apart during your fit? What will Tristan think?"

"He'll punish me further by forcing me to stay inside and watch you forever."

"You're supposed to be protecting me, little brother. You want to be a man, then act like one."

He looked ready to explode, upper lip curled back, face reddened, eyes narrowed.

Such a child. Diana crossed her arms and stood her ground.

He made an extraordinarily angry noise, then lost his fight. "I want to go outside."

"Fine. We can study in the courtyard as the children play."

"I hardly want to go outside to study."

"You want to take a ride?"

"No."

Her frown faded. If he didn't want to study or ride, only one thing remained. "Do you want to work in the fields or the stables?"

He jumped to his feet. "I want to be with Laure."

"Sit down and lower you voice."

"No. I want to be with Laure."

"Gavra's sister? Why?"

"Why do you think? I was with her last night, all right?"

No, it was not. By the color in Peter's cheeks and the way he couldn't look at her, Diana feared the worst. "My God, Peter, you're still a boy."

"The hell you say. I'm a man. You doubt it, speak to Laure; she'll tell you the same. And you know what? Tristan not only knows about this, he congratulated me on the matter. What do you think about that?"

Tristan had a lot of explaining to do. How dare he encourage such a young boy to become a man. He should have far more sense than Peter, who had none at all. "Are you actually leaving?"

He stopped in the doorway. "What do you think?"

"Come back here."

"No. I want to be with Laure. Stay in here until Tristan gets back."

"Peter!"

He'd already darted down the hall to his lady love.

* * * *

"Come on, man." Tristan smacked James's arm. "Where's your stamina?"

James lifted his head, then let it drop. His chin hit his chest. "My what?"

Tristan suppressed a smile. "Your endurance, or if you prefer, your fine spirit, your manly pride."

James's shoulders lifted to his ears. "Must you talk so loud?"

"Loudly. Didn't know I was. Are you all right?"

He sagged to his gelding's neck, his face pressed against horseflesh. "If I don't keep my eyes closed, they may fall out."

"Serves you right for drinking." Tristan wheeled his horse around and waited for James to notice and catch up. "Did you ever think to try a book to enrich your evenings?"

James laughed, then moaned. "I think I'm about to be ill."

"At the thought of reading?"

He swallowed hard. "When are we going home?"

"Soon as the sun sets, if our work's finished by then."

James groaned. "Perhaps one of the men can take my place."

The others were just now dragging into the fields and pastures. All had been at last night's celebration and looked as terrible as James did.

"Not likely." Tristan rode ahead and spoke over his shoulder. "Come on, we have a lot to do."

* * * *

Adamo frantically scooped sand aside, searching for the jewels and silks Canela had given him.

He couldn't find them.

Panicked, he clawed deeper, certain he'd buried them here, even marked them with a small wooden cross. The thing was gone now, most likely swept away by the wind or someone's feet.

He lowered his head, wanting to give up and go home. He needed to groom his horses, feed the pigs, store the grain, tend his garden. Tasks he should attend to, but if he came back without alerting the pirates, Canela would never forgive him. She'd hate him for losing her jewels and silks.

He wiped sweat from his forehead and dug furiously.

Small rocks fell off the rise and hit his hand.

Surprised, he lifted his face.

Gérard looked at him curiously. "What are you doing?"

Adamo's heart pounded so hard he could barely keep from shaking, but he forced a smile. "The other day I found a shell for Canela and hid it here. I wanted to make an ornament for her hair and surprise her, but now I cannot find it. Why are you here?"

Gérard stretched and yawned. "I was looking for you. Today, I keep watch. Philippe said you have the glass." He glanced around. "Where is it?"

With Canela. "Let me take your watch."

Gérard's bushy eyebrows shot up. "Why?"

Adamo breathed shallowly, terrified to say the wrong thing. "Because you and I are friends. You drank last night, but I slept. I feel fine and should keep watch."

Gérard smiled. "Merci." He stepped closer. "Can I help you search for the shell?"

"No. Go home and rest."

"I will. The next time you have a watch, you can count on me to take it. See you tomorrow." He climbed the path.

Adamo's pulse pounded wildly, his vision blurring. "Wait."

Gérard started back. "What?"

He wanted to tell his friend about Canela's plan, ask if he should do what she wanted, but hesitated. Gérard was also Tristan's friend and would surely tell him about this. If Adamo tried to stop Gérard from doing so, the man might fight or even shoot him. Canela would then be free to pursue the stone house and its riches because she wanted those things as she never had her husband. Adamo wasn't blind. She'd never love him, but it didn't matter. He wanted Canela so badly he'd do whatever she demanded to please her, even if that meant lying to a friend or betraying his people. "I hope you have a pleasant rest."

Gérard smiled. "I will, but only because of you, my friend."

He'd never been more ashamed but wouldn't betray Canela. Once Gérard had left, Adamo dug until he found what he'd buried. He couldn't turn back now. Not if he wanted his wife.

Pushing fear aside, he wrapped a silk cloth around the items, slung them over his shoulder, and ran to where his people hid the boats.

Committed to his plan, he rowed away from the island to the one on the left.

Chapter 14

"Well what do you know." Vincent kept the glass to his eye.

A young native man rowed this way. Minutes earlier, the savage had dug in the sand and pulled out a bright green cloth and items that sparkled like jewels. Unless they were colored glass. Vincent frowned, curious as to why the man had those things with him and why he'd bring them this way.

He checked the beach. No one watched, the bare-breasted girl gone. He left the stand and ran toward his crew.

One after the other struggled to a sitting position and stared at him, tearing down the beach like the devil was on his heels. Or there was a prize to be had.

Eighteen-year-old Howie Winters pushed to his feet first and helped Tom Ralston up. The others followed and exchanged quick glances.

Reaching them, Vincent gulped air and pointed behind himself. "A savage is rowing here from Tristan's island."

The men craned their necks to see past him.

Howie looked scared. "What do you think he wants?"

"We're going to find out. Come on, you lazy bastards, let's go."

"Glory be." Howie jumped from foot to foot. "Should'a worn me shoes. This sand's bloody hot."

Vincent pulled out his pistol. "Shut up or you'll speak your next words around a bullet in your mouth."

As he danced over the sand, Howie pressed his lips together and moaned softly.

When they were back to where Vincent had hidden, he gestured his men into the palms. "We'll stay here until the savage reaches our shore."

He stroked his brace of pistols. "Then we'll go out to greet him like the friendly men we are."

His crew laughed softly, except for Howie who still troubled over his burned toes.

Vincent glared at the young man.

Howie forgot his pain and forced a wide smile.

* * * *

Diana stayed in the library as long as she could, and finally stormed to Peter's room. She opened the door without knocking, hoping she wouldn't catch him and Laure sharing something other than a kiss.

They weren't in the chamber. She slammed the door and hurried to Canela's old room. The young lovers weren't in there, either, nor in the other bedchambers or dining area.

She ran to the courtyard. Young children darted past. The last bumped into her and tumbled to the ground. After soothing the little girl's tears, Diana crossed the courtyard to the stand where she and Tristan had made love last night. No one was there today. The women were at their usual places, working diligently, making soap, washing the men's breeches, nursing their infants.

Back in the mansion, she found Gavra in the dining room. Diana smiled briefly, hoping Gavra knew where the couple went. "Ah, Laure and Peter—that is Pierre?"

She looked at Diana expectantly.

Taking the easy route, Diana wrapped her arms around herself, puckered her lips, and made kissing noises.

Gavra giggled, nodded vigorously, and spoke hurriedly in French.

From the few phrases Diana understood, the converse was about Peter's conquest last night. Given his delight in being a newly made man, Diana suspected everyone but she had known the news. She struggled with the proper verb tense and sentence structure, then let loose. *"Avez-vous vu Laure avec Pierre?"* Have you seen Laure with Peter?

Gavra's smile faded. She shook her head.

Diana wasn't certain if Gavra hadn't understood the question, hadn't seen the two lovers, or was disturbed at the thought of witnessing them in the throes of passion. "Merci."

She rushed outside and crossed the courtyard to its walls. Forest, sea, and little else greeted her. Damnation. She was so frustrated she hoped Canela might happen by. At least the girl knew English and might reveal Laure and Peter's whereabouts. If Diana offered something in return, like her marriage collar.

Not bloody likely. She stopped at the forest edge. There wasn't any movement within the shaded areas. Perhaps Peter and Laure had gone to the beach.

Diana negotiated the path leading there, then finally slowed as she considered coming upon them if they were past kissing and really involved.

She made a face, guessing Peter would rail at her. Tristan too. He'd say the couple was none of her business, her brother was now a man, and had a right to indulge in carnal pleasure. No scolding from her would stop him.

Defeated, she retraced her steps to the mansion where she'd remain as Tristan wanted and Peter surely hoped.

* * * *

With Adamo well on his way to the other island, Canela left her hiding place and ran down the path to the beach. She lifted the glass to her eye and focused on her husband.

He looked troubled or afraid.

She shook her fist. "Do not fail me. Do not—what are you doing?"

He'd lowered his head and stopped rowing. The current turned the skiff, taking it away from the other island, killing her plans.

"Row!"

His face remained down.

Coward. Fool. She raced to the hidden boats, to take his place if necessary, then checked to see if anyone noticed her. Still alone, she focused one last time on Adamo.

He'd finally looked up and rowed, righting the boat to head for the other island. His movements were hesitant and cautious when she needed him determined and fearless, willing to do whatever was necessary to deliver the isle to her.

When his skiff reached the other shore, his courage no longer mattered. Men, perhaps thirty in all, ran from their hiding place to greet him. Each had a pistol.

* * * *

Tristan and James reclined beneath a palm to eat their grapes, cheese, and bread, though James had to force each bite down his freckled throat. On an anguished groan, he sagged to the ground and draped his arm over his eyes.

Poor man was a sorry mess. "You all right?"

"I will never imbibe again."

Tristan had heard his friend's solemn vow before and played along. "Sobriety will surely allow you more time with Gavra."

"Perhaps. Though I've hardly neglected her. She is with child."

Tristan grabbed another grape cluster. "Are you serious?"

"Found out last night."

"Well then, congratulations."

James winced. "Why do you keep shouting? Are you trying to kill me?"

"Sorry."

"What about Diana?"

"She stopped wanting me dead after that first night."

James groaned. "I meant her condition. Does she have one yet?"

Tristan lifted his face to the gentle breeze and inhaled deeply of its sweet, clean scent. The day was soft, his mood perfect. "I promised to keep the matter between her and myself. I'll say no more on the subject."

"There's no need. Congratulations to you, too, my friend. Are you hoping for a boy or a girl?"

"Six of each, eventually, if Diana can stomach me that long."

"How can she do anything but submit to her dangerous angel?"

Laughing, Tristan kicked James's leg.

The man smiled briefly, then readjusted himself on the grass. "Have you heard about Peter?"

Had he ever. Peter hadn't been able to stop gushing about his special night with Laure. "Had to happen. The boy will be fifteen next week."

"You're wrong you know."

"Peter's younger than he claims?"

"I'm not referring to his age but the fact that he's now a man not a boy."

"Quite right." Tristan enjoyed his cheese and rice bread. "There's no turning back for him now."

James slid his arm to his forehead. The whites of his eyes were as red as his hair. "Do you remember your first time?"

"I was thirteen, the lady was four-and-twenty, and I wore a smile on my face for five full days. What about you?"

"My story's similar. Though I must say I held my first love in my heart for a fortnight."

"Fourteen days you say. My, you are the romantic. Care to read some of my poetry volumes when we get back?"

James laughed, then clutched his head and moaned. "I'd tell you to give them to Peter, but I doubt he'll have time to read anything now. Unlike those ladies you and I first had, Laure's not about to deliver her charms to other men. She belongs to Peter, and I'd wager they're taking full advantage of it."

"To the detriment of everything else."

"Now you'll really have your hands full getting Peter to do his lessons."

"If pistols fail, there's always Diana's wrath."

"How right you are. Give me a shot to the head any day over a woman's fury." He struggled to a sitting position and kicked Tristan's leg. "Shall we get on with it? I'd like to be in bed with my woman before the moon rises."

Tristan pushed to his feet. "I agree fully."

* * * *

With countless pistols pointed at his chest, Adamo couldn't move or breathe. Two men pulled his skiff onto the sand. Another took his weapon. Although he'd done this for Canela, so she'd praise and respect him, he now feared he might die. "I have come to offer you treasure."

The pirate wearing the yellow scarf frowned, then said something in English to the man next to him.

He spoke to Adamo. "*Ce que vous chérissez parlant de?*" What treasure you speaking of?

Adamo inclined his head to the sack near his feet.

Yellow Scarf spoke to the other man. The pirate questioned Adamo. "What's in there?"

"Jewels, silks, combs, and more."

"Pick it up. Toss it to the man with the yellow scarf."

Adamo couldn't move. Once they had the jewels, they might shoot him, then row to the island and rape Canela. He should have considered such a possibility and spoken to Gérard or his other friends, asking them what he should do.

The pirate growled. "I said, toss it over."

Adamo stalled. "There is treasure in a hiding place only I know about."

The pirate spoke to Yellow Scarf who exchanged glances with the other men. They conversed in English before the one who knew French glared at Adamo. "Toss the sack over now or you're dead no matter how many treasures you know about."

He obeyed and steeled himself, expecting them to shoot.

The pirates' pistols remained trained on him as Yellow Scarf fell to his knees, upended the silk sack, and whistled at the gold, pearls, diamonds, rubies, and silks before him.

At last, he lifted his head and spoke.

The other pirate gestured to Adamo. "Where's a savage like you get a white man's treasure?"

He tensed at the insult, but the pistols reminded him to be humble and obedient. "Capitaine Kent."

Yellow Scarf stood and shoved his pistol into Adamo's temple.

The other pirate watched indifferently. "Where might we find Kent?"

Adamo couldn't stop trembling. "Kill me and you will never know."

The pirate spoke to Yellow Scarf who frowned and lifted his pistol to strike Adamo.

He shrank back. "Why do you want to harm me? I come to help you capture Capitaine Kent."

Yellow Scarf kept his pistol raised. The other pirate regarded Adamo closely. "Why would you be doing so?"

"He took my people's land. We want it back. If you help, we have gold, jewels, and silks you and your men may take to your ship, along with a white woman."

The pirate's attention jumped from Canela's jewels to Adamo. "White woman?"

"One who is called Diana."

* * * *

Diana sat on the windowsill, troubling over Peter's sudden manhood and her own future.

For the first time, she considered what might happen when her infant arrived, other than the expected joy. If the babe were male, that might fuel Canela's jealousy, encouraging her to do harm.

Diana considered the scenario and scowled. Canela's envy was causing her to worry about an infant not yet born, made her a prisoner in her own home, and left her concerned about Peter's safety. Given how besotted he was with Laure, he might not notice what went on around him. Canela might try to do him harm, simply because he and Diana were related.

She hurried to Peter's room, hoping he'd taken his pistol.

The weapon wasn't on the tables, his bed, or under the mattress. Diana supposed he was armed. Of course, to protect oneself with a pistol, one had to have their eyes open and their wits about them.

Poor Peter.

She considered having her own pistol for protection. After a thorough search, she found no spare weapons in the mansion for the women to use, and wasn't surprised. Peter had told her to let the men handle the danger because they'd been born to do so.

"You're handling this quite well. You left me here without any protection, and God knows if you've even thought to protect yourself."

She grabbed the largest knife she could find from the kitchen, the beach her destination. It was one thing to worry about coming upon Peter and Laure while they had relations. It was another to find them slaughtered because Canela had murdered them as they made love. After the incident on the point last night, most likely orchestrated by Canela, Diana didn't know what the she-devil was capable of.

In the courtyard, Diana stayed near the mansion walls to hide the knife from the others. An infant cried in one of the rooms.

"Shhh, shhh, *petit l'un*," Follie said.

Diana glanced in the window.

Follie's dark hair fanned over her arms. She kissed her son's cheek. He was perfect.

Diana cradled her belly, the new life inside. One she already loved and had to protect.

If anything happened to Peter, she'd never forgive herself. However, if she fell or Canela attacked her and Diana lost her unborn child, she'd surely die. She didn't have an easy choice to make, but Tristan's decision for her to stay within these walls finally made sense.

Peter was a man now with an obligation to protect himself and Laure. Diana's duty was to her husband and child. She'd probably been worrying for nothing. Surely, Peter was armed, Canela wouldn't attempt to harm him or Laure, and everything would be all right.

* * * *

Vincent had finally found Diana, Tristan, and treasure too. He couldn't believe his good luck. At least not enough to trust the savage who said his name was Adamo. Vincent spoke to Storley. "Ask him if there's anyone watching the beach."

Storley did.

Adamo shook his head.

"I see." Vincent stroked his pistol. "So absolutely no one's watching the beach?"

The savage looked confused.

Vincent brought his pistol butt down hard on Adamo's cheek. He wailed and sank to his knees, cradling his battered face.

There'd be more of that and worse if he'd lied. "Ask him again if anyone's watching the beach."

Storley did.

Adamo cried out in French.

Storley lifted his shoulders. "He says he was given the task. With him here now, no one's watching over there."

Vincent said nothing, did nothing, allowing Adamo's fear to grow. When he was certain the savage understood the gravity of his situation, Vincent told Storley to ask him about the bare-breasted woman who had held the glass. He demanded to know who she was and why she was on the beach.

Once Storley finished with his questions, Adamo lifted his bruised face but didn't answer.

Vincent struck him.

Blood poured from Adamo's split lip. He cowered, trying to protect himself, and finally spoke.

Storley translated. "The savage said she was only amusing herself with the glass. She's just a native girl."

Not likely. To Vincent, she'd looked far too intent. He gestured his largest men forward. The savage screamed from their relentless blows.

Vincent held up his hand. "Enough." He spoke to Storley. "Ask him again if anyone is watching the beach."

Storley did.

Adamo lay curled at their feet. Pain slurred his answer.

"He claims to be the only one."

Vincent finally believed him. No man would risk pirates beating him to death to keep such a secret. "Put the savage in the skiff. Get our boats and follow."

Vincent gathered the silks and jewels. Once he had the treasure safely beneath his arm, he climbed into the skiff beside Adamo, pressed his pistol to the man's temple, and spoke to Storley. "Ask him what to expect once we arrive on his island."

* * * *

As Adamo claimed, the beach and rise above it proved deserted.

No telling for how long.

Scowling, Vincent left the skiff hurriedly and ordered the others to pull Adamo to shore. They left the savage on the sand, then stowed their craft within the foliage. The other men arrived and hid the longboats.

A young woman came from behind the trees.

Vincent recognized her instantly as the one he'd seen in his glass. Only now, her odd collar was gone and he wanted to know why, worried that its absence held some meaning. A sort of advance warning.

Adamo reached out. "Canela, no."

"Quiet." Vincent struck the savage into silence and straightened, pleased the woman carried no weapons. "Canela. That's your name?"

She nodded despite his English, advanced, and stopped in front of him.

"You understand English?" he asked.

"Yes, though the others here speak French." Her accent was thick, voice lilting.

"So I was told. Where's the collar you had on before?"

She smiled. It was as cold as Christmas and said she knew what he didn't. Vincent grabbed her arm and pulled her to him. "What's the collar mean? Why ain't you wearing it no more?"

Despite his fierce tone, she remained calm. "It is only a marriage collar. I removed it as I am no longer wed. Now, I belong to you."

"Why am I so lucky?"

"You are the captain, are you not?"

"Why?"

She smiled, only this one was far warmer and promised a great deal of pleasure. "I belong to the captain who rules this land and has the stone house."

"Stone house?"

"Where Tristan Kent and his woman, Diana, live. She, you may give to your men. Him, you will hang. And then you and I will rule this land."

Chapter 15

Diana poured scented oil into her bathwater.

Something moved outside the windows.

Knife in hand, she hurried to the closest one.

Muted laughter sounded, the softer giggles belonging to a young woman. The foolish ones most certainly were her brother's. Relief and dismay flooded Diana. "Peter, is that you?"

He groaned, then sighed. "What are you bothering me with now?"

Throttling him would be delightful. She tossed the knife on the bed and strode to the window. After a brief hesitation, she looked out.

Peter and Laure jumped away from each other, him in his breeches, she in her cloth. Laure turned her back to Diana.

He screwed up his mouth. "Do you mind?"

"I might ask you the same. If you insist on this behavior, why not entertain the young lady in your room?"

He brightened. "That would be better."

He was still such a child, though one with a man's needs. With Laure's hand in his, he pulled her to his bedchamber window.

"Peter." Diana leaned out, wanting to irritate him a bit longer. "You should use the door like everyone else."

"Tristan prefers the window. He told me so."

He would. She would definitely have a word with her husband this evening. Given the sun's position, he shouldn't be much longer.

She stripped naked and lowered herself into the warm, fragrant water to prepare herself for him.

* * * *

The waning sun streamed across the men who worked in the vineyards. As they detailed their concerns about the crop, Tristan couldn't concentrate, agitated by Peter and Laure's newfound love. He had no idea why they would be on his mind and didn't understand why he was bothered by their relationship.

James elbowed him.

"What?"

"Are you going to answer the men?"

"About what?"

James gave him a strange look. "They just asked you about the grapes. They said this crop seems inferior to the last. Given how I imbibed last night, I know I'm not at my best, but what's your excuse?"

He had no answer except Peter's desire for Laure troubled him, though that was clearly mad. Earlier, he'd congratulated the boy on his new status. He regarded the men and asked them to repeat their concerns.

They did.

Tristan didn't listen this time, either.

"My God." James huffed. "What in the hell is the matter with you?"

Tristan frowned. "The boy's supposed to be watching her."

"Peter? Who's he supposed to be watching?"

"Diana, who else? He's supposed to be protecting her, not going off with Laure."

"Tristan, wait." James grabbed his arm before he could mount his gelding. "Who says Peter's with Laure?"

"Who says he's not? He couldn't stop bragging about her this morning. You were the one who said he'd be taking full advantage of her and not paying attention to his lessons."

"Diana's hardly a lesson, my friend, she's his sister. Peter also knows the trouble Canela can cause. Not likely he's taking any chances."

Tristan wanted to believe that. The other men were more tired than he, certainly as irritated, and needed to get on with this so they could be with their women.

"Come on." James smacked Tristan's back. "We have a bit yet to do. The sun's going to set soon and then we can go home."

Tristan nodded, chiding himself for his needless worry.

* * * *

On one knee, Vincent studied the sand drawing Canela had made, depicting a large house hidden within the forest. The drawing showed a courtyard surrounded by rooms, though Vincent was only concerned with the one belonging to Diana and Tristan. He swung his pistol to the right and pointed the muzzle at a bedchamber. "This is Diana's?"

Canela nodded.

"The room can be entered through a window?"

"Three."

Vincent smiled. "Is Diana in the bedchamber now?"

Canela's eyes narrowed. "Why do you want to know if she is in the room? What does it matter? You can capture her and give her to your men no matter where she is."

Vincent grabbed Canela's throat and squeezed, ready to wring the life from her.

She gaped in quick fear.

"Is Diana in the bedchamber now?"

She nodded.

He loosened his hold. "Why would she be there at this time?"

"The Englishwoman sometimes bathes at this hour."

He squeezed. "Sometimes?"

"Always."

"Where's Tristan when she's doing this?"

"Finishing his tasks."

"What tasks?"

"Those in the fields or the pastures."

"So he's not in the stone house at this hour?"

"Not until the sun goes down."

Vincent relaxed his grip but kept his hand about her throat and lifted his face to the remaining light. He had enough time to take Diana in her bedchamber, then await Tristan's return.

Grinning, he pushed to his feet, pulling Canela with him. "You're going to take us to the stone house and warn us of any danger. Do you understand me?"

She softened her gaze, her manner seductive. "I will do whatever you wish so Tristan and his woman are removed. Tonight, you and I will share their bed. I will bring you great pleasure."

"You'll bring me safety or else. Afterward, you go to my men. They like your sort. For myself, I'm going to have Diana, an Englishwoman. If you don't like it, it's best you remember this. The first sign of trouble from your people, and you'll get a bullet in your head for the problems you've caused me." He tightened his hold on her throat, forcing away her rage, replacing it with renewed fear. "Understand?"

Canela nodded.

"Good. Now go on and do as you're told." He pushed her away.

She stumbled into Storley. He slipped his arm around her waist and caressed her naked flesh. She glared at Vincent. "I helped you."

"So you did, you filthy savage. Now keep your bloody tongue or I'll cut it out."

Fury darkened her face. Tears filled her eyes.

* * * *

Diana rested her head against the back of the tub. Outside, lemurs rustled leaves, birds sang sweetly, and the sea hissed. In here, giggles and impassioned noises sounded from Peter's room, him and Laure experiencing no end of pleasure.

Diana covered her eyes. Come morning, she'd insist he move to a bedchamber across the courtyard. She was too English and civilized to fully accept this. At last, she hit the tub. "Will you be quiet?"

After several moans and grunts, they were, and the silence held.

She guessed he and Laure were asleep. If only Diana could be as lucky.

In an effort to relax, she closed her eyes, rotated her shoulders, and then lifted her legs from the tepid water to stretch.

The wind carried the children's shrill laughter, then a sudden shriek, one of them excited or upset about something.

She inhaled deeply and blew out her breath.

Leaves swished in the wind. Air whipped the silk sheets against the bedframe. An animal cried, or perhaps the sound was a newborn's thin wail.

A foot scraped ever so softly on the windowsill, its owner not wanting her to hear because he needed to surprise.

She smiled. Tristan had finally come back to her. Thank God. She opened her eyes to greet her husband.

A man wearing a yellow scarf grinned quite cruelly.

Diana screamed.

* * * *

Peter's eyes flew open. He sat up.

Diana screamed again.

"Damn you," Vincent said. "Be quiet."

Peter froze in surprise and confusion, not understanding how the man could be here.

"Pierre." Laure grabbed his arm. "Que—"

He put his hand over her mouth, his lips to her ear. "Don't say anything or make any noise. I'll see to my sister. Go to the vineyards and get Tristan and the others. Tell them our security's been compromised. Diana's in danger from his former crew. Do you understand?"

Laure nodded.

Vincent laughed and said something too muffled for Peter to hear. He released Laure. "Hurry."

With the silk cloth tied about her hips, she ran to the window, then pivoted and raced to the bed. "Men are outside. I have to use the door."

He grabbed her wrist. "Be careful. There may be more men in the hall."

Cautiously, she opened the door so the hinges wouldn't squeak. She looked out, then glanced back at Peter and mouthed 'be safe.'

He nodded. Once she left, Peter grabbed his pistol.

* * * *

Diana crouched in the tub, knees pulled to her breasts, hands protecting her marriage collar.

The pirate glared. "I told you to get to your feet and toss them diamonds to me. You'll do so now or I'll break your fingers one by one for the trouble you're causing."

Diana intended to cause far more. She'd only screamed to alert Peter, praying he'd escape and warn Tristan to protect himself. Rage, not fear, coursed through her. How dare this beast invade her home and look at her as though he had the right. She clenched her jaw and waited for his next move.

He plunged his hands into the tub, grabbed her ankles, and jerked her legs up.

She fell backward. Water covered her face. Panicked, she gripped the sides to pull up.

He pried her left hand from the metal.

She swung her fist but kept missing him.

He punched her right hand.

Holding on, she grabbed his shirt with her other hand, fear and fury giving her enormous strength. She pulled him down and lifted herself. Gasping for air and coughing, she dug her nails into his face and used the leverage to lift herself further.

He bellowed and tried to wrest her hand away.

She drove her other fist into his jaw.

He fell backward on the floor.

Cradling her belly and the new life inside, Diana rocked the tub and tipped it over. Scented water surged over the floor, carrying her with it, away from him. She crawled to her sodden gown, pulled it on, and rushed to the door.

He leaped up and used her wet hair to pull her into him. With one arm about her waist, he reached for her collar.

She yanked his hand to her mouth and sank her teeth into his flesh.

Shrieking, he fought to pull free.

She bit harder, then elbowed his ribs and kicked her heels into his shins. His arm dropped from her waist.

She bolted for the window and stopped at Canela, flanked by two pirates.

"You." Diana wanted to kill the girl for the danger she'd brought.

Canela looked past her.

Diana ran.

The pirate caught up, wrapped his arm tightly around her waist, and reached for her collar.

She twisted and fought.

"Release her at once!" Peter shouted.

Diana froze.

The pirate used her as a shield. "Go on. Fire. It will be your sister who gets the bullet."

"Peter, run."

The pirate gripped her neck.

She struggled to breathe, everything happening slowly.

Peter glanced from the man to her and back. Sweat dotted his forehead and upper lip. He looked ready to cry, a boy again.

"Mr. Vincent." Peter's voice trembled. "You must heed what I say. Release her."

In the hall, a pirate rushed into view. "Not bloody likely." He struck his pistol butt against Peter's skull. Peter dropped to the floor, unconscious.

Diana tried to scream, but Vincent's grip didn't allow it.

The pirate who'd struck Peter laughed. "Another prize to ransom to Bishop when we arrive in Mozambique."

"Many weeks from today." Vincent held on to Diana. "I intend to use them quite well, beginning now."

Diana fought as she never had.

Swearing loudly, Vincent dragged her across the room and flung her onto the bed.

She grabbed the knife.

He punched it away.

She rolled across the mattress and pushed to her feet only to come face to face with another pirate.

Fury battled with hopelessness and raw fear.

Vincent crawled across the bed to her. "Cause any more trouble, and your brother will get a bullet in his head."

A pirate trained his pistol on Peter's crumpled form.

Vincent gave her a disgusting smile. "You've kept me waiting too long. I intend to take you now, in front of the men. Let them know what they're missing." He slapped the mattress. "Come here."

Diana couldn't move.

Vincent looked over. "Kill the boy."

"No! I'll do whatever you want." Shivering uncontrollably, she padded to the bed.

Outside, a man ran to the window. "Captain, savages are on their way here from the fields. There are quite a few. They have pistols."

Chapter 16

A short distance from the mansion, Laure tore down the path toward Tristan and James, her eyes wild.

Worried, Tristan dismounted immediately and called out. "What happened?"

"No, you must be quiet." She glanced over. The path was empty. Gulping air, she turned back to them. "The pirates are in the stone house. Pierre said they were men from your old crew. They have your woman. We heard her scream."

Tristan could barely breathe. "Canela did this. She was looking into the glass."

"Wait." James gripped Tristan's arm. "You can't go back to the house now."

"I must." He yanked free.

James grabbed him again.

Tristan shoved him.

James regained his balance and blocked Tristan from his gelding. "If you ride to the house now, you'll surely be outnumbered. With you captured and murdered, how will Diana survive?"

"I must go. I have no bloody choice."

"First we round up the men. They're only a short distance behind us. With their help and numbers, we can free Diana. It's the only way, my friend."

"Please hurry." Laure bounced on her heels. "Pierre went to help his sister."

Mounting his gelding, Tristan prayed to a God he'd never asked for favors, though he did now. He offered his life for Diana and Peter's.

Laure rode behind James.

Tristan took off to gather the men needed for a counterattack.

Many streamed from the fields and vineyards. Others left the pastures.

All prepared to fight.

Tristan wheeled his gelding around and put his horse to a full gallop. Eighty islanders followed, providing a far greater force than the pirates they needed to defeat.

Tristan knew his former mates' desire for an easy prize. Only a determined and obsessive man could have found this island. Chadwick Vincent. The bastard was far too greedy. Vincent had most likely killed off quite a few of the pirates rather than share any prize with them. If he'd brought as many as thirty men with him, Tristan would have been surprised.

He tightened his hands on his reins as he'd soon do about Vincent's throat. "You harm Diana in the least, you so much as touch a hair on her head, not only will you die, you'll suffer greatly before doing so."

He drove his heels into his horse. Twilight approached. Despite the moonlight, it would be hard to follow the pirates if they escaped into the forest. Waiting until daybreak to strike wasn't possible. Vincent would have committed too many horrors by then.

"Just ahead." James pointed. "Islanders on the path."

Tristan put up his hand for the group to stop and reined in his horse near the men who'd stayed behind at the mansion today. The pirates had battered each. He asked if anyone got worse than them.

None had.

"Have any of you seen a man wearing a yellow scarf?"

The islanders shook their heads.

Vincent had most likely remained with Diana. Tristan lifted his face to the mansion on the rise. The forest protected him and the others from view.

"After the pirates beat you, did they go to the stone house?"

The men nodded.

"James, it appears Vincent and the others are still at the mansion. We need to surround them." Tristan pointed to the left. "Take half the men up that path. I'll take the other half up this one. Be careful."

"Always." He told the islanders the plan and led his group to the left.

The others followed Tristan.

The paths entered the grounds in seldom-used areas. Once they were near the mansion, Tristan and his men dismounted, tethered their horses, then ran to the courtyard walls. Past the opening, crying children and frightened women greeted them.

Follie said, "*Les pirates sont allés!*" The pirates have gone.

Tristan fought panic. "What of Diana and Pierre?"

"The pirates took her, him, and Canela."

James ran to Tristan's side. "Have you found them?"

"No. They must have run to the beach like the cowards they are to head back to the Lady Lark. Come on."

* * * *

Adamo could scarcely breathe, pain racking him.

Hurried footsteps sounded on the path. He didn't lift his head to see who approached. It didn't matter any longer.

Canela had betrayed him so cruelly, offering no comfort or outrage at the pirates for beating him. To her, he no longer existed. She'd torn her marriage collar from her throat and tossed it aside. In the moment before he'd shouted her name, wanting to believe in some small way he mattered to her, she'd looked at Yellow Scarf. Canela lusted for him as she had for Tristan.

Adamo forced down an angry cry.

Other footfalls joined the first. Yellow Scarf and his men spoke.

Adamo waited for the crack of a pistol, his death, blessed peace.

They strode past. There was a great deal of commotion. Sand hit his legs. Diana called Peter's name. She sounded afraid.

Adamo tried to open his eyes. The left had swollen shut, the right a mere slit. Two pirates pulled their longboats from a stand. The others held tight to Diana, Peter, and Canela.

Hatred for her warred with Adamo's love, or perhaps what he'd always felt had been nothing but lust. He no longer knew.

The pirate holding Canela ran his filthy hands over her breasts and spoke to her in English. She nodded, manner subdued, face lowered.

She'd traded her husband and people for the promise of a stone mansion, silks, and jewels. Luxuries she would never possess. Yellow Scarf didn't want her. His attention remained on Diana.

He forced her into the longboat. Peter followed, along with Canela and others in the crew. They cast off.

Adamo kept still until they were too far to notice or care what he did. Pain gripped him. Clenching his teeth, he lifted his head. The pirates' boats bobbed on gentle swells.

His temples throbbed so badly he couldn't focus and had to wait until the agony passed. At last, his vision cleared. Something glittered on the sand.

With great effort, he pushed to his knees and crawled to the sparkling object. Diana's marriage collar, Tristan's symbol of possession and love for his wife. Canela had deliberately torn hers off. Adamo couldn't believe Diana had done the same. The others had told him how she'd insisted on wearing the collar even after it hurt her. She adored Tristan.

Adamo closed his eyes, shame overwhelming him. If Tristan never saw Diana or Peter again, he was to blame. He struggled to his feet and staggered up the path to find Tristan, tell him what had happened. What he'd done. An anguished cry caught in Adamo's throat. His breathing hitched. He'd gone only a few steps when he had to rest.

* * * *

Diana wrapped her arm around Peter's shoulders.

He lowered his head, fighting tears.

She hugged him. "It's all right. Everything will be fine."

"Quiet." Vincent glared at her, then Peter. "The same goes for you. One more sound and I'll surely give you something to cry about."

Peter stiffened beneath her arm, but he kept his tongue like a timid cabin boy.

Vincent regarded Diana.

She stared him down, showing no emotion, yet inwardly she smiled. Moonlight revealed the bloody scratches she'd put on his hideous face.

He sneered. "You owe me a great deal of pleasure. You cheated me the last two times. Won't happen again."

It would if she had anything to do about it. She brushed her hair off her shoulders, wanting him to know what she'd done when they were on the beach, his error in not noticing.

Unfortunately, he was more concerned with the injuries she'd inflicted. He frowned at his bitten hand and touched his raked cheeks. "It appears you need taming before I take you." He bared his teeth at her. "Care to guess how I intend to accomplish it?"

"You will never do so."

"You think not?" He smiled. "Then you'd be wrong. Dozens of lashes to your brother's back ought to do the trick in getting you to bend to my will."

Peter tensed.

She squeezed his biceps, warning him to be still.

"It would appear you agree. You give me what I want or I give Peter the whip, after which I'll get exactly what I—what the bloody hell?" He seized her throat.

Diana froze.

Peter grabbed Vincent's wrist.

The pirate was deadly calm, the way a fiend is before he murders someone. "Tell your brother to remove his hand."

"Do it, Peter."

Tears sparkled in his eyes, but he dropped his hand.

Vincent squeezed Diana's throat.

Her ears buzzed, her vision growing dim.

He leaned toward her. "What did you do with the bloody necklace?"

She shook her head, unable to speak or breathe.

He released her throat. "Where is the damn thing?"

"On the beach where I dropped it."

He lifted his hand to strike her.

Peter cried out, "No."

Diana didn't cower. "Leave any marks on me and I assure you, Benedict Bishop won't pay your ransom."

Vincent's glare turned monstrous, his violent nature warring with his greed. He finally lowered his hand, avarice winning out. He spoke to the men at the bow. "We have to go back to the beach."

"Go back?" The pirate who'd spoken sounded as young as Peter.

Vincent pointed his pistol at the boy. "Another word and you die." He twisted around to the men in the other longboats. "We're going back to the beach for the jewels we missed."

They exchanged glances. One in the boat nearest them leaned forward. "What of Tristan and the savages?"

"They don't know we've left the island. They're most likely looking for us in the stone mansion or the forest."

The other men stopped rowing toward the Lady Lark and changed course for the island.

* * * *

Tristan ran down the path to the beach. Just below the point, he stopped at Adamo doubled over, his breaths shallow. Near the shore, water sparkled wildly beneath the moon. In the distance, the ocean was darker and less distinct. Without his glass, he couldn't see if the pirate boats were out there, Diana and Peter aboard.

"Tristan?"

Adamo lay face up on the path, lids black, nose bloodied, mouth swollen to twice its size. He lifted his fist.

James and the others raced down and halted abruptly.

Tristan pointed to the beach. "Get the skiffs and find the glass. Take care the pirates don't see you if they're watching with theirs. I'll be with you in a moment."

The men hurried to the boats.

Tristan dropped to one knee at Adamo's side. "Where did the pirates go?"

Tears rolled down the man's cheeks. "I brought them here. Forgive me. Your woman left this for you." Adamo opened his hand, revealing the marriage collar.

Pain tore across Tristan's chest. "Diana gave this to you?"

"No." He pulled in a strained breath. "She dropped it on the sand before the pirates took her and Pierre away."

"How long ago was that?"

"Not long."

"Where's the glass?"

"Canela had it before the pirates took her. She might have dropped it on the beach."

She had surely talked Adamo into this. His only crime had been in loving her too much.

Tristan pushed to his feet. "One of the men will take you to the stone house so Simone can treat your injuries."

"No. Let me die here. I betrayed you."

"You gave me Diana's marriage collar and told me what happened. You've helped more than you'll ever know. Now keep still, you'll be taken back shortly." Tristan pressed his lips to the diamonds. Once he'd run the collar through a buttonhole in his breeches, he fastened the clasp.

On the beach, Tristan found James behind a palm, the glass to his eye. "Do you see anything?"

"Vincent and the others are changing course."

"To where?"

"This beach it would seem." He offered the glass.

Tristan took in the scene and smiled. "Bravo, my love." Not only was his wife beautiful but crafty in the bargain, dropping the diamonds here so Vincent had to come back for them. He lowered the glass. "Tell the other men to take their positions on the beach but to hold their fire until I give the signal."

"What about Adamo?"

"I'll see to him."

Tristan bolted up the path, taking care to remain near the trees and within the shadows. He placed the glass to the side, helped Adamo to his feet, and led him into a stand where he'd be safe.

"No." Adamo held back. "The pirates took my weapon, but I still must fight with the other men."

"You're far too injured. Remain here."

"Please. If I cannot fight them, I am not a man."

Tristan gave Adamo a pistol. "Take care when using this. Your injuries may compromise your aim."

Adamo grabbed Tristan's wrist. "I will prove myself. Never again will I fail you."

"I know. Much luck to you in this fight, my friend."

"And to you."

Tristan retrieved the glass and rushed down the path to another stand. As he backed into the shadows, James and the others took their positions on the beach.

* * * *

Vincent pressed his gun muzzle against Peter's forehead, then spoke to Diana. "Think carefully before you answer me. Your brother's life depends upon what you say."

Terrified to make a wrong move or say something to set Vincent off, she nodded.

"Will Tristan be on the beach when we get there? Is that why you dropped the diamonds, hoping he'd waylay us?"

Of course it was, though she hadn't considered what her deception would mean to Peter. "The diamonds are a symbol of our love. I knew I'd never see Tristan again, so I wanted him to have a memory of me." Tears stung her eyes, her anguish true and overwhelming. "I hoped you wouldn't notice their absence. I never thought you'd go back for them."

His terrifying smile widened. "Then you don't know me at all, though you will before our time's over.

"Men!" He'd called to the ones in the other boats. "Stop rowing!" He turned to the pirates in front. "The boats aren't going to shore. Fletcher will swim to the beach and bring the diamonds back with him."

Peter stared. "What if I can't find them?"

"Then the island girl dies. After her, I'll shoot your sister, then you."

Canela's eyes widened.

Diana was past fear straight into outrage. "How can you do this?"

"I'll do whatever I damn please to get what's mine." He pulled her between his legs, using her as a shield. "If Tristan feels like taking a shot at his old friend Chadwick, it will be you he's killing, instead."

She wanted to be sick.

Vincent tightened his grip and pressed his lips to her ear. "We're nearly to our goal. In no time at all, you'll be mine."

Chapter 17

Tristan held the glass steady, barely risking a breath. Moonlight washed Diana's face. She pressed her lips tightly together. Vincent cowered behind her.

"Bloody coward." Tristan couldn't risk a shot now, nor could his men. He used a silver doubloon to reflect the moonlight, signaling for them to hold their fire.

James signaled back, indicating they understood.

Tristan raised the glass to his eye, readying for when the pirates reached shore.

They'd stopped rowing.

Peter left the lead longboat and swam toward the beach. A pirate held his pistol to Canela's head. Tristan guessed what would happen to her if Peter didn't retrieve the collar. The only solution now was to put the diamonds on the beach and allow Peter to discover them, leaving Tristan to his other plan.

He dashed past the trees and tossed the collar.

"Damn you!" Vincent's muted shout carried from the boat.

Tristan brought the glass to his eye.

Peter treaded water and faced the longboat. He swam toward it.

Tristan swung the glass in the same direction.

Diana rammed her upper body repeatedly into Vincent's. The pirates exchanged glances. One lifted his pistol. Hatred in their eyes, the others followed, training their weapons on Vincent rather than Diana.

They wanted him dead, but if their shots missed, she'd pay with her life.

Tristan dropped the glass. He pulled off the brace holding his pistols, tore across the beach, and dove into the sea. Even beneath the water, the first shot sounded clearly and deadly, then the next and the next.

Terrified, he broke water.

Peter had reached a longboat.

"No, Peter. Stop!"

The boy rocked the vessel and capsized it.

The men hit the sea, along with Canela, Vincent, and Diana.

Tristan swam as fast as he could toward her.

Vincent had the same notion.

Before the bloody bastard could lay a hand on Diana, Tristan slung one arm about Vincent's throat and pounded him into unconsciousness.

More shots rang out.

Tristan's men swam to the other longboats, overturned them, and captured the pirates.

Tristan shouted for James.

His friend swam toward him. "Want me to take Vincent?"

"Yes." Not seeing Diana, he shouted her name.

"Behind you." She treaded water and struggled to keep Canela afloat. "She hit her head."

Tristan swam to them and took Canela from her. "Were you hurt?"

"No." She craned her neck. "Where is Peter?"

Peter subdued a pirate with a skillful blow and grinned.

"He's quite well." Tristan hauled in another breath. "However, a farmer's life may never be to his liking."

"I refuse to accept it." She gulped air. "Laure will change his mind when he slips the marriage collar about her throat."

Love and pride filled Tristan to bursting. Despite the ordeal Diana had just been through, she was as confident as any man. "Your marriage collar's on the beach. Shall we fetch it?"

"I believe we should."

* * * *

On the beach, Tristan grabbed the collar and led Diana to a stand. They were well hidden from the others who'd reached shore. She lifted her hair and smiled when he fastened the collar on her throat, where the symbol would always remain.

He hugged her fiercely, emotion overtaking him. "I might have lost you."

She returned his embrace. "You didn't."

"I might have." His words were strained, his kiss hungry.

He branded her with his touch, scent, and far more, despite the others' proximity. He worked his stiffened cock from his breeches. She lifted her gown and bared her sex to him. Once she had her arms around his neck and her legs about his lean hips, Tristan thrust into her, possessing and filling her completely.

Diana pressed her face against his neck, quieting her breathing as he made her his.

While they were still trembling from pleasure, she snuggled closer. "That wasn't nearly enough. I want you until neither of us can stand."

He laughed quietly, his breath warming her throat. "Must I tie you to my bed again to get you to behave?"

"Please do. Promise me."

"You have my word to do so as soon as we see to the matter at hand."

* * * *

Diana joined the others.

Canela had regained consciousness. She eyed Diana's marriage collar, then Tristan, who was assisting the men.

Diana deliberately blocked Canela's view. "No one died. You should be grateful."

She regarded the water, indifferent as always. "What will become of me?"

"It's up to Tristan and the rest, including your husband."

Peter helped Adamo to the beach.

As dawn approached, the islanders voted to send the pirates to a distant island whose inhabitants were friendly with Tristan.

"I agree," James said. "Without a ship, these men can't cause us any more trouble."

"No trouble?" Peter scowled at the pirates who either cursed or moaned. "If they hang as they should, we can be certain of never seeing their ugly faces again."

Diana didn't know what to do about her little brother. Hours before, Peter had been scared witless. Now he acted too boldly. She exchanged a glance with Tristan.

He spoke to the boy. "There's never been a hanging on this island nor will there be as long as I draw breath. These men will go to the isle to live out their lives in service to the people there. It's more than a fitting punishment. They sought to rule islanders and now those people will rule them."

"I suppose." Peter glared at Canela. "What about her?"

Even with an ugly bruise on her forehead and everyone's rage to face, Canela refused to soften her stance, her bearing haughty, her attention at last on Adamo.

His handsome face was horribly swollen, his strong form bent in pain. A fate Canela had delivered him to with the false promise of love.

The adoring way she looked at him now sickened Diana. Canela seemed convinced the spell she'd woven around Adamo was so great, his passion so enduring, he'd plead her case, spare her from banishment.

Tristan faced her. "Adamo asked me to tell you what he's decided."

As James translated for the islanders, Canela tried to catch Adamo's eye. He kept his face down.

Tristan snapped his fingers to get her attention. "Adamo said you're no longer his wife. You removed the marriage collar."

"No!" She cried out to Adamo. *"S'il vous plaît. Vous devez* écouter. *Les pirates ont pris le collier de moi."*

Diana would have wagered Canela had told him the pirates removed her marriage collar.

Tristan stepped between Canela and Adamo so she couldn't see him. "You'll go to the island with the other captives. There you'll serve the islanders as you would have had your people serve you."

"No." She leaned to the side to look past Tristan's legs. *"Je t'aime,* Adamo."

That phrase Diana knew: I love you.

Adamo's back was to Canela.

* * * *

With the sun overhead, the men settled the fettered pirates and Canela in the longboats for their journey to the Lady Lark, after which James, Peter, and the others would sail for the island where the prisoners would spend their remaining days.

Peter joined Tristan and Diana. "We'll be leaving now."

"Take care." She hugged her brother more soundly than she was certain he wanted and kissed his cheek.

He squirmed. "You mustn't do that with the other men about."

"I shan't if you promise to become a farmer when you get back."

He made a face. "You women are all alike. Laure's already asked me to do the same."

"She's a bright girl and should be obeyed. Right, Tristan?"

He looked amused. "A man obeying a woman?"

Peter laughed. "There you have it. Tristan agrees with me. Women are the ones who—"

"Should be obeyed." Tristan winked at Diana. "At least part of the time."

Peter rolled his eyes and grumbled good-naturedly. "I best be going."

Diana wanted to hug him once more, but kept her hands to herself. "Return as quickly as you can."

"Less than a fortnight." He kissed Laure, then ran to the longboats.

As he, James, and the others rowed toward the Lady Lark, Diana softened against Tristan, her back to his front, his arms wrapped loosely around her waist.

She stroked his fingers. "Do we have anything to worry about?"

"Not at all. Peter will eventually come to your way of thinking. If he doesn't, I can assure you Laure will make him bend to her will."

"I wasn't speaking of them." She eased from Tristan's embrace and faced him. "Do we have anything to worry about as far as Bishop's concerned? Do you think he'll ever come here looking for us, or rather me, as the others did?"

"If he does, I'll be there to greet him with my pistols, cutlass, and fists, as will James, Peter, and the island men."

She rested her fingertips on his whiskered cheek. "I've caused you nothing but trouble."

"I know. It's been bloody hell."

She laughed softly, but couldn't push away her worry. "Never let me go." She slipped her arms around his neck. "That's an order."

"A what?"

"A request." She pressed her cheek to his, her dangerous angel. "One I'm begging you to grant."

"You were mine from the first moment I saw you. We both knew as much, even though you were reluctant to accept the truth."

She smiled at how she'd resisted him. "It was only because I wanted you to properly woo me."

"Have I?"

"Oh, yes." She brought his face down to hers. "First came desire." Her lips brushed his. "Then friendship and love. I would say you wooed me quite well."

THE END

Be sure not to miss Tina Donahue's erotic historical romance

PASSIONATE PURSUIT

Is their passion strong enough to break her chains?

Andalucía Spain, 1489: Innocent Beatriz is desperate to escape the threat of a miserable marriage to a cruel Marquis. Forced into the betrothal by her ruthless merchant papá, her only hope is to conceal her identity and become a servant in a nearby castle—a life drastically different from her comfortable upbringing.

Tomás doesn't know what to make of his well-spoken new servant girl. Her beauty and charm captivate the military hero; her mysterious nature intrigues him. And the desire she ignites burns brighter with each glance, as does his longing to claim her for his own.

Beatriz can't resist Tomás's passion, nor deny the heat of her own. But neither the lush countryside nor the walls of the opulent Moorish castle can entirely protect her—and if he were to discover her secret, she could be torn away from him forever. Yet how can she sustain his love if she's living a lie?

A Lyrical Originals novel on sale now!

Learn more about Tina at
http://www.kensingtonbooks.com/author.aspx/24772

Chapter 1

Andalucía, Spain—1489
The castle of Tomás de Zayas

The siege had begun. Not from bloodthirsty Moors. Oh, no. Tomás de Zayas would have welcomed such a prospect. He'd fought Spain's enemies with ruthless determination during his service to the Crown. Those battles were frequently grisly, but the conflicts had always ended. What he'd face in the coming hours however...

Two carriages approached his estate. The first of many, less than half a league apart, wheels kicking up dust clouds within the heavily vegetated land. Inside each conveyance was a scheming mamá and daughter with naught but marriage on their minds with him the unwilling suitor.

His gut churned. He refused to budge from the parapet until dragged away.

If only he could fly from his castle as jackdaws were doing, their wings outstretched on the mild breeze, sweet scents beckoning. Several birds dipped to spring flowers and lush vegetation shaded from the heavy sun. He longed to ride past the scene, laughing, loving...with the right woman.

The dark-haired beauty he craved was hopelessly out of reach.

He gripped the stone, despising circumstances, dreading the arriving females.

He'd held them off for months, declining invitations to countless gatherings. The mamás had persisted with endless requests to visit his estate, claiming they and their daughters wanted to see how he was doing after his brush with death.

He was hearty as ever and wanted to enjoy life again, though not with them. The woman he desired was already here.

Heat, unbidden and insistent, rushed through him.

"Here you are," Nuncio said.

Just what he didn't need. His manservant. An ancient fellow who'd been with the de Zayas family well before Tomás's birth. Despite Nuncio's sixty years, the man held himself as erect as a Spanish knight. While his bearing and white hair gave him a courtly appearance, his casual manner was more intrusive uncle than groveling servant.

Nuncio arched a bushy white eyebrow at Tomás's goblet.

Gleefully, he finished his wine, wanting more to fortify himself against the coming hours.

Clattering horse hooves and wheels quieted.

The first carriage had arrived. Mother and daughter left their conveyance, chattering endlessly. Their voices rang with excitement. Their silly giggles grated.

According to his brother, Enrique, and sister-in-law, Sancha, this was Tomás's proper future, with someone from his own world. His wayward passion for a woman not of his station couldn't amount to anything, ever, except trouble and heartache.

He slumped against the railing.

"Are you planning to throw yourself off?" Nuncio sighed tiredly. "Should I be alarmed?"

He would be when Tomás tossed him off the side. "You should do your duty and see to my desires." He held out his goblet. "I need more wine."

Nuncio remained planted to the spot, wrinkled hands folded in front, striking a lord of the manor pose. "Your guests might believe otherwise."

The carriage and footmen were off to the side, the women nowhere in sight. Presumably, mother and daughter were within the castle, waiting for what they believed would be a private visit with him.

Pity that.

He offered a pleased smile. "As they have no regard for my feelings, I hardly care what they think. If you remember, I politely declined their requests to come here, until you hounded me about my indifference to their marriage plans with me as their grudging victim. Now, I have a chance to tell the mamás I have no intention of wedding any of their daughters."

"By gathering all of them here at the same time."

"Clever, no?"

"Some might say reckless, considering their families are your political allies, though they may not be after today."

Tomás waved away Nuncio's comment. "Better to get this over with at one time rather than dragging the matter out through countless visits.

Besides, my public declaration will keep gossip to a minimum. None of the women will be able to say I rejected any señorita because of her shrill laugh, slow wit, poor shape, or dull converse. They were all equally lacking."

Nuncio looked heavenward. He might have even started to pray.

Tomás gritted his teeth. "Equally lacking in my desire for them. Never fear, I shall be unfailingly polite and let each lady know how wonderful she is. More beautiful than stars sparkling in the night sky, more promising than the hint of spring after a brutal winter, more—"

"Forgive me for interrupting, but one would hope they would still be listening at that point." He squared his narrow shoulders. "Cook prepared a feast for your guests. If any of them have an appetite after your pretty speech, I propose we hide the knives. For your safety, of course."

"I can take care of myself. And I refuse to settle for less than what Enrique and Fernando have."

"You mean the families they started."

Not entirely. However, Isabella had given birth to her and Fernando's first child, a daughter. They named her Juana after Isabella's late mother. Sancha hadn't yet delivered. Given what Enrique had repeatedly said, he didn't care whether she bore him a son or a daughter. He simply wanted her and the child's health and happiness.

Nuncio cleared his throat delicately. "If I may be so bold…"

"You will be, anyway. Get on with it."

"Very well. If you seek children, I advise you wed first as your brothers had."

"They fought for the women they wanted. Neither let convention get in his way."

"Your brothers wed women from their own backgrounds."

"They fell in love with them first and overcame numerous obstacles to be at their sides even though none were originally meant to be together. Have you forgotten Fernando's betrothal to Sancha was long before she married Enrique instead? What about Isabella pretending to be Sancha and wedding Fernando before he knew the difference between the two sisters? Despite such chaos, all are blissfully happy now."

"Miracles do happen, though in your case you best not hope for one."

Tomás shoved his hair back from where the wind had blown it. "As the youngest son, who I end up with, or if I end up with anyone, is of no consequence. Enrique inherits everything from Papá. Building upon the family dynasty is his duty. I can do as I please."

Nuncio looked off into the distance, his expression suddenly a mask, though the lines in his face seemed to have deepened. "Is this about Beatriz?"

Tomás's heart slammed into his chest. Lightheaded, he gripped the stone for support and pretended to drink from his empty goblet, since he was unable and unwilling to answer. Above, a jackdaw cried out. Below, wheels rattled against stone, announcing more guests. Three carriages drew near.

He wanted to run. His legs were too leaden to work properly. "Where is she?"

Nuncio shook his head.

Frustration oiled Tomás's limbs, allowing him movement. Fist clenched, he approached, prepared to thrash Nuncio to get an answer.

He stood his ground and kept his tongue.

Tomás crowded him further. "Answer me. Where is she?"

"Seeing to her tasks as the other servants are doing."

And would most likely finish her work before Nuncio offered anything more than he had. "Inform my guests I shall be delayed slightly."

"You plan to clean up a bit? Excellent. I suggest your dark green robe and doublet. The blue you have on hardly does you justice. As to your hose, one in peach, the other in white will work far better than the striped ones you chose. You should also have a shave."

Tomás slapped his goblet into Nuncio's palm and hurried down the steps, his shoes ringing on the stone. On the next level, he rushed through the castle once owned by a Moor, the same as Fernando's castle had been. Their service to the Crown had won them the reconquered estates. Although Tomás's new home was far smaller than Fernando's and certainly Enrique's, he still had to search numerous halls and countless rooms for Beatriz.

He wanted to see her. No. He needed to. A compulsion he couldn't seem to resist despite her being a servant. A matter important to Nuncio, Enrique, and Sancha, with them advising Tomás not to take advantage of his position and Beatriz, since a dalliance between them could lead nowhere.

He was well aware of the perils and hadn't done anything except watch her whenever he could.

She was remarkably different from his other servants, her air, manner, and speech refined. Intelligence shone in her eyes. She even seemed able to read. Weeks ago, he'd come upon her tidying his study. She'd regarded the book spines at length, the way one would when considering titles. Surprising and odd. If she were educated, he couldn't imagine why she'd willingly spend her days here in endless drudgery.

When he'd asked his housekeeper about her, Señora Cisneros said Beatriz came from one of the many villages Tomás owned and that she needed work to support her ailing mother. He hadn't bothered to check out the story, sensing Beatriz might have an ill parent, which drove her to seek work here. As to the other part of her background… Deep inside, he sensed she hadn't come from any village.

Not that he cared whether he was right or not.

Seeing her again, settling his overwhelming desire was his only goal. Today, he could compare Beatriz to the other women and determine if his desire for her was only a passing whim. Once he'd had another look at her, he might be able to dismiss his feelings as mere fantasy and have peace at last.

Where had she gone?

He strode toward the first hall and the bedchambers, this area open and airy, his face warmed by sun spilling through arched windows that stretched from floor to ceiling. Rays glinted off intricate Moorish mosaics, flashing blue, yellow, green, and red, turning the stone columns and floors milky and bright. He squinted.

Upon reaching the chambers, he checked room after room, each filled with rich wall hangings and Spanish furniture, the dark wood and leather carved with ornate designs. Every chamber was spotless and duly aired to smell quite fresh. Also empty. With only two more rooms to go, he sensed Beatriz might be elsewhere in the castle, tending to those rooms.

No matter. He'd run her down in time.

After a quick check of the remaining chambers, he turned.

Beatriz stood across the hall, holding linens heaped in a basket.

His mouth went dry.

Despite her red gown, white tunic, and linen cap, the same livery his other female servants wore, she might as well have been a queen.

She was certainly beautiful enough. Her skin was paler than most, the color of a fine pearl, features delicate, light brown eyes lushly lashed and softened with what appeared to be need.

His chest tightened, breathing became difficult, the air too thick suddenly.

Her plush lips, pink as an Andalucían dawn, parted in what seemed to be an invitation.

Everything grew quiet. Colors and the surrounding area faded into the background, leaving nothing except her to feast on. Dewy skin, sensuous mouth, full breasts, lush hips.

His shaft thickened and grew hard, craving her heated sheath damp with her excitement.

His for the taking. He merely had to cross the small space separating them.

The distance seemed wider than the ocean with too many warnings bombarding him. Sancha's advice that he not ruin Beatriz, leaving her few options for marriage to a respectable man. Enrique warning about the child Tomás would eventually sire with her. Nuncio's repeated admonitions about her peasant background that wouldn't allow them a future together no matter how much Tomás may have wanted one.

He shouldn't have sought her out. His plan to dismiss any feelings he'd had failed miserably. He wanted her far more than earlier.

He tipped his head. *"Buenas tardes."*

Pink bloomed in her cheeks. Her eyes cleared, no longer dreamy or aroused. She stepped back.

The distance between them was already too great. She didn't need to add to it. Although he understood her prudence, he hated that they had to resist their desire.

"Buenas tardes, *Patrón.*" She propped the basket on her hip and retreated two steps.

In another moment, she might bolt.

He prayed not yet. "Are the linens too heavy?" He wanted to help, needed to be near. "Do you want me to carry them?"

She shook her head, dark, silky tendrils dancing near to her cheeks.

He ached to wind the strands around his fingers and ease her closer. "Are you quite certain?"

She gripped the basket hard enough to make her knuckles white. "I can see to my duties. I can work all day and night if necessary."

"Have you ever needed to do so in order to finish?"

"No." Beatriz frowned, then made her face a mask, the kind servants show a master, leaving the poor fool no way to know what they thought. "I finish my tasks quickly. Without problems."

"How wonderful." He stepped in her way before she could get around him. "How is your mother doing? Does she need a potion or poultice?"

She stared, color draining.

Why? He only wanted to help. "Señora Cisneros mentioned your mamá's troubles in passing. How sad I am for you and her. However, I know a physician who may be able to make things better. Tell me the symptoms and I can bring you what she needs."

No matter what ailed the woman, Sancha could prepare a remedy. She was a healer. When Tomás had fallen ill at the *fortaleza*, she'd saved his life. A dangerous matter for her because of the Inquisition, which led to accusations claiming she was a witch. Thankfully, he, Enrique, and their brothers had handled the matter, leaving her free to practice healing in secret.

Beatriz hefted the basket and settled the thing more firmly on her hip.

"Those linens are too heavy for you." He grabbed them.

She held on.

Surely, she didn't think she'd win against him. He was a head taller, nearly twice her weight, and far stronger.

He tugged.

She let go.

He locked his knees to keep from staggering back at the weight. Far too cumbersome for such a delicate flower as her. He'd have to talk with Señora Cisneros about Beatriz's future duties.

Rather than offering a sweet smile for his help, she bit her lip.

Tenderness welled within him, along with unruly desire. "No reason to be afraid. Your position is safe. I merely want to help. Tell me what ails your mamá."

"Nothing at the moment. She recovered fully from her latest illness. I must get back to work." She reached for the linens.

He kept them away. "Is my housekeeper demanding too much even with you willing to work day and night?"

"Señora Cisneros is a lovely woman."

She had a mustache, hairs on her chin, weighed more than two women combined, and owned a high-pitched voice that set his teeth on edge. However, she did keep the castle running smoothly without being too overbearing. "I find her efficient in a slightly masculine way. Is that what you meant?"

Beatriz's mouth curled up, though she didn't allow herself to smile.

Making her laugh meant everything to Tomás without him understanding why. "Do you promise not to tell her I said such a thing?"

She gripped her skirt. "We rarely speak. Work keeps us busy."

"So you do promise. Wonderful." He grinned and lifted the basket to his shoulder, showing off his strength. "Where did you plan to take this? I can bring the linens to whatever room you—"

Loud throat clearing flowed down the hall.

Either Señora Cisneros or Nuncio had just entered from behind. Hard to tell which, since they both made the same noises when displeased with the help. He looked over.

Nuncio.

Beatriz pulled the basket from Tomás with surprising strength, though she did totter.

"Careful." He reached for her.

She twisted away.

Nuncio cleared his throat once more.

Tomás frowned at him. "Did you inform the guests of my delay?"

"Several times. They still await your presence. Every one of them in the same room."

Surely without knives if Nuncio had anything to say. Tomás gentled his mood for Beatriz. "If your mamá should fall ill again, please tell me. I can help."

Her attention remained on Nuncio.

Wanting to speak softly to her, Tomás leaned closer, catching her seductive fragrance, freshly washed clothes and clean skin. He reeled, finding speech difficult. "If Nuncio rails at you for keeping me here, let me know. I shall thrash him soundly."

Laughter bubbled from her, which she quelled without pause.

Her joy, no matter how brief, was a balm for everything wrong with today. How marvelous if they, at least, became friends, speaking freely, laughing, enjoying themselves. An odd notion for any man when faced with such a delectable woman. However, he didn't see many other options at this point.

He strode to Nuncio. "Shall we go?" Halfway down the hall, Tomás spoke. "Make certain the ladies' carriages, drivers, and footmen are ready to depart. I trust no one will be staying long once I give my speech."

"As you wish. Whatever you wish. Whenever you wish."

Tomás rolled his eyes. If wishes were his for the asking, he'd still be speaking to Beatriz, inviting her to ride the grounds with him, having a late supper with her on the hillside overlooking his estate, finally carrying her into his chamber for some much-needed passion with them discovering wondrous things about each other.

He surely wouldn't be facing women who might want to harm him once they understood he had no intention of wedding anyone.

* * * *

Beatriz González y Serrano sat on a guest bed when she shouldn't have. She should bolt from the estate and Tomás.

Her legs wouldn't support her. If she left, she might not be able to secure work at another estate. No one in the villages would hire a house servant to toil in the fields. Even the children would fare better than she at the backbreaking labor. The few merchants in town would do the work themselves or have family to help. Returning to the city was far too dangerous unless she wanted to live out her life imprisoned by a man she loathed who'd use her in the vilest ways possible.

Hopeless, she did the only thing she could, savoring the few moments she'd spent with Tomás. Magical and enticing snatches of time that shouldn't have happened.

She hadn't meant for him to see her, prepared to duck into a room so he'd never know she'd spied on him. His purpose in searching bedchambers hadn't occurred to her. She'd been too taken with his size and promise of the warrior he was, all lean muscle and man. Too many nights she'd dreamed of her lips pressed to his rich mouth, fingers buried in his thick, blond hair, drowning in his heat and strength.

Her nipples tightened, the tips hard enough to sting. The soft folds between her legs were damp and ready for him. A nobleman with countless women who wanted to share his life and bed, each desiring his looks, wealth, and position.

She adored his gentle teasing. How easily he'd made her smile and laugh, despite her caution and lies.

She buried her face in her hands, ashamed at what she'd said about her mamá. When he'd brought up her supposed illness, Beatriz hadn't recalled telling Señora Cisneros about an ailing mother in order to secure a position here.

Tomás seemed to believe her falsehood. Unless he'd pretended with her as she had with him.

Shoes slapped against stone. She pushed to her feet and froze.

Nuncio stood in the doorway, taking in the scene.

Quickly, she smoothed the bright red counterpane where she'd sat. "I was just finishing here."

"You were sitting. I saw you." He closed the door and approached.

Fearing the worst, she backed away. "I can work an extra hour or two to make up for the few seconds I sat on the bed. I can go without food for the rest of the day. I can—"

"Your silence is all I ask. And for you to listen to me. Do you think you can do such a thing?"

She didn't want to hear anything he had to say but nodded readily.

Nuncio folded his hands behind his back and paced, his tapping shoes sounding horribly loud.

"Don Tomás is our master." He stopped and glared. "He never carries linens."

"No. I mean, I agree."

"Then why was he holding your basket?"

"He wanted to help."

"Were you bent over from the weight of the linens? Had you fallen because the basket was too heavy? Could you not breathe? Were you in danger of swooning or dying?"

"No. Of course not." Forgetting herself, she frowned.

Nuncio narrowed his eyes.

She hid her feelings as any intimidated servant would. "I had no trouble with the work. I was merely standing in the hall when he came upon me and offered to assist."

Nuncio inhaled deeply but didn't argue the point as she'd expected. Surely that couldn't mean Tomás was wont to help all servants when seeing them in hallways.

"You should have told him you were busy." He straightened even more. "Then went on your way."

"I tried. He blocked me."

Nuncio frowned hard, making terrible dents in his face.

She wanted them gone. Him too. "Don Tomás merely asked about my mother's health. I told him she recovered. Everything is fine." She grabbed her basket. "I should go back to work."

He approached more quickly than his age should have allowed and stood between her and the door. "You must stay away from our master. If you see him, go in the other direction. If he comes upon you, do not smile sweetly. I know you can as I saw the one you gave him. Forget that. Move to another area in the castle even if you have to leave your work. Never fear, I will have a word with Señora Cisneros, letting her know if you fail to finish your duties, the fault is not yours. Do you understand me?"

All too well. If she'd been in another position than the one she was currently in, she would have laughed in his face and gone after Tomás on her own. Given her precarious situation, she could only agree. "*Sí*."

"About Rufio."

He was also a house servant, close to her age. His duties took place in the kitchen or dining hall, not the chambers as hers did. "What about him?"

Nuncio observed her carefully. "I see how he is when the two of you are near. Make certain you never encourage him."

She bristled. "I never have or will. I keep my distance from him and all the men."

"Make certain you continue to do so, especially with our master."

"Does Don Tomás behave with the other female servants as he has with me?"

Nuncio remained turned away but did look over. "His habits are not yours to know."

"Did you tell those servants the same?" Did those women obey and stay away from him?

On a loud sigh, Nuncio faced her. "The monarchs granted Don Tomás this land quite recently. Before that, he was away for years fighting the Moors. I have no idea what he did at the fortaleza. This castle is my only concern."

Then Tomás hadn't behaved with the others as he had with her, or Nuncio would have said so, warning her what became of those women. Beatriz's spirits soared until she recalled her and Tomás's impossible situation. Hopeless because of their positions, as long as she remained a servant and never revealed her past. There was also Nuncio's dogged determination to protect Tomás from himself.

Nuncio opened the door.

She joined him. "One last thing."

He regarded her warily and closed the door. "What?"

"Even if I flee every time I see Don Tomás, what do I do if he follows and catches me?"

Nuncio gave her a cold stare. "If he does, your days at the castle are over. I should make you leave this second, seeing the trouble you could cause. However, I know Don Tomás far better than you ever will. If anyone stands in the way of what he believes he wants, he craves it even more, making everyone as miserable as he is. Long ago, I learned to let him reach the proper conclusion on his own, which he always does. Therefore, you may remain here unless you force my hand by making yourself available to him on purpose or accidentally. The burden to avoid any trouble is upon you. No one else."

He left without a backward glance.

Meet the Author

Tina Donahue is an Amazon and international bestselling novelist in erotic, paranormal, contemporary, and historical romance for traditional publishers and indie. Booklist, Publishers Weekly, Romantic Times and numerous online sites have praised her work. Three of her erotic novels (Freeing the Beast, Come and Get Your Love, and Wicked Takeover) were Readers' Choice Award winners. Another three of her erotic novels (Adored; Deep, Dark, Delicious; Lush Velvet Nights) were named finalists in the 2011 EPIC competition. Sensual Stranger, her erotic romance, was chosen Book of the Year 2010 (erotic category) at the French review site, Blue Moon reviews. The Golden Nib Award at Miz Love Loves Books was created specifically for her erotic romance Lush Velvet Nights. Deep, Dark, Delicious received an Award of Merit in the RWA Holt Medallion competition. Take Me Away captured second place in the NEC-RWA contest. And The Yearning was honored with an Award of Merit in the RWA Holt Medallion competition. She's featured in the 2012 Novel and Writer's Market. Before penning romances, she worked in Story Direction for a Hollywood production company. You can find her online at http://tinadonahuebooks.blogspot.com/, twitter.com/tinadonahue and https://www.facebook.com/DonahueTina1/.